LISTEN

RENE GUTTERIDGE

TYNDALE HOUSE PUBLISHERS, INC.

CAROL STREAM, ILLINOIS

Visit Tyndale's exciting Web site at www.tyndale.com.

Visit Rene Gutteridge's Web site at www.renegutteridge.com.

TYNDALE and Tyndale's quill logo are registered trademarks of Tyndale House Publishers, Inc.

Listen

Designed by Mark Anthony Lane II

Edited by Lorie Popp

Published in association with the Books & Such Literary Agency, 52 Mission Circle, Suite 122, PMB 170, Santa Rosa, CA 95409-5370, www.booksandsuch.biz.

Scripture quotations are taken from the *Holy Bible*, New Living Translation, copyright © 1996, 2004, 2007 by Tyndale House Foundation. Used by permission of Tyndale House Publishers, Inc., Carol Stream, Illinois 60188. All rights reserved.

This novel is a work of fiction. Names, characters, places, and incidents either are the product of the author's imagination or are used fictitiously. Any resemblance to actual events, locales, organizations, or persons living or dead is entirely coincidental and beyond the intent of either the author or the publisher.

Library of Congress Cataloging-in-Publication Data

Gutteridge, Rene.
  Listen / Rene Gutteridge.
    p. cm.
  ISBN 978-1-4143-2433-3 (pbk.)
  I. Title.
  PS3557.U887L57 2010
  813'.54—dc22   2009038254

Printed in the United States of America

16 15 14 13 12 11 10
 7   6   5   4   3   2   1

To those whose lives have been forever altered by words

Acknowledgments

I've had this book on my heart for quite some time, and it's so thrilling to have it completed and ready to offer to readers. I knew when God put this story in my heart that it would strike a chord with many people. I wrote it for everyone whose lives have been touched, either negatively or positively, by words. Everyone has his or her own personal story, but I believe we can agree that words are powerful, whichever way they are used. I have been hurt by words, and I have been forgiven for words that have hurt others. But I have also been lifted up and encouraged by words, and I hope that I have lifted and encouraged too.

I'd like to thank the magnificent team at Tyndale, who believed in this story from the beginning: Jan Stob, Karen Watson, Stephanie Broene, and Lorie Popp, plus everyone else from Tyndale who contributed to this book. You are a talented and lovely group of people, with great vision and purpose!

Thanks to the Kansas Eight, who encouraged me through some difficult rewrites. Also special thanks to Janet Grant, my agent and constant guide, and Ron Wheatley, my loyal friend and technical adviser.

As always, I cherish and adore my family—Sean, John, and Cate, who stand by me and lift me up daily with their words. To my friends and family, thanks for your loyalty and love.

Thanks also to my readers, some of whom have followed me for a decade now! I appreciate each one of you and thank you for taking the time to read this offering. I pray that God moves in your heart and that you will be encouraged to use your words with grace, discipline, and love.

And thank You, Father, for all that You do inside me so that I may write for Your glory.

Prologue

MEREDITH SAT QUIETLY in the center of her room on the carpet that had been freshly steam cleaned for the party. Against the far wall sat all the gifts she'd received, still in their fancy sacks.

The wind rattled the windows as the evening news, barely audible from another room, reported a blizzard on the way. She loved snow and the sound of haunting wind ushering it in. The house creaked against the gusts, and she closed her eyes, listening to the invisible. She liked that things unseen could be heard.

Her mother would be gone for exactly thirty-two minutes to take home the toddler and infant she babysat three times a week to earn a little extra cash for the family. Her brother was at work, his third job, to try to make ends meet.

Such small problems, money and food.

Meredith wanted to keep listening to the wind, but time was running out.

She placed the baby monitor and its receiver in front of her. Sky blue plastic, both with long white cords. She stared at them . . . portals to reality, a reality that told her who she was. What she was.

Her friends still didn't know she had heard them when she'd gone to the back bedroom to get a sweater. But she heard everything through the baby monitor. Every word.

She didn't know she embarrassed them by how she dressed. She didn't know her hair was ugly.

She'd clutched the sweater she'd gone to retrieve, the one with the small hole in the sleeve, and listened for a long time. She didn't come out of the room until they left.

The wind howled, reminding her that she had better hurry.

Meredith took the end of each unit, where the plugs were, and tied them together, pulling them as tight as possible. Then, with the rope to the toy horse her grandfather had made her when she was four, she added more length, closing the knots. She stood and tugged against the rope, tightening each knot one more time.

Her knees shook, which surprised her because until now she had felt calm and peaceful. Nearly euphoric, which made her realize she had indeed chosen wisely. But the piercing whistle of the wind through the house caused her to shiver. She never questioned whether she had the guts to do it. Other people questioned things about her, though.

She stood for a moment in her room, reconsidering the closet. The high bar would hold, but she knew her mother and knew she would need a place of solace when this was over. So she went to the garage.

The garage door shook against the wind, its metal rattling as if someone were outside shaking it furiously.

Her father's workbench stool would do. Something without wheels but unsteady enough to kick over.

Meredith studied the steel tracks bolted to the ceiling. Their family was the last on the block to still have the manual roll-up garage door, but she respected that about her dad. He wasn't a sellout. She always wanted to be like him. He was charismatic, likable. But her brother got all those traits.

She carefully climbed onto the stool. The last thing she needed was to fall and break her arm or something. That'd be just her luck.

She stood erect, looking down at all that was in the garage. Her gaze fixed on the oil stain her dad had been trying to remove for a week now. He scrubbed and scrubbed but couldn't get rid of it.

Stains are permanent, Dad.

From her back pocket, she pulled the rope and notes she'd copied from the library yesterday. She glanced over the drawing she'd made. It was pretty self-explanatory. She stuffed the paper back in her pocket and felt her other pocket for the small envelope, a note to her parents and brother telling them she loved them and she was sorry. She pushed it in deeper.

Meredith tied the noose like she'd studied, then lifted the other end and tied it twice around a thin, sturdy beam on the track above her. It didn't have to hold forever. Just long enough.

Her heartbeat reminded her that this was not going to be an easy task. She never expected it to be. But the euphoria had vanished.

Her hands started shaking. Tears fell against her cheeks. She'd prepared for this.

She'd decided on a countdown. After all, she was blasting off to somewhere far better for her and everybody else. She'd settled on starting at twenty, because that was her age and that seemed like a decent number. Not too long, not too short.

She had one more test. She took a deep breath and then yelled, "Can anyone hear me?"

She listened. But all she heard were those awful words from the girls. Over and over. She couldn't get them out of her head.

She tried one more time, this time louder, to give it a fair shot. "Can anyone hear me?"

Nobody answered. Nobody ever would.

Meredith pulled the noose around her neck and turned to see out the garage door windows. Her favorite tree, the weeping willow her father had planted when she was born, was in sight. She tightened the noose one more time so that the cord pressed deeply into her neck.

"Twenty. Nineteen. Eighteen. Seventeen. Sixteen. Fifteen. Fourteen. Thirteen. Twelve. Eleven. Ten. Nine. Eight. Seven. Six. Five. Four. Three. Two." She clenched her fists. "Can anyone hear me?"

She thought she heard a voice nearby. Then another sound, like a door shutting. She stopped breathing to hear better. But it was only the wind teasing her. Tears bled down her cheeks. She fixed her eyes on the dark stain below her.

"One."

1

PRESENT DAY

Damien Underwood tapped his pencil against his desk and spun twice in his chair. But once he was facing his computer again, the digital clock still hadn't changed.

In front of him on a clean white piece of paper was a box, and inside that box was a bunch of other tiny boxes. Some of those boxes he'd neatly scribbled in. And above the large box he wrote, *Time to go.*

This particular day was stretching beyond his normal capacity of tolerance, and when that happened, he found himself constructing word puzzles. He'd sold three to the *New York Times*, two published on Monday and one on Wednesday. They were all framed and hanging in his cubicle. He'd sent in over thirty to be considered.

He'd easily convinced his boss years ago to let him start publishing crosswords in the paper, and since then he'd been the crossword editor, occasionally publishing some of his own, a few from local residents, and some in syndication.

The puzzle clues were coming harder today. He wanted to use a lot of plays on words, and he also enjoyed putting in a few specific clues that were just for Marlo residents. Those were almost always published on Fridays.

A nine-letter word for "predictable and smooth."

Yes, good clue. He smiled and wrote the answer going down. *Clockwork.*

He glanced over to the bulletin board, which happened to be on the only piece of north wall he could see from his desk at the *Marlo Sentinel.* Tacked in the center, still hanging there after three years, was an article from *Lifestyles Magazine.* Marlo, of all the places in the United States, was voted Best Place to Raise a Child. It was still the town's shining moment of glory. Every restaurant and business had this article framed and hanging somewhere on their walls.

The community boasted its own police force, five separate and unique playgrounds for the kids, including a spray ground put in last summer, where kids could dash through all kinds of water sprays without the fear of anyone drowning.

Potholes were nonexistent. The trash was picked up by shiny, blue, state-of-the-art trash trucks, by men wearing pressed light blue shirts and matching pants, dressed slightly better than the mail carriers.

Two dozen neighborhood watch programs were responsible for nineteen arrests in the last decade, mostly petty thieves and a couple of vandals. There hadn't been a violent crime in Marlo since 1971, and even then the only one that got shot was a dog. A bank robbery twenty years ago ended with the robber asking to talk to a priest, where he confessed a gambling addiction and a fondness for teller number three.

Damien's mind lit up, which it often did when words were involved. He penciled it in. An eight-letter word for "a linear stretch of dates." *Timeline*. Perfect for 45 across.

So this was Marlo, where society and family joined in marriage. It was safe enough for kids to play in the front yards. It was clean enough that asthmatics were paying top dollar for the real estate. It was good enough, period.

Damien was a second-generation Marlo resident. His mother and father moved here long before it was the Best Place to Raise a Child. Then it had just been cheap land and a good drive from the city. His father had been the manager of a plant now gone because it caused too much pollution. His mother, a stay-at-home mom, had taken great pride in raising a son who shared her maiden name, Damien, and her fondness for reading the dictionary.

Both his parents died the same year from different causes, the year Damien had met Kay, his wife-to-be. They'd wed nine months after they met and waited the customary five years to have children. Kay managed a real estate company. She loved her job as much as she had the first day she started. And it was a good way to keep up with the Joneses.

Until recently, when the housing market started slumping like his ever-irritated teenage daughter.

The beast's red eyes declared it was finally time to leave.

Damien grabbed his briefcase and walked the long hallway to the door, just to make sure his boss and sometimes friend, Edgar, remembered he was leaving a little early. He gave Edgar a wave, and today, because he was in a good mood, Edgar waved back.

Damien drove through the Elephant's Foot and picked up two lemonades, one for himself and one for Jenna, his sixteen-year-old daughter, who had all at once turned from beautiful princess or ballerina or whatever it was she wanted to be to some weird Jekyll and Hyde science experiment. With blue eye shadow. She never hugged him. She never giggled. Oh, how he missed the giggling. She slouched and grunted like a gorilla, her knuckles nearly dragging the ground if anyone said anything to her. A mild suggestion of any kind, from "grab a jacket" to "don't do drugs" evoked eyes rolling into the back of her head as if she were having a grand mal seizure.

So the lemonade was the best gesture of kindness he could make. Besides offering to pick her up because her car was in the shop.

He pulled to the curb outside the school, fully aware he was the only car among the full-bodied SUVs idling alongside one another. It was a complete embarrassment to Jenna, who begged to have Kay pick her up in the Navigator. Some lessons were learned the hard way. But his car was perfectly fine, perfectly reliable, and it wasn't going to cause the ozone to collapse.

She got in, noticed the lemonade, asked if it was sugar-free, then sipped it and stared out the window for the rest of the ride home. It wasn't sugar-free, but the girl needed a little meat on her bones.

"Your car's ready."

Finally, a small smile.

* * *

"Have a seat."

Frank Merret shoved his holster and belt downward to make room for the roll of belly fat that had permanently attached itself to his midsection. He slowly sat down in the old vinyl chair across from Captain Lou Grayson's cluttered desk.

"You got a rookie coming in this morning."

"I thought we had an agreement about rookies."

"You ticketed Principal MaLue. We had an agreement about that too."

Frank sighed. "He was speeding in a school zone."

"He's the principal. If he wants to hit Mach speed in the school zone, so be it. The rookie's file is in your box." Grayson's irritated expression said the rest.

Frank left the captain's office and killed time in the break room until lineup, where the rookie stood next to him, fresh-faced and wide-eyed. He was short, kind of stocky, with white blond hair and baby pink cheeks like a von Trapp kid. There was not a hard-bitten bone in this kid's body.

Frank cut his gaze sideways. "This is Marlo. The most you can hope for is someone driving under the influence of pot."

Lineup was dismissed, and the kid followed him out. "That's not true. I heard about that bank robbery."

"That was twenty years ago."

"Doesn't matter," the rookie said. "I'm on patrol. That's cool. I'm Gavin Jenkins, by the way."

"Yeah, I know."

"Did you read my stats from the academy?"

"Not even one word."

Gavin stopped midstride, falling behind Frank as he made his way outside to the patrol car. Gavin hurried to catch up. "Where are we going? Aren't we a little early?"

Frank continued to his car. Gavin hopped into the passenger side. Frank turned west onto Bledsoe.

"Listen, Officer Merret, I just want you to know that I'm glad they paired me with you. I've heard great things about you, and I think it's—"

"I don't normally talk in the morning."

"Okay."

So they drove in silence mostly, checking on a few of the elderly citizens and their resident homeless man, Douglas, until lunchtime, when they stopped at Pizza Hut. The kid couldn't help but talk, so Frank let him and learned the entire history of how he came to be a Marlo police officer.

Gavin was two bites into his second piece and hadn't touched his salad when Frank rose. "Stay here."

Gavin stared at him, his cheek full of cheese and pepperoni. "What? Why?"

"I've got something I need to do."

Gavin stood, trying to gather his things. "Wait. I'll come."

Frank held out a firm hand. "Just stay here, okay? I'll come back to get you in about forty minutes."

Gavin slowly sat down.

Frank walked out. He knew it already. This rookie was going to be a thorn in his side.

2

A SOFT HAMMERING sound filtering through the ceiling meant Hunter was home, probably tinkering with something electronic. If he wasn't rebuilding a hard drive, he was writing software or designing software to write software.

Computers irritated Damien. They cheapened society, caused social unrest, not to mention contributed to the butchering of the English language and the rendering of grammar obsolete.

He had no love for technology and used it only when necessary. A cell phone hung off his belt, only to satisfy his wife. He refused to learn anything except how to answer it. Watching people text back and forth was like driving a stake through his heart. He'd once tried it, just for kicks, but it took ten minutes to type two sentences, and he refused to send something with a typo. Plus, the English language wasn't meant to be condensed into abbreviated substitutes, like *LOL*. He constantly told his children *LOL* meant "love of language." They never got that joke. Maybe it wasn't that funny to them. Or maybe the joke was on him.

He set his briefcase down, slid his blazer off, and went to the kitchen. It was his night to cook. Kay would be home at seven sharp. At least twice a week they made sure the entire family ate together, which so far hadn't paid the dividends the parenting magazine had promised.

But they'd been doing it for only eight years. Maybe he needed to give it more time.

Hunter stalked through the kitchen, his backpack hanging off his shoulder. "I'll be back."

"Dinner will be ready in a few—"

"I know. I know. It's family dinner night. I'll be back."

Damien sighed and turned to tend to the broccoli. The teen years were like a chasm—huge, black, swirling, sucking—a gulf that separated him from his kids. He missed them.

Jenna's cell phone conversation filtered down the stairs and into the kitchen. He could hear only snippets, but it sounded like high drama, which was one of only two moods she was capable of. The other was a blend of sneer, seethe, sulk, and snarl.

The timer indicated the rolls were done. Outside, the Navigator's purring engine sounded through the windows.

Soon the back door opened. Kay walked in, looking exhausted but happy to be home. She dropped her things and hugged him from behind. "Hi."

"Hi." He'd fallen for her the second they'd met. Tiny

dimples pulled through each of her cheeks. Her eyes shimmered like expensive jewelry. A short pixie haircut showed off her delicate features.

And she always smelled like fresh flowers.

Kay went to change, Jenna continued to sound overly frantic, and Hunter finally came back home, ten minutes after the lasagna was ready.

"Dinner is served," Damien called.

The kids took their sweet time getting there.

Kay didn't wait but filled her plate while saying, "Mike and Jill are getting a divorce."

"I thought they already were divorced."

"Separated. They filed this week."

"Oh. That's too bad."

"You know, Jill's really hard to get along with. I can't imagine being married to her."

"Well, they say it takes two to tango. Or tangle, whatever may be the case."

"I got to know Jill better a couple of weeks ago when we worked on that fund-raiser together. She's just so abrasive, but maybe I'll warm up to her."

"Maybe she's having a hard time with the div—"

Kay shushed him as the kids arrived at the table, whispering, "Natalie's in Jenna's grade."

Damien could only assume Natalie was Jill and Mike's daughter, but he wasn't sure. He didn't even know their last name. He actually didn't even know Jill and Mike at all, though Kay swore he'd met them before at school functions.

Damien got comfortable in his chair and served himself. Then he said to anyone who wanted to listen, "I'm going to talk to Edgar about my position at the paper."

Kay looked up. Hunter tossed a roll in the air and tried to catch it behind his back. Jenna stared at her broccoli.

"What for?" Kay asked.

"I've been writing the op-ed and issues column for five years now, and I'd like a change of pace."

"Like what? The comics?" Hunter twirled his knife between his fingers until Kay snapped at him.

Damien tried to smile and acknowledge that at least Hunter was participating in the conversation. "I thought I might like to be an investigative reporter. I'd still be dealing with issues, but I'd have a lot more facts to work with, and I could get out of the office more."

Kay set down her fork. "Why would you want to do that?"

"I don't know. I guess I'm getting a little bored."

"You always said what you did was important," Hunter said. "People's lives are changed by your column and what you have to say about things and all that. Words, words, words."

"Shut up," Jenna said. "He's a grown man; he can do what he wants."

Kay chewed her food, staring at him. "How can you be bored? We run 24-7. Most nights I don't even get to bed before midnight."

"It was just a thought. I'll still be doing the crosswords

of course. Couldn't give that up. But sometimes you need to shake things up a little, you know?"

Kay shrugged. "Ask Mike and Jill. I'm sure they'd rather be bored."

3

KAY WATCHED THE whites-only scramble she was making for her eldest child, Jenna, who had somehow converted from a lover of all things fried and fat to a near vegetarian. Except there was one problem with that—she really hated vegetables.

She fried up some turkey bacon, hoping her husband and son wouldn't complain too much. She thought it actually tasted pretty good.

Damien came into the kitchen, kissing her on the cheek. "Good morning."

"Morning." She smiled.

She served Hunter, who, with earbuds in, was busy playing his DS. He wasn't supposed to play it at the table, but enforcing the rules she once had in place for him at nine was getting harder at fourteen.

"You seem stressed," Damien said, sitting at the table.

Kay sighed. "Yeah . . . being a mom isn't what it used to be. I mean, you should see them."

"Who?"

"The high school moms. They're nipped and tucked and tan and skinny. It's ridiculous how much money they spend on themselves. Shameful, really."

"Kay . . ."

"I'm serious. It's like being in high school all over again, except I'm battling varicose veins instead of acne."

Damien took her hand. "You look beautiful. Classy."

"Maybe that's what I have on them. Class. I'm not showing up in a tank top, you know?"

Jenna bounded down the stairs, her backpack swung over one nearly bare shoulder. Kay's eyes widened as she noticed her outfit.

"Whites only?" was the only thing she asked as she threw herself into a chair.

"Yes." Kay put a double helping on the plate and added two slices of bacon. She set the plate in front of her daughter and then went to pour some orange juice.

Jenna ate in silence while Damien read the morning newspaper.

Kay sat down across from her. Jenna glanced up and asked, "What? Why are you staring?"

"I thought we talked about ripped jeans."

Jenna set her fork down and glared, folding her arms. "No. I think you did all the talking, as I recall."

"We agreed you weren't going to wear those kinds of

jeans to school. And if I'm not mistaken, I don't believe spaghetti-strap tanks are allowed either."

"Everybody wears them and nobody gets in trouble. Besides, these jeans are ripped only at the knee. So don't freak out."

Kay was about to retort when she noticed something on Jenna's wrist. It looked like white string. She remembered reading something about what these string bracelets meant. It was some sort of code for—

"I've got to go. We've got that cheer thing today," Jenna said.

Kay glanced at Jenna's eggs. Hardly touched. "All right. I'll see you there."

Jenna paused. "You're coming?"

"The cheer moms are supposed to be there, aren't we?"

"Yeah, I guess. Whatever." Jenna grabbed her backpack.

Kay stood. "Why don't you take a light sweater? or one of those cute hoodies I bought you last month? It's December and—"

"I've got something in my backpack," she mumbled. And she was gone.

Kay nodded toward the doorway. "You think she's okay?"

"I don't know. Probably just hormones."

"I miss her. I mean, the old her. She was so bright and sunshiny."

"She'll pop out of this."

"You should talk to her," Kay said, sitting back down

at the table. "About how she's dressing. She'll listen to you."

"Honey, she's a teenager. All parents hate how all teenagers dress. It's just the way it is. Didn't your parents hate your clothes?"

Kay sipped her coffee, trying to calm the nerve that struck. She wanted to explain that Jenna was giving off a lot of promiscuous signals with those kinds of clothes. And that string . . . she couldn't get her mind off it.

They both noticed Hunter had taken his earbuds out and was staring at them.

"Sweetie?" Kay asked.

"I'm not really hungry anymore. Can I go?"

"Sure. Go ahead. I'll see you tonight." She checked her watch. "I probably should go too. I need to stop by work before going to the school."

"Hey, I've got that thing with Frank tonight," Damien said, wiping his mouth and looking at the bacon like it had personally insulted him. "Is this real meat?"

"What thing?"

"That whole ritual we do. Yesterday was his ex-anniversary with Angela. You know how he gets."

"So you're ordering chicken wings and beer and watching something violent on TV?"

"Exactly."

She squeezed his hand. "Have fun."

"And, um . . . wish me luck. I'm going to talk to Edgar today."

Kay, halfway out of her seat, sat back down. "You're sure this is what you want? Because for years all you wanted to do was write op-eds and crosswords. Why the change of heart?"

"Maybe I always wanted to change the world. Or at least my little square mile of the world. Op-eds aren't what they used to be. People don't read a lot anymore. But maybe some investigative journalism could change people's lives. Hold people in power accountable."

Kay couldn't help but smile at him. He was a good man. Honorable. Always an optimist. "Whatever you want to do, sweetheart. You think Edgar will go for it?"

"I'll probably have to threaten an op-ed piece about him."

* * *

Damien actually put on a tie. Usually he just wore a blazer and a semipressed shirt to work. Dressing up was more about self-dignity than anything else. He'd once read about a novelist who got up and put a suit on before writing every day to put him in the right mind of a professional. So maybe the tie would help.

He let a couple of hours pass in the morning. Edgar was hardly tolerable before ten. But if you waited until too close to lunch, then his blood sugar dropped and you had a whole new set of problems.

So at 10:17, according to the digital clock that was set by satellite or nuclear power or something, Damien knocked on Edgar's door. The grunt meant "Enter."

Edgar glanced up from a pile of papers on his desk, a strained expression almost in permanency. Everything looked strained on Edgar, from his undersize sweater to his blood-shot eyes. But usually, when he saw Damien, all that seemed to melt away.

"You got a second?"

"I never have a second," Edgar glowered, but a hint of a smile gleamed in his eyes. "I'm going over the numbers. It's not good. People don't read. Why don't people read?" Then he held up the crossword from Thursday, half-finished in blue ink. "This one's a doozy. Some of these clues are ridiculous." He set the paper down. "Anyway, people don't read."

Damien ran his hand down the synthetic silk of his tie. "They do read. Blogs are a huge hit."

"That is a curse word around here. Nothing but someone's opinion. Hardly ever backed up by fact."

Damien smiled to himself. Edgar was already making his point for him. "So I wanted to talk to you about that very thing."

Edgar's face dropped. "Please tell me you're not going to start a blog. We have eight going already. Not to mention a bunch of people Tweetering, which honestly seems like the quickest way to lose testosterone, but that's just me."

"No, no. Not interested in all that. In fact, it's the opposite. I was hoping to do more investigative pieces."

Edgar blinked, that strange sleep apnea sound he made during waking hours the only noise in the room.

"So that's a yes?"

"It's your generation. Never happy with where you are. I've been a newspaperman all my life. Done nothing else."

Damien sat down. "That's admirable. You know how much I admire that. And you. But I think it's also healthy to venture out, not stay in the same place. I wouldn't ask if I didn't think I had something to contribute."

"But people like what you do. You're a popular column. Controversial. Thought-provoking. People write in about it all the time. Don't you read those?"

"Of course. And I'm glad to do what I do. But maybe it's time for a change. Like . . . like the clocks. Digital as of 2006, right? So now we're right on time with the universe. See? I'm going from analog to digital; that's all."

"That sort of nonsense might work in your op-ed pieces, but it won't work with me. What is it? You want a raise?"

"No. It's not about money."

Edgar scratched his double chin. "I don't know. Bruce runs the investigative pieces."

"He's a sportswriter. He just does that because we're trying to cover all the bases since you cut Jim's position. I could help Bruce cover some of that."

The leather office chair creaked as Edgar leaned back, staring first at Damien, then at the ceiling, and then at the clock. "It's not even noon yet. This is going to be a long day." He slapped both hands on his desk. "I don't want the op-eds to stop. That's your first job, and they better keep coming. If you want to throw in a few investigative pieces, we'll see how it goes."

Damien jumped up. "Thank you!"

"Bruce is not going to take this well."

"I'll handle Bruce. I'll talk to him right now. He'll be fine."

"Okay. Hey, you want to go grab a sub for lunch?"

"Sure. In about an hour?"

"Yeah, sounds good."

Damien raced out of the office and headed for Bruce's desk, which sat across the room from his.

Bruce looked up from his *Sports Illustrated*. "Hey, Damien. What's going on?"

Damien lowered his voice. "Edgar's going to let me do investigative pieces."

Bruce's magazine dropped to his lap. "What?"

"Yeah, I just talked to him. Figured he wouldn't go for it, but he said to go ahead, except I gotta keep doing the op-eds. So basically I'm doing twice the work for the same pay, but at least I'm not dying a slow death at my desk."

"So . . . you're doing the investigative pieces? Not me?"

"Kind of. He still wants you to—"

Bruce threw his magazine to the floor, jumped out of his seat, and tackled Damien, backing him up several feet before managing to wrap his arms around him and pick him off the floor a good two feet. "My man! My man! How did you manage that?"

"I'll tell you as soon as my feet are on the ground."

"Sorry." Bruce let go and Damien dropped straight down. "Dude, this is amazing!"

"I can't believe he went for it. But look, you're going to

have to play up some disappointment. The man was nervous, certain you'd be devastated."

"I only intimidate Edgar because I'm six foot three and can quote sports stats." Bruce high-fived him. "I owe you big-time. Let me know if you want tickets to the game or something."

"All right. See you later."

"Hey, Damien?"

"Yeah?"

"Frank okay?"

"Why?"

"It's his ex-anniversary, right?"

Damien smiled. "He'll be fine. I'm feeding him chicken wings tonight."

*　*　*

Kay put on another coat of light lipstick and got out of her Navigator. She tugged at her T-shirt, which must've shrunk in the wash.

Once inside, she checked into the office, then went to the gym, where the ladies were setting up the cheer moms table. "Hi. How can I help?"

Nobody bothered to look up. Nobody responded. All five women continued their conversation as if she wasn't there. Which wasn't unusual. It was like no one had ever taught them any social skills. She decided to start arranging the brownies on the platters.

"I wouldn't do them like that."

Kay looked up. Jill Toledo, dressed in a tight tank and a tighter miniskirt, stood above her, hands on her hips. "Do what?"

"I'd arrange them more stacked, so people will see them."

"They might get knocked over or off the plate." Kay tried to eyeball how many inches Jill's skirt was from her knee. Six, maybe? The woman looked ridiculous.

"I've been doing this a long time since I've had three daughters in cheer, and I'm telling you that if you don't stack the brownies, people will walk right on by. These are kids. They have no attention span."

"What about these balloons we've got tied here? That'll draw attention."

"Yeah. Right. Like this is fourth grade."

Kay glanced behind Jill at two of the other moms who were watching. She tried a smile, but they just stared. This was her first year as a cheer mom. She'd been against Jenna trying out for cheerleading, but Damien had convinced her Jenna was really good at it. She hated how pressured the girls were to wear those tight, belly-exposing uniforms. "All right. I'll stack the brownies. No problem."

Jill spun around. "Who has the change bag?"

"Nobody's picked it up," one lady said.

"Can't anybody do anything around here?" Jill threw her hands up. Fifteen bracelets clanked against each other. "I'll be back."

As Jill stomped away, Kay took in a deep breath. All this

drama over brownies? She began taking the brownies, which she'd laid in a perfectly acceptable circle, off the platter and started over.

"Don't worry about her." An attractive woman with a sleek ponytail and darkly lined eyes stood next to the table.

"Oh, um . . ."

"I've done cheer moms with her twice, and she's a total control freak. I'm Shannon Branson, by the way."

"Kay Underwood."

The blonde behind leaned in. "She's having an affair."

Shannon glanced at her. "Kelly, you're serious?"

"Totally serious. Susan told me."

Susan popped up from a box she was digging through. "Nobody really knows what's going on, except she's coming home at two in the morning. That's what her neighbor told me."

"How do you know her neighbor?" Kelly asked.

"We go to church together."

Kay tried a casual lean against the table. "All I know is she and Mike are getting a divorce."

Shannon's eyes widened. "No kidding."

"Yeah, um, she told me herself." Not exactly true. She'd heard something about it while eavesdropping on one of Jenna's phone conversations.

"Maybe that explains her mood," Kelly said, then looked at Kay, putting a hand over her arm. "Well, whatever. Don't mind her. She's a brat and always has been, which is probably why she's getting a divorce. Did she say anything else about it?"

Susan said, "The day we were making the posters, I went to the bathroom and she was on her cell phone in there, really upset and crying."

Kelly roared with laughter. "I see where Natalie gets her drama-queen genes. According to my Madison, Natalie cries at the drop of a hat." She checked her watch. "The kids will be here in about fifteen. Kay, you want to come with me, grab some Starbucks for us?"

"Yeah, we'll definitely need Starbucks," Susan said. "You'll be our lifesaver and forever friend!"

Kay smiled. "Sure, I'll go with you." As they walked off, Kay grinned and looked over her shoulder. "But, Susan, whatever you do, stack those brownies."

The women howled.

4

FRANK DEVOURED FOURTEEN chicken wings before he spoke a word to Damien, who never kept up, though he tried hard. The problem with Damien was his aversion to gristle, which slowed him down considerably.

Frank downed another bottle of beer and turned the sound up on the television, which had picture-in-picture going so they could watch the ESPN highlight show and the NFL game.

Damien popped open another can of Mountain Dew. "So, how'd it go?" he asked, wiping his mouth and reaching for a few more wings.

"Okay."

"Okay?" Damien leaned forward. "That's different."

"It's a hard day for me, but I made it through."

"That's good, right?"

"That's good. Maybe it's getting easier."

"It probably helped that you didn't look through your old photo albums."

"Yeah. Thanks for taking those."

"Have another chicken wing."

"My tongue is on fire," Frank said. "Just the way I like it. You know, the first sign that Angela and I might not make it was the day I ordered chicken wings to surprise her for our anniversary."

"A good woman loves chicken wings."

"I know, and I totally thought she was that kind of woman. I really did. I mean, she smokes cigars sometimes. How can she hate chicken wings?"

"I don't know, dude. Women are hard to figure out. Kay's going through some sort of high school crisis with the cheer-leading mothers. And she's got a weird aversion to anything Jenna wears that doesn't look like she stepped off an Amish buggy. I don't get women, even my own."

"You're lucky to have 'em."

"There are other women out there, looking for some-one as loyal as you. In fact, there's a woman at the office who—"

Frank held out a saucy hand. "Don't want to hear it."

"All right, fine. I tried."

"It's practically part of our yearly tradition now."

"Speaking of traditions, let's get War started."

Frank hopped up. "Hold on. I gotta show you something. Follow me." He led Damien downstairs to the basement, where his computer was.

"Aw, man. No, no. Let's not do this tonight. I was in such a good mood," Damien moaned.

"It's not what you think."

"That's what you always say, and then the next thing I know, you're showing me how to install a webcam or a wireless device. And although I appreciate the coolness of GPS, I just don't want it."

Frank sighed. "How do you even live in this world? Honestly. It's not like you have to program anything. I think you must be still scarred from the early days of the VCR. Computers are easy to use."

"You're not going to be saying that when they take over the world and start hunting us for food."

"Funny. If that happens, they're going after you first because you don't even know how to turn one off."

"Now you're being mean."

Frank laughed. "You'd score huge points with Hunter if you showed him you were at least open to the idea of computers."

"Computers are doing nothing but dumbing down our society."

"Well, at least you're keeping the resource department open at the library."

"You should darken the door of a library once in a while. You might like it."

"Yes. The Dewey decimal system is infinitely fascinating. Pull up a chair."

Damien sighed as Frank yanked the string on the lightbulb.

"I promise I'm not going to try to sell you on anything. But I found this on the Web and thought it was interesting."

"Of course the Antichrist is interesting. That's what makes so many people fall for him."

Frank rolled his eyes. "No matter how many ways you spin it, *www* does not add up to 666. Now, stop fearing Armageddon and check this out."

Damien leaned in. "What is it?"

"It's called a Web site."

Damien cut him a look.

"Just read it for a second."

Damien moved in closer and silently read for a minute or so. "Okay, not really getting it. Is this a blog? Because it seems like endless nonsense."

"I'm not sure what it is," Frank said. His tone seemed a little more subdued. "It appears to be people's conversations. They're typed out, like transcribed or something."

"What people?"

"That's the question. But look at the top of the page. It's a warning to our town. It specifically says Marlo."

Damien squinted. "I've got to get glasses. What is that type, eight point?"

I have listened to you for a long time now, Marlo. Longer than I should. I have tried not to listen, to tell you the truth. I've covered my ears, but your words are like flaming arrows. They pierce through anything, including, maybe, my good judgment.

I have hoped for more from you. I have given you the benefit of the doubt. I have stood near you and watched your faces, hoping to see light. Goodness. Anything.

But there are only words. So many. Too many. Or maybe not enough. I'm not sure. All I know is that they hang over all of you like the eye of the storm. It seems peaceful, doesn't it? Like blue skies and calm winds?

The storm is coming, and it will sweep you away. The destruction will not end. Even when you call for help, it will not come. Because you have not listened.

My words are finished here. I will not speak again.

From this day forward, all you will hear are your words.

Life and death are in the power of the tongue.

www.listentoyourself.net

"It seems like somebody in Marlo is going around randomly recording conversations and then posting them to this Web site." Frank looked at Damien as if waiting for him to say something.

"Terrific. I'm going to eat more wings."

"Wait." Frank grabbed his arm. "Seriously, this is weird."

"There is no normal on the Web. It's where every freak in the world is celebrated."

"Look, I know you hate the Web. But don't you think

this is strange? I mean, posting people's personal conversations? Sometimes there are five or six posts a day, and it's just conversation after conversation."

"Which was exactly what I was hoping for tonight. Mountain Dew and good conversation with my lifelong friend, Frank, who continues to faithfully mourn his ex-wife every year on their ex-anniversary and then celebrate, with his best friend and a bucket full of wings, the fact that he's still rolling along." Damien turned. "So let's go."

Frank sighed and followed him upstairs. "You're in kind of a bad mood, aren't you? I'm the one supposed to be sulking."

"I'm actually in a good mood," Damien said, returning to the couch. "I got promoted to investigative reporter."

Frank stopped, his hand halfway to the bucket of wings. "You're kidding."

"Why would I be kidding?"

"Because you love your opinion and you love writing about your opinion."

"I know. And I'll still be doing that. But I thought maybe trying something new would put some life back into my work. It's not quite as exciting as yours. I don't get to hang out in school zones and wait for the principal."

"You heard about that."

"Surprisingly, news also travels the old-fashioned way these days. It's called gossip."

Frank grinned. "It was a fine moment."

"I wish I could've seen the look on his face."

"Back to your big news. So what does this mean? A big raise?"

"Actually it's twice the amount of work for the same pay."

Frank groaned. "That's just like you, to get excited about something like that."

"Words excite me. What can I say?"

Frank's mood dampened. "Maybe I'm not as fond of words as you are."

"Yes, well, words on the Internet are substandard words, Frank. They're like the ugly stepchildren of all things literary."

"Just shut up and take a chicken wing before I threaten to destroy all your eight-tracks."

* * *

Damien arrived home to a quiet house, but he knew Hunter was upstairs by the glow of his bedroom light from outside. He dropped his things and pushed the answering machine button. They had to buy an answering machine because Damien refused to get the voice mail off the phone.

"Hey, it's me. Jenna and I are still at the game. Went into overtime. Not sure when we'll be home. Hope you had fun at Frank's."

The iron wall clock in the living room said fifteen minutes after ten. He climbed the stairs and tapped on Hunter's bedroom door before swinging it open.

"Dad!" Hunter shot up, hit his leg against his desk,

toppled the chair over, and tumbled to the floor. "What are you—?" From the floor, he reached up to his computer and clicked the mouse.

Damien froze, his legs spread wide, one hand on the doorknob and the other raised like something dangerous might be flying his direction. But no, all the excitement erupted from a speedy entrance into his son's bedroom. Which caused Damien to instantly think the worst.

It was probably showing on his face by the way Hunter suddenly grinned wildly. "Sorry. You just scared me to death."

"Oh? How would I do that?"

"I wasn't expecting you; that's all. I was . . . uh . . . concentrating on something here."

"What?"

"Some math stuff. There's a . . . uh . . . Web site that we can get on for math help."

"Need some help right now? I'd be happy to—"

"No thanks. I got it figured out. I was just going to bed." Hunter pulled off his socks and hopped onto his bed, fully clothed. "So, good night."

A sudden sorrow swept over Damien. It was unexpected and frightening, as if his son were miles away and he couldn't reach him. He and Kay had discussed not allowing Hunter his own computer in his room, but Kay had argued that they should trust him. Plus, the kid's life revolved around computers and technology. Damien figured Hunter would probably make a great living at it someday.

If he didn't turn out to be a reprobate. Damien whimpered as the word crossed his mind. How could he even think that? He glanced at Hunter, who stared at him from his bed all the way across the room. Maybe he was being too hard on the kid. After all, he didn't have cold, hard facts. If he was going to be an investigative reporter, he needed to have the facts.

He slowly let go of the death grip he had on the doorknob and smiled, about three and a half minutes too late. Now he just looked awkward or intoxicated. But a determination set in. No, he was not going to let Hunter fade away into the screen-saver sunset. He and his son had always been close. He took a few steps into the room.

"Need something?" Hunter asked, clutching his pillow against him.

"No. Just wanted to say hi. Hadn't seen you all day. Guess your mom told you I'd be over at Frank's."

"I know. It's Frank's ex-anniversary, right?"

"Yeah. Had some chicken wings and stuff."

"Cool. Chicken wings are good."

"Yeah."

Silence again.

Then, like a magnet pulling his face, Damien turned his head to the right to glance at the computer. Now he looked like a snoop! But shouldn't he be snooping? Shouldn't he be wondering? He had to save face quickly. "Hey, Frank showed me something interesting tonight. Can I borrow your computer?" He sat down in front of Hunter's computer.

Hunter swung his legs around and his feet hit the floor. "Show me something on the computer?"

"Yeah. Believe it or not, I do know how to use one of these things. I just need you to get me on the Internet."

Hunter walked over, took the mouse, clicked on something, and up popped a picture.

"Is this where I type in the World Wide Web thing?"

"The address. Yes."

Damien's hunt-and-peck method drove his son crazy, but he managed to get it all typed in and push Enter.

"What are you doing?" Hunter asked.

"Someone has started a Web site about our town. It's kind of weird. They're posting conversations. Only conversations. Frank says it's not a blog. Take a look."

Hunter leaned over Damien's shoulder, then said, "Yeah. Okay. Cool."

Damien spun in his chair, trying to act enthusiastic. "What do you think about it?"

Hunter shrugged. "I don't know."

"I don't know either. It's a little strange. Why would someone want to post conversation after conversation? Is that something new? Like a clog?"

"Clog?"

"Conversation log." Damien laughed. "Sorry. Just being funny." He spun back around to look at the computer. "Anyway, I just thought you might find it interesting. But maybe not. It's probably pretty boring to you. But you know me . . ."

"You love words."

"I love words. Words are important. Words—"

"I know, Dad. Connect us." Hunter stood next to him, looking at the screen. "Somebody has too much time on their hands. But maybe there's a point to it."

"Maybe." Damien stood and pushed the chair against the desk. They were connecting here. This was good. "I got the investigative reporter job today, so I'm probably going to have to start using a computer more for research and things like that. I was wondering if maybe you could show me a few things this weekend, like how to do research using search engines."

"Sure. No problem."

Damien grabbed Hunter's shoulder and pulled him into a quick hug, then went to the door. "You know you can always come talk to me. About anything. You know that, right?"

Hunter nodded.

"And that I'm always proud of you. You're a good kid, and I'm amazed at how much you know about computers. I know you're going to go places."

Hunter's dull eyes of late brightened a little. "I kinda want to do what you do."

"What I do?"

"Yeah. I think it's cool how you write stuff and people respond and how you can change people's minds and make people think about things. Like that."

Damien couldn't stop the smile on his face if he wanted to. "Really? I had no idea you even thought about it."

"Not all the time, Dad. Just sometimes. Don't get carried away."

Damien grinned. "Good night, Son."

Damien quietly shut the door and glanced down the hallway. Kay was coming up the stairs and going into their bedroom. Damien followed her in.

"There you are!" she said. "I was looking for you."

"Just chatting with Hunter."

"Oh. Everything okay?"

"Why do you ask that?"

"Usually you two talk if there's something wrong."

This probably wasn't the time to mention their son might be looking at porn, especially after that little bonding moment they had back there. Maybe if he spent more time with Hunter on the computer, Hunter would have less time to dwell on other things. "How was the game?"

"The other moms were really nice to me."

Damien paused. "I meant, did we win?"

"Yeah, yeah. We won. But I'm telling you, Jill has mental problems."

"The one getting a divorce?"

"She's very up-and-down with her emotions and very insecure. She actually confronted me and asked if I'd gotten someone else to keep track of the money after I'd already asked her. I'd simply said . . . Oh, never mind. It's a long story. You wouldn't understand. The point is, she's a real pain to be around. We're going to see if we can figure out how to get her uninvolved."

"We?"

"And she can't seem to dress her age. The miniskirts are outrageous." Kay disappeared into the closet and emerged with a blouse. She held it up to herself in the mirror. "What do you think?"

"Looks good."

Kay turned to him. "Wouldn't it embarrass you if I wore a tank top and a miniskirt?"

Damien smirked. "Embarrass? Not sure that would be my first reaction." He winked and tried to pull her close.

She batted him away. "I'm being serious."

Damien didn't say so, but he thought it was strange she was thinking so much about what people were wearing. Usually she just reserved that for their daughter. "Jenna home?"

"No. Told her she could go out with some of her friends for a little while."

"It's a school night."

"I know. I know. But she's been so depressed and moody, it's hard for me to say no to things she wants to do. I told her to be home in forty-five minutes. She'll live. Plus, I know these moms. They're normal. They have the audacity to wear pants, for heaven's sake."

"All right. But I don't want this to become a habit. We haven't spent sixteen years enforcing rules so she can pout her way out of them."

"I totally agree. It's just that these girls make good grades, and I think they'd be a good influence on Jenna."

Damien wasn't sure what there was to influence. Jenna

had always been a good kid and still was. Sure, she'd been moody, but she was a teenager.

Damien tickled her ribs. "Okay, so let's talk again about that tank top and miniskirt you're going to be wearing."

Kay shot him a hard look. "I wouldn't be caught dead wearing that."

5

"YOU'RE COMING ONTO the force at a good time," Frank said as they walked into the only Starbucks in town.

"Why is that, sir?" Gavin asked.

"Used to, it was only free coffee at 7-Eleven. Now we get the mochas. When I first started, police were treated even better. Free breakfasts if you'd been on all night. Lots of different perks. But that kind of faded until we were left with free 7-Eleven coffee and discount day-old donuts. That is, until Starbucks arrived." Frank leaned on the counter. "Yeah, I'll take a grande macchiato, upside-down, double caramel, whipped cream. Two of 'em."

"But I don't really like coffee."

Frank eyed him. "I'm already suspicious of you, kid. Don't tell me you're an abstainer."

"An abstainer?"

"Are you?"

"I, uh . . . I don't even know what that means."

"You eat organic?"

"No."

"You eat meat?"

"Yes."

"All right, fine," Frank said. "But you better start liking this stuff. It'll be your lifeline some days."

"It can't be that boring. I mean, a police officer's job is to—"

"Frank Merret?"

Frank turned to find Patti Gable, one of Angela's old college friends, standing in line behind him. "Hi, Patti. Good to see you." He looked at Gavin. "Why don't you go see if our coffees are ready."

Gavin left and Frank looked at Patti. "How's Dale doing?"

"Fine. And the kids are doing great too."

"Good to hear."

"I'm glad I ran into you. Have you talked to Angela lately?"

"Why?"

"I've been leaving her messages. She won't return my calls. That's not like her."

Gavin returned with the coffees.

Frank said, "I'm sure she's fine, Patti. Maybe busy?"

Patti nodded. "Yeah, sure. We all get crazy busy sometimes, don't we? Well, if you see her, tell her I wanted to talk to her about a Tri Delta reunion."

"Will do."

Frank and Gavin walked out of the coffee shop and got into the car. Frank headed north. "What do you think?" He glanced at Gavin.

"I , uh, well . . . very nice-looking for an older woman."

"About the *coffee*."

"Oh. I don't really taste any coffee. It tastes like whipped cream."

"Keep drinking." Frank turned west on Forty-eighth Street. He was force-feeding a rookie coffee. That was funny.

"Where are we going?"

"Just taking the long way."

"Why? Don't we have to be—?"

"Taste the coffee yet?" He glanced at Gavin, who was dutifully sipping, taking breaks only to let the steam escape from the small hole in the lid.

"Yes. I think so."

"What do you think?"

"Good."

"Good? Come on. Use some intelligent words, Jenkins."

Gavin held the cup to his mouth. He seemed to be thinking hard. "Robust and um . . . hearty?"

Frank turned into the First Bank parking lot and pulled to the curb. "See? There's a real difference in quality. Sure, you can get forty-eight ounces of coffee at 7-Eleven, but does it taste like that?"

"I don't . . ." Gavin glanced out the window. "What are we doing?"

Frank checked his watch. "Something's wrong."

Gavin's back went erect, and for a moment he seemed unsure what to do with his coffee. His free hand slid over his holster. "Is it the homeless guy?"

"She's late."

"Who?"

"Angela."

"Who's Angela?"

"Just shut up for a second. You talk too much." Frank pulled out his cell phone and checked the time against his watch and his dashboard clock. The small parking lot in front of the bank was half-full. He scanned it again, hoping maybe he'd just accidentally missed her PT Cruiser. "Why isn't she here?"

Gavin bit his lip, then sipped his coffee, looking out each window.

"This isn't good. Something's wrong."

"Sir, what's going on?"

"Come on. We have to check on her. She's always on time. Always."

"Maybe she's sick."

"She doesn't get sick."

Suddenly the radio crackled to life. "Unit 8. Do you copy?"

"Copy."

"We've got a situation. It's a signal 7."

"Whoa!" Gavin shouted. "That's the code for dead body."

Frank grabbed the radio. "Repeat. Did you say signal 7?"

"Well," the dispatcher's voice said in a softer tone, "we don't really have a code for a feline death."

Frank and Gavin exchanged glances. "An animal? A cat?"

"The address is 1559 Greenway. The woman is hysterical."

"We're on our way." Frank pulled out and looked back one more time to see if Angela's car had arrived.

*   *   *

"What's going on?" Kay said as Damien came alongside her in the long hallway of the high school. Her heels clicked furiously against the waxed and buffed linoleum, echoing off the long line of metal lockers.

"I don't know. I got the same call you did."

"She has never gotten in trouble at school! Not once!"

"Let's not jump to conclusions. Maybe it's not as bad as we think. We need to hear what's going on first."

Kay felt her face flush. "I hate when you're calm like this. It drives me insane. Whatever it is, it's not good. They don't call both parents to the school to pat us on the back." She lowered her voice. "It's probably that stupid outfit she had on this morning. They do have a dress code here, you know."

Kay swung open the door to the school office. A large desk divided the room. Two secretaries, who didn't look like they wanted to be bothered, sat behind the desk. Behind them, a long, semidark hallway led to Mr. MaLue's office. Some potent vanilla candle mixed poorly with the pungent smell of the cafeteria.

Kay straightened her suit and combed her fingers through her hair. Her hand slid over her ear as she said, "Yes, hi, we're here to see—"

"Yes, I know," the woman with a bun on top of her head said. "Go on back."

Kay grabbed Damien's hand. The vibe in the office wasn't good.

Damien wrapped both hands over hers and whispered, "Don't panic. It'll be fine."

The door stood open to Vincent MaLue's office. Kay had never been in it before. It was large, with plenty of bookshelves, a window, and framed prints of the ocean. The sea foam–colored walls made Kay feel sick to her stomach.

Mr. MaLue stood, towering over them in such a way that a long shadow was cast right between them. Kay guessed he was well over six feet. His legs looked like small rods under his black pants. A plain tie hung from his skinny neck, and a suit jacket was thrown over one side of his leather chair. She'd only seen him from a distance at school functions. This was the man Frank wanted to kill for taking his wife, and then the relationship only lasted eleven months. Kay couldn't imagine what Angela had seen in Vincent MaLue. But she had to push those thoughts out of her mind now.

"Mr. and Mrs. Underwood, please have a seat." His hand stroked his tie as he sat down behind an overly organized desk. "Thank you for coming."

"We're very worried," Kay said, hating herself for showing her hand, but she couldn't take it. She pulled out a pad and a pencil.

"Don't be alarmed," the principal said with a small smile that did nothing to reassure Kay. "Jenna is not hurt."

"Hurt?" Kay gasped. "What are you talking about?"

"There was a fight."

Kay wrote that down only to buy time, holding back the tears.

Damien's calm demeanor was fading as he leaned forward. "A fight? What happened?"

"Jenna hit another girl in the hallway this morning."

Jenna? Kay didn't even know Jenna knew how to hit. She accidentally snapped the eraser off the end of the pencil with her thumb. "Our daughter has never been in trouble before. I'm having a hard time believing—"

"There were several witnesses who all saw the same thing. Jenna hit this girl."

"Is the girl okay?" Damien asked, and Kay put a hand on his knee. It was a good, appropriate, sensitive question, one that Kay would never think to ask.

"Bloody nose, but that's about it. Nothing broken. But we did call her parents."

"Where's Jenna?" Kay asked.

"She's in detention hall right now. But she'll be suspended for the rest of the day."

Kay began to tremble. "Jenna is a great student. You know that. She has never been in trouble. Honors student. We are very normal people. Abnormally normal. Don't you think this is out of character for her?"

"Not lately."

"What does that mean?" Damien asked.

"Jenna isn't the same person I knew when she came to this school. I realize kids change, but Jenna, especially this year, seems particularly angry. Is everything okay at home?"

Kay leaned back into her chair. "At home?"

"Any problems? Marital, perhaps? Something else?"

Kay and Damien both shook their heads. "Nothing," Damien said. "We have noticed that she has been out of sorts, but we just assumed it was the teen phase."

"Maybe it is. It's hard to tell. You might want to have Jenna see the school counselor when she returns."

"But we're normal people," Kay said, scribbling the word *normal* on her little pad.

"Mr. MaLue," Damien implored, "please reconsider suspending her. This is the first time she has ever been in trouble."

"Which is why she is suspended for the day, not the week. We have a no-tolerance rule for violence. I'm sorry. And you might want to express to Jenna that next time she'll be suspended for the entire semester." He stood, causing Kay to shoot out of her seat for no particular reason except perhaps to not look like she was falling behind in etiquette. "Right this way."

They followed Mr. MaLue down a hallway and then left to another hallway. Kay studied the walls as they passed.

Bright, neon posters hung every few feet, announcing bake sales and contests and student leadership conferences. It all seemed so innocent—what school was supposed to be.

"In here." Mr. MaLue opened the door and gestured for them to enter.

Kay rushed in, nearly knocking Damien over. Jenna sat at a desk in the back of the room, completely alone, staring out a window that faced the back side of another building. At the sound of the door opening, she turned her head. Her expression didn't change. She picked up her backpack, slung it over her shoulder, and walked toward them.

"Jenna," Kay said, "first, you owe Mr. MaLue an apology. Then you have some explaining—"

"Sorry," she said and walked right past them and into the hallway, disappearing around a corner.

Kay shook her head, giving Mr. MaLue an apologetic glance. "You will be getting that apology in written form."

"Have a nice day," the principal said and walked the other direction.

Kay hurried to catch up with Jenna, which wasn't until she reached the front door of the high school, where Jenna was already hurrying down the steps.

"Young lady, wait! Right now!"

But Jenna didn't wait. Instead she kept her pace and went straight to Damien's car. But it was locked.

Kay, nearly out of breath, stopped short of plowing into her. "What is the matter with you?"

Jenna stared through the window of the car.

Kay grabbed her arm. "Jenna! Talk to me!"

"Talk to you? Really, Mom? Talk to you? Give me a break." Jenna yanked her arm away. "Unlock the stupid car!"

"No!" Kay clutched her purse. "Not until you tell me what's going on."

"I got mad. I hit a girl. Clear enough?"

"No. I want to know why you would hit someone. That's a very irrational, irresponsible thing to do. You've never been violent. We're nonviolent people."

Damien hurried around Kay, stepping between them. "Maybe we should finish this at home."

"I can't go home! I have to show a house in—" Kay looked at her watch. "I'm late!"

Damien put a hand on each of them. "Okay, let's calm down. Kay, I can take Jenna. She can come to work with me."

"To work with you?" Jenna moaned. "Just kill me right now, would you?"

Damien smiled at Kay. "You owe me one."

Kay couldn't smile or think anything else except that her world had suddenly fallen apart. Her baby girl, the sweetest she ever knew, had hit someone. On purpose. Kay took a tissue out of her purse and pressed it against her eyes. She watched Jenna get into Damien's car. She could only stare at that stupid white string bracelet she kept wearing. Had someone called her a name? insinuated she was . . . loose?

Kay hurried to her SUV. She started it and peeled out, the frustration of the day coming to a head.

Then, like a slow-motion dream, someone stepped in front

of her SUV. Two people. Kay slammed on the brakes, her tires squealing like a frightened pig. Her body lunged forward and then snapped back as her seat belt locked. Instinctively she held out her hand to the passenger's empty seat.

"Watch out!" a woman yelled.

Kay had missed them by ten feet or more, but it was still a close call. She tried to catch her breath as she watched the woman and her teenage daughter cross. The woman had a protective arm around the girl. As Kay leaned forward for a better look, she realized the girl was holding . . . her nose. A bloodstained rag poked out from her hand. Kay slid down in her seat. Should she say something? apologize? do nothing?

The girl, a brunette with a glittery headband on, was crying and shaking her head. Her mother was rubbing her back as she assisted her along the pavement. That was the girl? Kay had pictured the other girl being Goth or something.

They finally made it across and Kay inched forward, daring to look one more time. They seemed so . . . normal.

* * *

A crowd had gathered on the front lawn of the home when Frank and Gavin arrived. Frank got out and immediately saw the cat, black as night, swaying from a limb in the slight breeze, a stark white rope around its neck.

He wanted to turn away, but he couldn't. He hadn't expected this. The dispatcher said nothing about the cat hanging from a tree.

"What do we do?" Gavin said, suddenly beside him.

Frank tore his eyes away from the cat. "Where are the home owners?" he said loudly, above the noise of the crowd.

"Over there!" someone shouted.

Frank saw a couple standing on the porch, holding each other.

They met Frank in the driveway. "I'm Reverend Ted Caldwell. This is my wife, Beth."

"Is this your cat?" Frank asked, his back to the tree.

"Yes, it is," Reverend Caldwell said, glancing at it. "His name is Riddle."

"When did you discover the cat?" Frank asked.

"We know he wasn't there this morning."

Gavin took out his pad, started writing notes.

"Our daughter left for school, and we surely would've noticed him."

"When did you notice him?" Frank asked.

"Maybe around nine thirty," Mrs. Caldwell said. Tears dripped down her face. "I was leaving for the grocery store."

"Jenkins, go ahead and cut the cat down." Frank didn't want the freaks to start showing up, though there were plenty of people gawking already, with their cell phone cameras out. "There are some tools in the trunk." He grabbed Gavin's arm and said quietly, "Don't let it drop to the ground. Do it carefully, considerately. Do you understand me?"

Gavin's eyes widened. "Yes."

"And make sure it's really dead."

"Don't you need to keep it there . . . for evidence?" the wife asked.

"No, ma'am. We don't do crime scene investigations on animal cruelty cases, but we do take them very seriously." Frank pulled out his own notepad. "You didn't see anybody?"

"No, sir," the reverend answered. "Nothing unusual."

"You're a pastor. Of what church?"

"Redeemer's."

Frank asked all the standard questions, his voice calm and collected, but inside an uneasiness started to set in. Marlo was not the kind of town where you found cats hung in trees. He was having a hard time focusing on the Caldwells. "Can you think of anyone who would want to do this to you?"

"Actually, yes." Mrs. Caldwell glanced at her husband, then back at Frank.

Frank raised an eyebrow, his attention on the reverend, who suddenly looked uncomfortable. "Really? Someone has a grudge against you?"

"*Grudge* might be too hard of a word," he said. "We just recently learned this."

"Who is it?"

"His name is Tim Shaw. He's a deacon at our church," Beth Caldwell said.

"What is the nature of the disagreement?"

"Church, apparently," Reverend Caldwell said.

"You're not sure?"

"Not exactly."

"Has Mr. Shaw confronted you?"

"No. Not directly."

"How do you know he's angry with you?"

The reverend glanced at his wife, who gave a small nod. "Well, um . . . there's this Web site. It's . . . I don't know really what it is. But it's got conversations on it from our town. One of them is Tim talking about me."

Frank quickly jotted down notes. A slight stirring of the crowd and a timid scream caused them all to look toward the tree. Gavin hung from a limb, sawing the rope. It snapped and the cat fell to the ground. A poof of dust rose up around it.

Frank turned and marched toward Gavin, clutching his pencil like a weapon. Gavin was climbing down the tree. Frank grabbed him by the shoulder and yanked him off.

He fell to the ground and jumped up, looking angry and scared. "What?"

"I told you not to let that cat drop!" Frank yelled.

Gavin breathed hard. "I tried. Honest. But I couldn't hold on to the limb, cut, and hold the cat. I would've fallen out."

Heat flushed through Frank's face. "Give me your coat."

"What?"

"Your coat!"

Gavin took it off and handed it over.

Frank turned to the cat and crouched, searching carefully for any signs of breathing. He put two fingers to the small of its neck, then stood and laid the coat over the cat. And glared at Gavin. "You better learn to follow orders, son." He walked back to the Caldwells, trying to compose himself.

Mrs. Caldwell looked away from where the cat lay, shaking her head. "How are we going to tell Gabriella?"

"Where might I find Mr. Shaw?" Frank asked.

Mrs. Caldwell pointed through the crowd. "That's him. Standing on his lawn across the street."

The reverend grabbed Frank's arm. "But I know this man. He wouldn't kill my cat."

Mrs. Caldwell glared distantly. "Yeah, well, we all thought we knew Tim. Until we heard what he was capable of saying about you."

6

DAMIEN DROVE TOWARD his work, glancing at Jenna every few seconds, trying to figure out what to say. She only leaned against her window, gazing out, seemingly not even there. "Do you want to tell me what happened?"

"No."

"This is unlike you. You're not one of those kids."

"And what kind of kid would that be?"

"A kid that hits other kids. You were a pincher in pre-school, but you got over that phase." Damien smiled, but Jenna didn't. "Look, why don't you just explain it. I want to hear your side of the story."

"It won't change anything. I'm suspended. Probably grounded." She looked at Damien.

"Well, um, yes. Of course. But still, you need to tell me what happened."

A long, strong sigh escaped from Jenna, and she finally sat

up. "It goes down like this. A girl was being mean. To another girl. So I hit her."

Damien didn't react. He wanted to listen, hear her out. "Okay."

"That's it."

"That's it?"

"This isn't some epic tale."

Damien took a deep breath, trying not to lose his patience.

Jenna turned the radio on, switching the channel to some horrid sound called alternative rock.

Damien pushed it off. "I don't think so. I don't know what's going on with you and your attitude, but it's not acceptable."

"You want to give me some speech about the power of words, Daddy? Something about how I should've tried to use my words? You know what? Sometimes words are the problem. And sometimes they can't fix things."

Damien nodded, alarmed at her tone, but glad she was at least talking. "Okay. I understand that."

"No, you really don't."

"Then help me understand."

"Just ground me. And let's leave it at that."

"Fine. You're grounded."

"From what?"

"You pick, since you want to go this thing alone."

Jenna's scowl couldn't hide the surprise. She attempted a halfhearted shrug. "Whatever. Fine. The Internet."

"Perfect. One week."

"Thank you," she mumbled.

* * *

Frank told the Caldwells to go inside and wait there. He backed the crowd away to give them their space. Gavin was calling animal control and covering the cat with a sheet so he could take his coat back. Frank turned to cross the street.

Tim Shaw stood still, watching the scene.

A nearby man approached Frank before he got to the other side of the street. "I have some information."

"About the cat?"

"Yeah."

"What is it?"

"I work at Al's Hardware Store. Tim's a frequent customer."

"Uh-huh."

"Well, he was in the other day. And he paid with cash."

"He paid for what in cash?"

"His items."

"You're saying he bought a rope?"

"No. He didn't buy a rope. He bought some weed killer. But he paid in cash. He pays for a lot of things in cash. You know, maybe trying to cover something up."

Frank glanced at Mr. Shaw, who was still standing there, looking worried. "All right. Thank you." He started to walk off.

"It's just, you know, there was a conversation."

"On the Web site."

"Yeah. Something about getting even."

"How do you know it was Mr. Shaw talking about Reverend Caldwell?"

The guy shrugged and pointed to the tree. "The cat kind of says it all, doesn't it?"

Frank continued across the street. As he neared Mr. Shaw, the man looked more and more alarmed. "You're Tim Shaw?"

"Yes."

"Let's talk inside."

He led Frank inside the house. A woman, presumably his wife, stood near the large front window, like she'd been peeking out the country blue curtains. She walked across the country blue carpet and stopped by the country blue couch. A collection of rooster images, from framed prints to metal-and-wire cutouts, hung on a far wall.

"I'm Officer Merret."

"Darla." She gave a limp handshake and sat down. "What's going on?"

"You don't know?" Frank asked.

"We went over this morning when we heard all the commotion, and Beth yelled at us to get off their lawn," Tim explained. "I'm not sure why they're so upset with us. We're friends."

Frank sat down in a dark blue recliner. Through the kitchen he saw two poodles anxiously panting at the door. "You're aware their cat was hung—" he cleared his throat— "from a tree."

"Yes," Darla said, squeezed close to her husband on the couch. "That's awful."

"Did you have anything to do with it?"

Darla's mouth dropped open, and Tim's eyes widened. "They think we hung their cat?"

"That's what they said." Frank gave them a moment to process it, closely reading their reaction.

"Why would they think that?" Tim said, anguish in his voice. "I'm the head deacon at their church. We've known Ted and Beth for years."

Frank wasn't sure how to broach the next subject. He took his time figuring out how to say it right. "Okay, look; they mentioned a Web site. Are you aware of it?"

"A Web site? What Web site?"

"It's called Listen to Yourself."

"Never heard of it," Darla said and looked at her husband. "Have you?"

"No. What is it?" Tim asked Frank.

"I'm not sure. I only recently discovered it myself. A fellow officer told me about it. Apparently someone is going around town recording conversations and posting them on the Internet."

Tim and Darla stared at each other, then at Frank. This wasn't sinking in.

"According to the Caldwells, there is a conversation on there—you're talking about them. I don't know the specifics because I haven't seen the actual conversation. But whatever it was, they've concluded that you're angry with them."

As if guilt had cloaked Darla, everything about her changed, from her expression to her posture. She turned to Tim, who still didn't seem to follow.

Tim asked, "What do you mean, our conversation?"

"Like I said, I don't know that. But this Web site is called Listen to Yourself and—"

Tim walked over to the breakfast bar, where a laptop was open. He cleared the screen saver and typed quickly.

"What are you doing?" Darla asked.

But Tim didn't answer. He seemed to be scrolling. Then he stopped.

Beyond the hum of the refrigerator, silence hung as Tim leaned toward the computer, reading. Frank looked at Darla, who continued to glance between Tim, Frank, and the front window.

Then Tim turned. "Oh no."

Darla stood. "What's the matter?"

Tim didn't seem to know what to say. He stared at the floor, shook his head, his hand on his cheek.

"Tim! What's the matter?"

"It's . . . it's the conversation . . . the other night, when I was mad."

"About the vote?"

"Yes, yes. About the vote. The whole conversation is on there. Except there are, uh . . . The, um, curse words. Aren't."

Frank had noticed that too. Whoever was recording these conversations seemed to be taking out the cusswords.

It felt like the air in the room disappeared. Frank said, "Why don't you both sit down."

Tim made his way to the couch, his eyes distant. Darla looked totally stunned. They sat down, this time a small space between them. Both stared at Frank as if he had an answer.

Finally Tim spoke, his face tightly drawn. "They think we hung their cat just because I was mad at him?"

Frank decided to take it a different direction. "Sir, do you go to the hardware store? Al's?"

"Yes. All the time. Why?"

"Were you there this week?"

"Yes."

"What did you buy?"

Darla's face looked like it hadn't seen the light of day in a decade. She tried to keep her composure, but her hands were shaking. "Weed killer, wasn't it?"

Tim nodded.

"Did you pay cash for it?"

"You really don't think we did this, do you?"

"Did you pay cash, sir?"

"Yes, we pay cash for everything."

"You pay cash for everything?"

"Yes."

"No credit cards or debit cards? What about checks?"

"No. Cash. Except for bills."

"Why?" Frank asked.

"It's the envelope system," Darla said.

"The what?"

"It's a method for getting out of debt, living within your means," Tim said. "You pay cash for everything, like clothes, groceries, things like that."

Darla hopped up and grabbed her purse, pulling out a small, yellow book. "See? Here." She handed it to him. Inside were small envelopes filled with cash. Each envelope was labeled differently: *Groceries. Dining. Date night. Pharmacy.*

Frank handed it back and scribbled a note about it.

"It's Dave Ramsey's idea," she said.

"Who's Dave Ramsey?" Frank asked.

Darla pointed behind Frank and he turned around. There, standing in the darkness of the far corner of the room was a life-size cardboard cutout of a man, balding, fiftyish, pointing his finger toward Frank.

"He's a financial guy. Writes lots of books," Tim said. "To help us stay on track, we took him and had him blown up."

"Enlarged," Darla said quickly. "What Tim means is that we had him enlarged. We don't blow things up, of course. Or people. Or hang things."

"Look, Officer, I don't know what's going on or how they heard our conversation, but we did not kill the Caldwells' cat. I was angry when I was speaking to my wife. But that was a private conversation, and the next day I was over it. Ted has not mentioned a thing about it to me. I didn't even realize he was upset. He canceled coffee early this week, but he said he was busy. I didn't think twice about it."

Frank stood and closed his notepad. "All right. We may

need you to come in and answer some more questions later."

Darla seemed to be in full-blown panic. "Do we need a lawyer?"

"No," Tim snapped. "Of course not. We've done nothing wrong."

"I can't answer that question, ma'am. Do what you need to do. But for now, I'd advise staying away from the Caldwells until this thing is sorted out."

Tim seemed sad more than anything. He walked to the window and looked out, his back slumped. "I can't believe this is happening."

7

"FRANK, I'M SO glad you could stay for dinner," Kay said, putting the pot roast in the center of the table.

"Thanks for inviting me," Frank said. As Jenna and Hunter slowly made their way to the table, Frank leaned forward, engaging Damien. "Maybe I should call her."

Damien sawed into the meat. "I don't think that's a good idea."

"This is not like Angela. She doesn't not show up for work."

Damien plopped some potatoes onto his plate as Kay returned with the salad. "There are a billion reasons she wouldn't show up. Sick. Family emergency. Had to go neuter a pet. You're overreacting."

Frank sighed and sank back into his chair, crossing his arms and staring at the food. "I don't expect you to understand. It's just that she never gets sick. And she never misses work. When we were married, she never missed one day of work. Not one. For anything. She's dependable and a vitamin C addict."

Jenna and Hunter took their seats.

Frank put on a smile. "Hey, kiddos."

"Hey," Hunter said.

Jenna offered only a small smile. Damien cleared his throat, and she made another attempt with a slightly bigger smile.

"What's going on these days?" Frank asked.

Hunter grinned. "Jenna's grounded."

"Shut up," Jenna said. "So is he. From his cell phone. For racking up, what was it, three thousand minutes?"

"From the Internet," Hunter added. "For beating a girl—"

"I'm going to shove this roast beef up your—"

"Okay," Damien said, meat knife in hand, waving it between the two of them. "Let's try to be civil while Uncle Frank is here."

"Then tell the rodent to shut up," Jenna said, jabbing her fork across the table at Hunter.

"Right in the nose—"

"Hunter! Enough," Kay said. "It's not up for discussion."

Damien took a deep breath and served himself some peas.

Jenna suddenly stood, grabbed her plate, and headed upstairs.

Kay passed Frank the salt and pepper. "I'm sorry about that. She's going through a stage. I think it's just hormones."

Frank nodded and looked at Hunter. "What about you? How's school?"

"Fine, I guess."

"Built any more computer programs?"

"Nah. Too busy."

"I finally got the Wii. Maybe you can come over and play it this weekend."

Hunter's face lit up. "Really?"

When Frank's cell phone rang, he reached to his belt to grab it. "Sorry. It's my work phone." He frowned as he checked the caller ID. "Huh. It's the captain. Excuse me." Frank left the table.

Damien glanced at Kay. "I think we should tell Jenna to get back down here and stop being rude."

Frank returned to the table. "I have to go. Kay, I'm sorry to leave in the middle of dinner. It's a work thing."

"You're not even on," Damien said.

"I can't talk now. I've got to—" Frank stopped himself and turned to Damien. "You want to come with me?"

"What?"

"Come on. You're the investigative reporter now. And this is going to be quite a story, I think."

Damien looked at Kay, trying to look appropriately desperate and remorseful all at once.

Kay smiled. "Sure. Go on. Hunter and I can eat three pounds of roast beef all by ourselves, can't we, Hunter?"

"Thanks!" Damien jumped up from the table. "Hold on. I gotta run upstairs and get my briefcase and a tablet and

pen. And a recorder." He raced upstairs and flew into his bedroom, gathering his soft leather briefcase, which contained
everything but a recorder. Nearly out of breath, he hurried
to Jenna's room and knocked.

"What?"

"I need a favor."

"Come in," the sulky voice said.

Damien opened the door. The first thing he noticed was
the room was littered with clothes, shoes, papers, and empty
fast-food boxes. It stunned him into silence because Jenna
was normally compulsively neat. When was the last time he'd
been in her room? How long had it been like this?

"What, Dad? You're standing there like a moron." She
eyed his briefcase. "Going to work? At night?"

"I'm running to a crime scene or something with Frank.
He says it's a big story. I need a recorder. Do you have
one?"

Jenna shook her head.

"Surely you have one, with school and everything. It usually takes a little tape and you—"

"They're digital, and no, I don't have one." She sighed
loudly, rolled her eyes, and got off her bed, walking toward
him. She pulled his cell out of his shirt pocket, pushed a
few buttons, then handed it to him. "You can record on this
thing."

"I can?"

"Just go to the utilities menu and there's a recorder under
there. It's so unfair. You hate cell phones, and you've got the

top of the line." Back on her bed, she wrapped her arms across her chest.

Damien set his briefcase down and tiptoed over the junk to join his daughter on the bed.

"What are you doing?"

"Believe it or not, I'm concerned about you. You're not acting like yourself."

"Really." Deadpan expressions came easy to Jenna these days. As a little girl, her face would light up with all kinds of expressions. Her eyebrows rose high on her head. She blinked when she got very excited. She grinned, even when she was doing something wrong.

"Tell me what's going on," Damien said, daring to reach out and pat her foot, which she quickly retrieved and stuck under her pillow. "You know you can talk to me. You've always talked to me about everything."

She stared at her pillows. "It's nothing. Just hormones, as you keep saying."

"Do you want to see a doctor for that?" Damien asked.

Jenna looked at him, her eyes narrow and scornful. "Is that it? You think a pill is going to solve all this? solve me?"

"That's not what I'm saying. At all. You're taking it wrong."

"Yes, well, that's my calling card these days. I'm overly emotional and taking everything the wrong way, so you better leave now while you can escape with your life. When my hormones get disheveled, I've been known to eat people alive."

Damien smiled. *Disheveled.* He loved when she used

words in unique ways. *Disheveled hormones*. Now that was a word picture.

His smile faded as he met her eyes. Nothing but contempt seemed to live inside them. He wanted to hug her, hold her in his arms, but she could hardly stand to be touched. He was left with nothing else to do but get up and go. At the doorway he turned and said, "Thanks for the help on the recorder."

She didn't look up.

"Take your dishes downstairs when you're finished and help your mother clean up."

That, at least, evoked something. Disdain? Who cared. He needed her to be something more than absent.

Grabbing his briefcase, he hurried downstairs, stopping by the dining room. He found Kay sitting alone at the table, her hands folded and her chin resting on them. It was as if she'd prepared a huge feast for only herself and didn't have the stomach to eat it.

"Where's Hunter?"

Kay nodded to the window. "He wanted to walk Frank out."

Damien stared out the window. The two of them leaned against Frank's truck, talking. He turned back to Kay. "I won't go if you don't want me to."

"Why? Of course I want you to go."

"You look sad."

"I'm okay. Go. Get those facts. Write a killer story."

Damien laughed. "I don't even know what I'm going to, but if Frank thinks it'll make a good story, he's probably right."

He pecked her on the cheek and hurried out the front door and down the sidewalk. Hunter, upon seeing him, stood erect and stepped away from Frank, shoving his hands in his pockets and taking a sudden interest in the dead winter grass.

Frank regarded Damien as he went around the truck. "I don't think breaking news is your forte." He glanced deliberately at his watch. "It usually means you have to be quick on your feet."

Damien waved at Hunter as he got into Frank's truck. "Sorry. I'm ready now." He snapped his seat belt on. "What were you and Hunter talking about?"

"You always hovering over your kids like this? No wonder they're going berserk."

"Is Hunter going berserk? Is that what you're sensing? Because I think I caught him with porn the other night."

"He was just getting some Uncle Frank time, okay? Sometimes it's easier to talk to people outside your family."

Damien sighed. "Yeah, okay. I guess. But you have to tell me if he's getting into something he shouldn't."

Frank pulled the truck onto the neighborhood street. "You shouldn't worry so much about him. He's a good kid. He's got a good head on his shoulders."

"I know he is." Damien pulled out his notepad. "So what is it that we're going to?"

Frank gripped the steering wheel and focused on the road ahead as they turned onto Shelton Street. "You should prepare yourself. This might be disturbing."

8

FRANK PARKED HIS extended cab at the curb and got out of the truck, searching for Captain Grayson among a crowd of emergency personnel mingled with the curious neighbors. Damien came up beside him.

Frank spoke quietly. "I can't say much here, okay? Just walk around, see what you can find out, ask a lot of questions. I'll see you in a little bit."

Frank walked along the street, the flashing lights of the cruisers leading the way to the house. An ambulance was parked on the other side of the roadblock, its back doors open and its bed empty.

The Shaws' house bustled with activity. Several officers from the night shift milled around outside. Crime scene tape, tied from one tree to another, fluttered against the cold north wind. Frank followed the sidewalk and was about to enter the house when Detective Dean Murray exited.

"Hey, Frank," he said. "Grayson's looking for you."

"What's going on in there?"

"They're working on the lady right now. Not sure if she's going to make it."

"What happened?" Frank asked, glancing behind him toward the reverend's yard across the street. The couple stood by the tree where their cat had hung just hours before. "Are those two suspects?"

Detective Murray looked up to see what Frank was talking about. "No. The husband confessed. He's in there right now. They're taking him in for more questioning."

"The husband? Tim?"

"Yeah," Murray said, checking his notes. "That's his name. Tim Shaw." He continued down the sidewalk.

Frank gathered himself, unsure of what he was going to find.

Upon entering, he noticed the enlarged photo of the finance guy was tipped to the side, leaning against the drapes of the large window. Tim sat on the couch, crying, a night shift officer on either side of him.

"What have I done?" Tim moaned, shaking his head, hiding his face against the handcuffs around his wrists. He looked up at Frank.

Frank noticed movement and shouting near the kitchen. He squeezed around a small crowd of firefighters to where two EMTs were hunched over someone.

He assumed it was Darla. Her feet, shoeless but with pink socks, were barely visible at the moment. Her left hand outstretched on the kitchen tile, frozen in a clawlike grip.

"Save her! Please!" Tim's shrill voice punctured through tense noises of the room.

What could've happened here?

"Frank," said a calm voice behind him. Grayson.

"What in the world is going on?"

The captain's tone was somber. He glanced at Darla on the floor and then at Tim. "He lost his temper. That's what he's telling us. He was asking for the officer he first talked to. He couldn't remember your name."

Frank turned back to Darla. As the EMTs moved around her, he saw glimpses of her shirt, bloodied. Her chin also bloodied.

"He apparently threw a remote control. It hit her skull. He claims it was an accident, that she stepped right in his line of fire." Grayson pointed to the remote, shattered into pieces on the kitchen floor.

"Is she going to make it?" Frank whispered, still trying to get a better glimpse of Darla.

"I don't know. She's going into seizures. They're trying to stabilize her."

Suddenly Tim was pulled off the couch and to his feet by the officers.

Frank faced Grayson. "Let me have a couple of minutes with him, will you? Before Murray gets to him?"

Grayson looked hesitant.

"I won't interfere. I just want to talk with him for a second. He did ask for me."

"All right, but make it quick." Grayson motioned for the officers to leave Tim.

Frank sat on the couch and pulled Tim back down. "What happened?" Frank asked.

Tim gasped for air, but no words came out.

"I need you to tell me the truth."

"Is she going to be okay?" Tim asked, unable to take his eyes off her.

"I don't know. They're trying their best."

Suddenly the EMTs lifted her onto the stretcher and raised it. "Clear the way!" one of them shouted. They rolled past them in the living room, one of the EMTs holding up an IV bag. Frank still couldn't get a good sense of how bad it was, but by the way they were rushing her out, it couldn't be good. They both watched through the front window as she was rolled down the sidewalk and quickly put into the ambulance. The sirens blared through the house, but soon enough the sound was distant.

"What happened?" Frank repeated.

Tim sobbed into his hands again, and Frank could barely make out what he was saying. "I just lost it. I thought . . . I thought Darla told."

"Told what?"

Tim finally looked up at Frank, his face a splotchy mess of emotion. "I thought she told the Caldwells what I'd said." His bloodshot eyes glared at the handcuffs. "How else could anyone know what we said?"

"What did she say?"

"She denied it. She said she would never do that. But," Tim said, his voice lowering to a whisper, "what was on that Web site . . . it's exactly what I said. Exactly. Verbatim. She was the only person in the room. How could that be?"

"Tell me what happened here tonight."

Tim tried to gather himself, taking two deep breaths and squeezing his handcuffed hands like he was accustomed to using them when he talked. "We got into an argument. I accused Darla of telling the Caldwells. She said she didn't. It just got more and more heated. She accused me of some things . . . of never knowing when to shut up." He sniffled. "Which is true. My mouth and my ego, they kind of get in the way sometimes. And . . . people are talking. About us. About me."

"Then what happened?"

Tim covered his eyes as if he were being forced to watch it all over again. "I wasn't thinking. I was so enraged. I couldn't imagine how all this was happening." He looked toward the kitchen, his gaze glued to the floor where blood was smeared across the white and gray tile. "There was the remote sitting on the coffee table. I picked it up. Darla said something—I can't even remember what now—and I turned and threw it. I think she had moved; I'm not sure. It hit her . . . right . . ." Shaking fingers moved to his skull, just above his right ear.

"Did you call the police?"

"Yes."

Grayson walked back in. "Let's get him to the station, Merret."

Frank helped Tim to his feet and handed him over to two officers behind Grayson. They led him out of the house.

"What a mess," Grayson said. "That guy's going to do some heavy time. All for losing his temper. Did you get anything useful?"

"He definitely did it. But it sounds like he didn't mean to hit her with the remote."

"Yeah, well, he can explain that to a judge. I'm going home."

Grayson and Frank walked out of the house. Frank tried to find Damien in the crowd, then noticed Reverend Caldwell walking straight toward him.

"Reverend Caldwell," Frank said.

The reverend put his hand on Frank's shoulder, lowered his voice. "I've known this man for a long time. I know what he did in there, but that's out of character."

Frank sighed, searching the reverend's pleading eyes. "I understand, sir. But this is not working in his favor. He assaulted his wife."

"I know. I know. This is very bad. All of it. But I know this man. And I know he's not what everyone is saying he is."

"What is everyone saying?"

"Empty words. Accusations." A sadness swept over the reverend's expression. "We're neighbors. We're supposed to look after one another." He gestured toward the Shaws' house. "All this over a conversation. We humans can tame animals, birds, reptiles, and fish, but no one can tame the tongue."

Reverend Caldwell's words crawled over Frank's flesh. All that could be heard was the low, fretful murmuring of the nearby crowd.

"Officer? Are you all right?"

"I'll be in touch."

* * *

Damien stood in the middle of the street for a moment, taking it all in. He wanted a complete picture for the story, which included the setting—a quiet neighborhood in Marlo, just two blocks from their world-famous chocolate shop, erupting in violence on what on any ordinary day would be a playful, tranquil street. Damien noticed a crowd gathered on the lawn directly across from where the incident took place, whatever that incident might be.

A stretcher with medical personnel around it had made a hasty exit out of the home on the left. He caught a glimpse of a woman lying on it as they wheeled her toward the ambulance. The EMTs were in a hurry to get her loaded. A couple of firefighters helped lift the stretcher.

Damien took out his notepad and wrote down a few words to help him remember the moment. Yeah, he knew, this was supposed to be investigative reporting, but cold, hard facts don't always tell the complete story.

At least, in his opinion.

The wailing sirens of the ambulance caused him to shiver. Whatever happened here, it wasn't good. Wasn't right. Through the glowing front window of the home where the lady was taken from, he saw Frank pass by, hands on his hips, a strangely fierce look on his face.

He decided to see if someone from the crowd would talk to him. He pulled his newspaper ID badge from his wallet and clipped it on his shirt. Just a few short steps toward them already drew attention. They all stared as he approached.

He smiled pleasantly but not eagerly. "Hi, folks. I'm Damien Underwood from the paper. Can I ask some of you a few questions?"

An elderly woman with a tight expression sized him up. "From the paper, you say? Underwood? Don't you write those opinion pieces?"

"Yes."

"And crosswords," someone else said. "A little easy for my taste."

Damien held up a hand before anyone else wanted to give an opinion. "Folks, listen. I'm here to talk about what happened tonight. What's going on over there?"

A bald, overweight man with motorcycle pants on said, "All we heard was that the husband nearly beat his wife to death."

"They just brought her out on a stretcher. She looked half-dead," the elderly woman said.

Damien quickly took notes. The recorder would've been better, but people were talking. Now. It would take him several minutes to figure out how Jenna got to the right menu to bring up the recorder on the phone.

"I always thought that man had a mean streak in him," a woman wearing a dirty apron said.

Another woman scoffed. "Whatever, Ginger. I've seen you over there flirting."

"What are you talking about?" Ginger said, her eyes white-hot.

"You and Sara are always talking about him."

"Shut up, Pam. No we're not."

"Really? Because the Web site says differently."

Ginger suddenly lunged at Pam, who gasped and stumbled back into the crowd.

Damien stepped out of the way and observed the two women shouting obscenities at each other while others kept them from swinging punches. He carefully wrote down what he'd heard, but there was such a ruckus he wasn't sure he was going to get any more quotes.

He glanced across the street and noticed Frank talking to a man. They wrapped up their conversation, and Frank headed to his truck. Damien decided he'd better get there too before a full-blown riot took place over who flirted with the man who beat his wife.

"Dad?"

Damien turned as he heard a young voice, much like his daughter's. A teenage girl shoved her way through the crowd.

The man Damien saw Frank talking to rushed over to her. "Come on, Gabriella. Let's get you inside. You don't need to see this."

"Dad, what's going on?"

Their conversation faded into the crowd noise as they tried to make their way to the house.

"You're a jerk!" someone yelled.

Damien and Frank both turned around.

A man, presumably Tim Shaw, was being led away in handcuffs. His head hung low, and he never looked up, not even once he was in the cruiser.

Damien scribbled more notes. Behind him, he heard a man say, "Come on. Let's go home. I want to see this Web site they're talking about." The crowd began to disperse.

Frank unlocked his truck and climbed in.

"What a night," Damien said, joining him.

Frank started the engine.

"Heard he beat his wife half to death."

Frank backed up, swerving around cars and people, into a driveway so he could turn around. "You better get your facts straight. He threw a remote control and it hit her."

Damien smiled. "Can I quote you on that?"

Frank didn't laugh. He just drove.

"So you believe him?" Damien asked.

"I don't know. I'm just telling you what he told me." Frank turned left on Arberry Street.

"Where are we going? My house is that way."

But Frank didn't answer.

9

"Frank!"

Lineup was about to start when Frank's name was hollered through the headquarters.

It cut Gavin off as he bemoaned missing some real police action last night. "You should've called me! I would've wanted to be there. I—"

"Frank! Now!"

Frank looked at the kid, who was shaking his head like he'd just heard the news of a relative's death. "We were off duty. I went in as a favor to the captain."

"Frank!"

"Looks like he appreciates it," Gavin said in a flat tone.

Frank sighed and lumbered down the hallway to Captain Grayson's office. The door was wide open, so he walked in. "Angela?"

She stood straight, just to the left of the captain's desk, her arms crossed tightly in front of her slender body. The light pink jacket and skirt, matched perfectly to her lipstick, were not doing much to make her scowl look any softer. Her glare hit Frank like sunlight beaming off a mirror. He knew he was in trouble but with whom? Her or the captain?

"Frank, sit down," Grayson said.

"You stay right there!" Angela barked, pointing her finger at him.

The captain skittishly ducked.

Frank froze, unsure what to do. He tried a small smile. "I'm glad you're okay. I was worried."

"Worried? How can you be worried?"

Frank glanced at Grayson to get a read on him. Yep, he was fuming. "It's not like you to not be at home. Then work. And then last night, not at home. Again. And—"

"You came by my house last night?"

"I was with Damien," Frank said with a shrug. "I just thought I'd check on you, and when you weren't there, I, um . . ."

She grabbed a piece of paper out of her purse and waved it in the air. "A missing person report? Really? Really?" She crumpled it up and threw it at him. It hit his chest and dropped to the floor, where he was looking anyway. "Do you know how humiliated I am? I'm at work, a professional place of business, when two cops show up this morning and start asking me all these questions."

Frank tried to keep it in but couldn't. "Where were you?"

Angela gasped. "You're an idiot! I can't believe you would

even stand there and ask that!" She yanked her purse off the chair and swung it over her shoulder. "You have to stop this. Do you understand me? I am a grown woman. We are not married anymore. You have no business being in my business. You need to move on. Why do you even care whether I'm at work or home or elsewhere?"

Frank glanced at the captain, then back at Angela. "Because I still care about you. That's why. Some weird things are happening in town, and I wanted to make sure you were okay."

She stepped closer to him, her brow so furrowed that the skin between her eyes turned purple. Her finger jabbed his chest. "Leave me alone or I'm going to file a restraining order on you."

"Please don't do this. I, um, overreacted—"

"You've crossed the line. You always cross the line. Heard you gave MaLue a ticket. When are you going to get over *that*? Get a life. Please. Get a life." Angela brushed past him and out the hallway. Her stilettos clicked and clacked until he heard the back door open and close.

Grayson said, "Close the door."

Frank closed it and decided to sit down. "Well, I'm glad she's okay."

Grayson's expression didn't change. "Captain Stephens sent out his guys on this. Gave it preferential treatment because you're one of our own. Said you sounded frantic when you were filling out the form at the station last night."

"I couldn't find her."

"Yeah, but don't you think this is a little extreme?" Grayson asked. "We all know the divorce was hard on you. I realize it's been difficult to let her go, but—"

"It's not about that," Frank snapped. He drew in a quick breath. "It's not about the divorce."

"Then what's it about?"

"I just . . . I overreacted. That's all. I mean, we've got dead cats hanging in trees and deacons abusing their wives. Stuff like this doesn't happen in Marlo."

"If she were to press criminal charges against you, you'd lose your job. You understand that, don't you?"

Frank leaned forward, trying to relieve the strain on his chest caused by all the emotion that wanted to bubble up and out. None of this would be happening if she hadn't insisted on a divorce five years ago. He could protect her.

There was nothing for Frank to say. He froze in his own humiliation. It was one thing for the captain to come down on him, but another for Angela to. He saw the hate in her eyes. It was the same look she'd had for him that morning at breakfast when she announced she wanted a divorce.

Grayson pulled a folder off his desk. "The woman from last night, the deacon's wife, she's not pressing charges. Says it was an accident."

"So I guess she's going to live."

"Fractured skull but the bleeding has stopped and the doctors said she'll make a full recovery. So the case is closed. I don't know if the neighbors are going to press charges about the cat. I need you to write up your part of the report. Murray will fill in the rest. Now, go on. Get out of here."

Frank stood slowly. His knees hurt today.

"By the way, I told Gavin to report if you go anywhere near Angela."

"Is that really necessary?" Frank asked.

"I don't know. You tell me."

Frank went to the door. The day hadn't started and already he was exhausted. "Captain?"

"Yeah?"

"What about this Web site?"

"What Web site?"

"The one where all this information is coming from. It's got this ominous message on it about our town, and now apparently we've got someone recording private conversations and posting them there. Look what it's already caused."

The captain sighed. "There's always going to be things to get mad about. Any guy that would throw a remote control at his wife doesn't need a Web site to set him off. It could've been anything."

"It's stirring up trouble in our community."

Grayson nodded, but his focus had turned to a file on his desk.

"Aren't you curious how this person's doing it?"

"Doing what?"

"Listening to people's conversations?"

Grayson lifted his hands as if he were at a loss for words. His focus went back to the file he was trying to read.

"I think we should investigate it."

"Come on. We can't get involved in this."

"The Shaws aren't the first. There are days' worth of con-versations on there now. Some of the conversations are mun-dane and meaningless. Others have more of a . . ."

"A what?"

"There are words. There are words on there that are going to change people's lives."

"Just let it drop. If it becomes a big deal, then it becomes a big deal. Marlo doesn't need anything else to worry about right now."

Frank tried to walk out but he couldn't. Wouldn't. "I think that it's in the best interest of the town to find out at least how the Shaws' conversation was recorded."

"Frank," the captain said in a heavy tone, "we've got two detectives working all of our departments. Our budget was slashed last year. We don't have the resources for . . ." His tired expression grew stern. "This is about a man assaulting his wife with a remote control. Whatever caused him to go off isn't our problem."

"But if we could just check their house for bugs—"

"You mean bring the state in on this? You know we don't have the resources for that, and the last thing we want is the state involved in our town." Grayson gave him a hard look. "Now leave this alone. That's an order."

* * *

"This is great stuff," Edgar said, skimming the notes Damien had handed him. Edgar sipped scalding black coffee, blowing the steam off the top. "Yeah, I like this. I like the direction this is going." He tapped the paper. "And this Web site. That's intriguing."

"The Web site? Well, yes, I suppose it is. But I'd like to focus on the Shaws and their—"

"Oh yes, definitely. Did they or did they not hang the cat? But this Web site. Where did it come from? Who's doing it?"

Damien feigned interest by nodding and rubbing his chin, but that wasn't the story he wanted to cover. He had plans to interview Darla Shaw, then Tim, the neighbors . . . try to figure out how a deacon of the church could end up nearly killing his wife with a remote.

"You say here that it all started with a conversation that was posted on this Web site, right?" Edgar asked.

"I guess, but—"

"So the conversation was about their neighbors across the street, good friends?"

"Yes."

"Then these neighbors find their cat hanging from a tree."

"Yes."

"And by evening, the deacon has almost killed his wife."

"I called the hospital and talked to my cousin so I could get some info. Turns out she's going to be fine and she's not planning on pressing charges."

Edgar looked delighted. "Even better. Everyone's fascinated with the wife who'd stay with the abuser. Oprah makes a killing off stories like this. And now it's our turn." He stood and grabbed the coffeepot in the corner of his office, pouring himself another cup. "This Web site, though. I want you to do some digging. Let's follow it regularly in the paper."

"Sir, with all due respect, do you think that's a good idea? What good could come of drawing people's attention to gossip?"

Edgar held the coffee near his lips but didn't drink. "So you're back to editorial opinion pieces now? If you want to be an investigative reporter, you've got to stop thinking about people's feelings. And your own opinion, for that matter. I want facts. They're not called cold and hard for nothing."

*　*　*

Thirty more minutes of office time and then Kay had a showing. Probably the only showing of the day. The economy wasn't bad in Marlo, but it was all about perception. Nobody wanted to make any big financial moves, including buying a house they couldn't afford. But truth was, when it came to Marlo, nobody could afford what they were living in. Or driving. Or vacationing to.

She decided to check on some properties that went up for sale yesterday. But before her hands hit the keyboard, an unfamiliar female voice floated down the hall, asking where Kay's office was. Soon, Shannon, Zoey's mom, stood in the doorway.

"Look at you, all professional and snazzy." She sauntered in wearing really expensive jeans and a cozy sweater. Long earrings stretched her lobes down, and a small Gucci purse dangled off one shoulder.

Kay stood because that was the professional thing to do. Normally she might extend a hand to shake, but moms didn't shake hands. They just gave one another the once-over and an either approving or disapproving look.

Shannon's finger traced the air. "Girl, you are rocking it in that pink number."

"Oh, uh, thank you. How are you?"

"Sit; sit." Shannon flopped herself into the single chair on the other side of Kay's desk. She kicked her feet up. Ugg boots. Of course.

"So what's up?" Kay asked.

"I had to come talk to you. So we're at Kelly's last night, right? Doing the whole scrapbooking thing for the girls. By the way, cuuute picture of Jenna in her cheer outfit. Anyway, guess who stops by? Jill! Exactly. Uninvited as usual. Well, she's a mess."

"A mess?"

"First of all, she should not be wearing those awful Juicy outfits. Really. She looks ridiculous. Especially when she's got mascara running down her face."

"What was wrong?"

"It took us fifteen minutes to get her calmed down to even tell us. According to her—and this, mind you, is according to her—Mike is the one having an affair. At least she's suspecting it. I don't know why she's devastated. I mean, she's divorcing the guy. Cut your losses. Move on. She claims that she's upset for Natalie's sake, but come on. The woman is a total codependent. You know what I mean."

"Yeah, sure. It's written all over her."

Shannon twirled the hair from her ponytail around her index finger, snapping her gum and seemingly sizing Kay up for a moment.

"So, what happened?"

Shannon sighed. "The same thing that always happens. We listen to her drone on and on about her problems. We tell her it's going to be okay. And we push her out the front door so she can go hit the liquor shop before it closes."

"She drinks?"

"Honey, she doesn't just drink. She guzzles. Not for pleasure or party either. She can't get through a day without knocking the hard stuff back." Shannon stopped twirling her hair. Popping her feet off the desk, she leaned forward, locking eyes with Kay. "I'm sensing something here. You knew Jill before we knew you. I'm not crossing the line, am I? You're not still tight with her, are you?"

"Jill? No."

Twirling. Again. "All right. Anyway, just wanted to update you. Warn you. In case she starts calling you. I seriously wouldn't even answer the phone. You'll get stuck for like an hour." She crossed her long legs, picked at the fuzz on her pants. "So, how's Jenna? Heard she had to put one of the girls in her place. But hey, sometimes that's what it takes."

"Jenna? Oh, she's fine. Great."

"Yeah? Liking cheer again?"

"Loves it. She's totally happy."

"Good. It's all about keeping the girls happy." Shannon

rose and went to the door. "We'll probably get together next weekend, plan the sleepover. I'll call you."

Kay stood and leaned casually against her desk. "Sounds good."

"See ya."

Kay smiled and waved, then slowly sat back down in her chair, pulling her suit jacket closed. Mike was the one having the affair? That was hard to believe. She'd known both of them since Jenna and Natalie were in the fifth grade. He didn't seem the type.

She wondered what kind of influence Natalie would begin to be on Jenna, especially if she was acting out. Kay always suspected it was Natalie who influenced Jenna's style. For the worse. She'd have to keep an eye out for more problems.

She'd have to keep an eye out, period.

10

"WHAT, UM, ARE we doing?" Gavin stared at Frank like he might radio in.

"I'm just looking into something. Don't have a cow." Frank got out of the cruiser, and within seconds, Gavin was right by his side. They both looked up at the large black sign hanging over the strip mall store. *Spies Are Us.* "Ever been in here?"

"Why are we going in here?" Gavin scurried after Frank, who opened the front door and walked inside. "What are you doing?" He took a moment to glance from wall to wall.

"Cool stuff in here," Frank said.

Gavin's face twitched. "Um, I'm not trying to be . . . It's just that—well, the whole thing with your ex-wife. The captain said I'm supposed to . . . you're not supposed to do that thing anymore."

"What thing?" Frank asked, his hand gliding along a glass shelf piled high with spyware. He really loved messing with this kid.

"Be around her and stuff."

Frank stopped and turned to him. "I don't see Angela here. Do you?"

Gavin actually glanced around as if she might suddenly appear.

"Well? Do you?"

"Um, no," Gavin said. "But we are at the spy store."

"So?" Frank picked up a pair of night-vision goggles.

"Look, Officer Merret, you can't do this, okay? You're not supposed to be around her."

"I'm not around her."

"But," he said, dropping his voice to a whisper, "you're going to spy on her?"

Frank only smiled at him—a long, prideful smile that caused Gavin's eyes to widen. Then he continued to the next wall, where they sold the small listening devices one could plant underneath a coffee table.

"You need to just leave it alone or you're going to get in trouble."

"Trouble? By who? You? You going to rat me out, Jenkins?"

Gavin tried to maintain a stoic expression. "The captain asked me to report anything to him."

"You know what happens to rats in the department, don't you?"

Gavin's expression wouldn't hold. Fear flitted across his face. "He gave me the orders."

"Uh-huh. And what you do with those says a lot. You're

going to rat to a guy that sits behind a desk all day, or are you going to cover for the guy that could keep you from getting killed. The guy that would risk his life to save you if he had to."

Gavin scratched his cheek, seemingly thinking this over. He followed Frank as he moved to another part of the store. "Okay, fine. I won't say anything. But don't you think you're taking this a little far? Spying on your ex-wife? What makes you think she's not going to wig out again?"

"Well, the very idea of spying is that you don't get caught."

A man, skinny and pale, came around the checkout counter. "Hi. I'm Corbin. What can I help you with, Officers?"

Frank said, "I'm looking for a sweeper. I need something that's at a professional level, something with a high RF sensitivity."

"All right. We keep that kind of thing in the back. Give me a second and I'll bring a few models out."

Gavin turned to Frank. "What do you need that for?"

"Look, I'm done messing with you. This isn't about Angela. It's about that Web site."

"Listen to Yourself."

"That's the one."

"So what are you doing?"

"I read the Web site last night. Lots of posts but it's hard to know exactly who is speaking. Except we know for sure that the Shaws' conversation was recorded because Mr. Shaw admitted that he'd said everything that was put onto the Web site. I'm going to ask if the Shaws will let me do a sweep, see if we can find some hidden transmitter or something."

Gavin seemed interested. "So you think that someone is going around planting these things and then listening in on the conversations?"

"I don't know. But we've got to start somewhere."

Corbin returned to the front counter and beckoned them over. He set an armload of boxes down and arranged them in a line. "Here's what we got. I'll start with the top gun of the bunch." He opened a box and pulled out a machine about as big as a toaster. "This, my friends, is the CF-900. It has total RF spectrum coverage and can locate audio transmitters as low as 1 MHz. It's got a built-in audio filter, search and/or monitor mode, LCD bar graph, and full carrier current detection."

Frank lifted the machine, looking it over. "All I want to know is, will it pick up bugs in a sweep."

"You betcha. If it's in there, it'll find it."

"How much?"

"Twenty-five hundred, normally. But it's on sale for a hundred dollars off today."

Frank set it down.

Corbin continued. "This is what the professionals ask for. Same brand as what the FBI uses."

"Over my budget. You got anything cheaper?"

Corbin pointed to the box at the end of his line. "Got that thing. A miniature battery-powered scanner for five hundred."

"That sounds better," Frank said. "A little."

"You'll be lucky if this thing picks up a fax machine," Corbin said, handing the box to Frank.

Frank decided on a different approach. "Have you seen a recent interest for listening devices here at the store?"

Corbin smirked. "Is there love and jealousy in the world?"

* * *

"Dad? What are you doing here?"

"Surprise!" Damien smiled and opened his arms.

Hunter just stood there, blinking.

Damien lowered his arms. Surprising Hunter in elementary school got a way better reaction. "Hey, I just thought I'd take you out for lunch today."

"Oh."

"What? Don't want to go to lunch with the old man?" Damien tried not to look as insecure as he suddenly felt.

"Um . . ."

"You got plans or something? A cute girl?"

Hunter grabbed his arm and swung him around, pushing him out of the office. "Yeah, fine. We can go to lunch. No big deal."

"Great!" Damien wrapped an arm around his son's shoulder as they walked out the front door of the school. "So how's your day going?"

"Fine."

"Tell me something, anything."

Hunter cast him a forlorn look. "It's eighth grade. The highlight of my day was that we had a sub in calculus."

"You have calculus in eighth grade?"

"Yes, if you're an honor student."

"Right."

Inside the car it was mostly quiet. Outside, the high school was letting out for lunch. Kids yelled and hung out the windows of their cars, blaring their horns at one another. Damien headed for Mack's Ribs. He reached between the console and pulled out a piece of paper. "Brought you my new puzzle. We'll publish it next week, but I thought you'd like to take a crack at it."

"Pretty Amazing is the theme?"

"Yeah."

"Okay." Hunter studied it for a moment. "Twenty-two across is too obvious. It's Pamela. As in Anderson."

Damien smiled. "Yep."

"Two down. Desirable Berry." He scratched his head. "Halle?"

"Wow! You're good."

Hunter shook his head. "This is weird. You're, like, doing all hot women?"

Damien swallowed. It was strange to hear his baby boy say "hot women," but he kept the smile on his face. "Try some more."

"Simpson, without googly eyes . . . seven letters." Hunter laughed. "Jessica?"

"You're good. I thought I'd made it more difficult."

"So you sat around today and thought of nothing but hot women?"

Again, the "hot women" remark made him clench his jaw. "Well," Damien said slowly, "I am a, um, man. And men do like . . . hot women."

Hunter was in a full-fledged stare now. "Is Mom on here?"

"What?"

"Are you having an affair?"

"What? No! No! Why would you think that?"

"Because not once in my whole life have I heard you say 'hot' and 'women' in the same sentence. You don't even use those words. You tell Mom she's beautiful."

"It's just a . . . I thought—" Damien stopped himself. "Okay, look, I haven't really ever had the birds-and-the-bees talk with you."

Hunter's eyebrows shot straight up. "Dad! Yes, you did. Wait . . . no, you didn't. Mom did. She bought a picture book that explained it all. I was nine. It came with a coloring book." He glued his gaze to the road.

Damien took a breath and tried to remain cool. This was much harder than he anticipated. Were the windows fogging up? "I know that you know 'technically' how it all works, but there are some other things you need to know, things that every father should teach his son."

Damien noticed Hunter's knuckles turning white as he gripped the denim on his jeans. Maybe he was going about this wrong. At the time, a crossword puzzle seemed like a good way to broach the subject of how women and hormones and all that could be, well, puzzling. But things seemed to be backfiring. Quickly.

"What I'm trying to say is that I'm here for you if you ever need to talk about anything. Anything at all, even if it's difficult or you think it's wrong. Whatever it is, I'll listen. Okay?"

Nothing. No reaction.

"What I mean is that you know right from wrong because we took you to church. That's what I'm trying to say. Not that you're doing anything wrong. Are you?"

Hunter finally looked at him. "We haven't been to church in, like, two years."

"Well, we've been busy and you've had soccer tournaments on the weekends and all that. Hunter, just hear what I'm saying. If there's something you need to talk about, I'm here for you."

"Maybe I could talk to Uncle Frank."

That stung. But he trusted nobody more than Frank. "Sure, buddy."

Hunter let go of his jeans. "Yeah, okay. I get it. Thanks."

Damien turned into Mack's. "Now, let's dig into a big ole slab of meat!"

Hunter smiled. "Can I get double ribs?"

"Definitely."

They walked in and sat down at a table near the window. Hunter gazed out for a little while, then apparently got bored with the view. "So what's going on at work?"

"Just trying to get this investigative reporting down."

"I heard a cat got hung."

"The news is making its way around, is it?"

"Gossip travels fast."

"You hear anything else?"

"What do you mean?"

"I don't know. Kids talk. We're trying to figure out if the neighbors did it."

"No, I didn't hear anything."

"What about this Web site I showed you the other day? Anyone talking about that?"

Hunter shook his head. "Not that I've heard."

Suddenly Damien got an idea. He leaned forward. "Edgar wants me to check this whole thing out. The Web site. Try to figure out where it's coming from. You can do that, can't you?"

"You mean hack into it and try to find the host and therefore find the person responsible?"

"Can you do that?"

"I can try. It's not easy. Or, um, legal."

"How about after work, I'll join you upstairs, and we'll see what we can dig up."

Hunter pitched a thumbs-up.

11

THE SUCCULENT SMELL of pork chops wafting into the dining room did nothing to add any ambience to the chilly atmosphere at the dinner table. Kay brought in scalloped potatoes and returned to the kitchen for the rest of the food. She wasn't in the mood for the moods. Not today. But she faked a smile and returned to sit with her family. If she couldn't have the happy family, the next best thing was the illusion of one.

"Pork?" Jenna moaned, leaning over the platter. "What is it with you and pork? Do you know how fattening this is? And then you have the carbs with the potatoes."

"It's a lean cut of pork," Kay said, serving Damien and then Hunter. She tried not to focus on the paper-thin T-shirt Jenna wore. It barely covered her stomach. "It's high in protein. It's not like I'm serving up bacon here." She stabbed the last chop and plopped it on Jenna's plate. The sauce splattered onto her shirt.

"Mother!" Jenna barked, grabbing her napkin.

"It was an accident," Damien said, handing Jenna another napkin. "Calm down. It washes."

Jenna glared at Kay as she furiously scrubbed her shirt. "I'm not hungry," she said and started to rise from the table.

"No ma'am," Kay said sternly. "Sit your rear end back down right now."

All movement froze, Damien holding the scalloped potatoes, Hunter with a big bite of pork bulging in his cheek. Jenna's glare cut through the steam coming off the lima beans. But she finally sat, grabbed her knife, and started sawing at her pork as if she intended on murdering it had it not already been dead.

Kay cleared her throat and passed the bread basket. "Hunter, how was your day?"

"Good. Dad came to eat with me."

Jenna looked up briefly, studied her brother for a moment, then went back to her food.

"Yeah, I'm going to need Hunter's help for my first investigative piece. Edgar wants me to do some digging, see if we can figure out where that Web site about Marlo is coming from."

"What Web site?" Kay asked.

"It's called Listen to Yourself. Apparently it's recording private conversations of the citizens of Marlo."

"Are you reading it?" Jenna stared at Damien.

"Not for pleasure, no. But it's a little eerie. And newsworthy. Not to mention illegal if the person doing it is indeed eavesdropping."

"Or maybe it's more like Robin Hood. You know, stealing from the rich, giving to the poor." Hunter shrugged. "Except with words."

"That's stupid." Jenna's attention returned to Damien. "What kind of stuff's on there?"

"Just weird, random conversations. Some are harmless and some are . . ."

"Are what?" Kay asked.

"Well, damaging. You two haven't heard about this?"

"No," Kay said. She looked at Jenna. "Have you?"

Jenna continued eating one lima bean at a time.

Kay watched her daughter for a moment, trying to read that mind of hers. When she was little, she'd worn every emotion on her sleeve. She became glassy-eyed at a moment's notice if something didn't go her way, or anyone else's way for that matter. She had the biggest heart, always concerned for other people, including her little brother, who often made her life difficult if not embarrassing.

Then, as if a switch had been flipped, the emotions were gone and in their place, nothing more than sulky, disapproving expressions that went no deeper than the gobs of makeup she smothered her face in. She had the most beautiful freckles sprinkled across her nose, but they hadn't seen the light of day since she'd discovered a high-priced foundation that promised to cover up all flaws. So what once had been a bright sign that summer was here was now like a shameful secret that was not allowed out.

Kay really missed those freckles. And so much more.

Jenna was like a whisper of who she used to be. Friends told Kay not to worry. Jenna would come out of it one day. It was what you were to expect with a teenage girl. But Kay had never expected it to be like this.

And then there was the way she'd suddenly started dressing. *Sleazy*. That was the only word for it. She hated to say it, but it was true. Cleavage when at all possible. Jeans tight and low. Shirts flimsy and revealing. Damien didn't seemed concerned, but Kay knew what it meant.

Kay cleared her throat and focused her attention on Jenna. "Hey, so who are you hanging out with this year? I haven't heard you talk about anybody in particular. What about the girls on the cheer club? Zoey. Caydance. What about Madison?"

"Just because I cheer with them doesn't mean I have to hang out with them," Jenna said.

Damien added, "What about Natalie? She used to be a good friend."

Jenna's gaze darted from Kay to Damien as she stopped chewing. "What is this, twenty questions?"

"We just like to know who your friends are," Damien said, his voice kind in tone like it always was with Jenna. Kay, for some reason, could never quite find the right tone.

Jenna sighed, picking at her dinner roll. "Yeah, fine. Natalie. We still hang out some."

Kay lowered her fork. "You do?"

"What? You don't approve of Natalie now?"

Damien frowned. "Nobody said that. Natalie's a perfectly fine—"

"She's not."

Everyone stopped and looked at Kay.

"What I'm trying to say," she said, forcing a calm tone on top of a tight smile, "is that Natalie seems troubled."

Jenna placed her fork onto her plate and put her elbows on the table just like Kay hated. "What are you talking about? No, she's not."

"I'm just hearing some things—"

"What things?"

"Her mother is . . . well, there's some trouble at home and—"

"So what? That doesn't mean there's anything wrong with Nat. Her parents are screwups. But it's not fair to say she is."

Damien held up a hand to each of them. "We're not saying that. Not at all. I think you're reading what your mom is saying wrong; isn't she, Kay?"

Kay bit down hard on her lip, casting a measured look at Damien. "I think that she should be careful when choosing friends. Sometimes kids can act out when their parents are going through something and can be bad influences on other kids."

Jenna gripped the edge of the table. "So you think Caydance and Zoey are good examples?"

"They seem like nice girls."

"Do they. Hmm."

"And Madison in particular. She's a straight-A student."

"So let me get this straight. You want me to hang out with Caydance and Zoey and Madison because they're popular and straight-A students, and you don't want me to hang out with Natalie because her parents are weird."

"That's not what your mother is saying," Damien said, shooting Kay a look that said *stop talking*. "You've always chosen your friends wisely. We don't question that at all. I think what your mother is trying to say is that if Natalie becomes a bad influence, think twice about hanging out with her."

Jenna took in a deep breath, looking the slightest bit relieved. "May I be excused now?"

Kay started to stop her but Damien said, "Of course. I'll get the ice cream out later."

"Yum. Ice cream. That's all I need, more fat on my hips," Jenna growled, throwing her napkin onto the table. She disappeared up the stairs.

"Can I have her pork chop?" Hunter asked.

Damien scooted the plate toward him but stared at Kay. "What was that all about?"

"What? I'm just trying to figure out who she's hanging out with."

"It seemed like you already had an opinion about whom that should be."

"Don't give me the third degree on this. I happen to know the mothers of those girls, and it's better for us if we know the parents of the girls she's hanging out with."

"She doesn't seem to be a big fan," Damien said, continuing with his meal.

"Well, sometimes at this age they don't know what's best. Can't you see what's happening with her? Didn't you see her shirt tonight? Papier-mâché thin."

"You know Jenna. She's never been drawn to the most popular girls. Even when she was younger, she was able to choose quality over quantity. I think we should trust her on this one."

Kay looked down, everything on her plate suddenly unappetizing. "She just can't see . . ."

"See what?"

The doorbell rang and Damien scooted his chair back. "I'll get it."

Kay watched him go around the corner to the door, then looked at Hunter.

But Hunter didn't look back. "May I be excused?" he asked and didn't wait for an answer. Before she knew it, she was totally alone.

The table, overcrowded with dishes and plates of uneaten food, caused her to push away and leave the room. She wandered to the office, where a bright screen saver of a rolling hillside greeted her. With one click she was on the Internet. Ten seconds later, she was immersed in a dark world of insinuation and accusation, but she couldn't tear her eyes away.

She searched for anything that could be about her.

* * *

Damien smelled her before he even opened the door. That was some kind of dousing to be able to instantly kill the smell of pan-seared pork chops. He braced himself for the overwhelming scent of jasmine and the intrusive eyes that would undoubtedly focus on him.

He'd once complained to Frank that Angela wore too much perfume. He made that mistake only once.

Swinging open the door, he feigned surprise while managing to say, "Angela!" and hold his breath. "What are you doing here?" He stepped out onto the porch for some fresh air and privacy. He didn't want Kay involved in this conversation, whatever conversation it might be. When Angela dumped Frank, Kay remained friends with her but not for long. They got into a fight and hadn't spoken since. To this day, Kay wouldn't talk about it or her again. Damien never even knew what the fight was about.

His nose twitched, fighting off a sneeze. He turned a little toward the breeze.

"I want to talk to you." Her voice was low, breathy.

"I'm here. What can I do for you?"

"It's about Frank."

"I figured it was."

"You know he filed a missing person report on me, don't you?"

"I haven't talked to Frank today."

"Surprising. I thought you two were attached at the hip. And also, you went with him."

"I don't know what the report was about. Honestly I don't really care. The thing is—the thing you've never understood—is that Frank loves you and will never stop loving you. He does crazy things because of his love for you. And his love has been tested in a variety of different ways. It's still holding."

"Don't you dare bring up the affair."

"I didn't say a word about it."

"A lot of people blame me for that. But nobody knows what it was like. Frank was not an easy person to live with."

"I can only imagine."

Angela kept her eyes locked on Damien's, stepping forward. "I've put up with a lot from that man, but he's crossed the line now. And I'm not talking about the ridiculous missing person report he filed on me."

"Okay . . ." The muscles in his shoulders began seizing up. He didn't like talking about Frank, not in this way, where all his vulnerabilities and shortcomings were exposed. That tended to happen a lot when Angela was involved, but Damien never questioned it to Frank. Daresay a bad word about Angela, and that was the permanent end to the friendship.

Again, she stepped forward, backing him toward his front door. Not only was he drowning in the scent of jasmine, but he was also now suffocating from lack of personal space. He had nowhere to go. He blinked rapidly as if a fly buzzed near his face.

"And I know something," Angela said, her voice lowering again. "I know that you don't like to hear that Frank isn't the perfect guy. Nobody likes to hear that. But you have to hear this."

"First of all, I know Frank's not perfect. None of us are. Nobody ever said Frank was perfect."

"That's the thing that always got under my skin," she said, her eyes narrowing. "Despite the immense personal failings of this guy, nobody was more liked than Frank Merret. The guy has the social skills and the self-awareness of a baboon, yet most people think the world of him."

"That's because he's a good guy. Something you could never see about him. Despite all his flaws, at the end of the day, he'd do anything for anybody. And he'd do more than anything, above and beyond, for you."

It seemed whatever words Angela was about to speak halted at the tip of her tongue. She stared at her feet for a moment, her fingers twisting around her lips and her chin, scratching her skin as if she were attempting to fend off whatever it was she thought she needed to say.

She finally looked up, a half-baked resolve set in her eyes. She didn't look directly at Damien. Her gaze shifted to the left to the point that Damien wanted to lean over into her line of sight. "I'm seeing someone," she said.

"All right. What does that have to do with me?"

"We're getting serious. Very serious."

"Good for you. You're afraid this is going to upset Frank? He's been down this road a time or ten."

Angela scowled. "You're painting me like I'm a . . . Maybe this was a mistake. I came over because I figured Kay wouldn't answer the phone if she saw it was me calling." She took a few steps back.

Damien drew in a big breath that probably sounded like a heavy sigh, at least judging from the sour expression on her face. "I'm just saying that Frank cares for you and whatever he may or may not be doing all stems from his feelings for you."

"Does that include listening to my private conversations?" Angela folded her arms.

"What are you talking about?"

"He's listening to me. Listening to my private conversations."

Damien shook his head, still not understanding.

"There's a Web site called—"

"Listen to Yourself."

"He told you!"

"He told me about it, but Frank's not the one doing this."

"Oh, really? Already defending him."

"What makes you think it's Frank?"

"Because a conversation I had with the man I'm seeing was posted on there." Suddenly the harshness in her voice was gone.

"I know about this Web site. Lots and lots of conversations from the town have been recorded and posted."

"Yes, well, the only one that matters to me is mine."

"So what does this have to do with Frank?"

"I caught him. He was behind the house near the sidewalk, peeking over the fence, on the same day that I had that conversation."

"You don't have a fence."

Angela bit her lip. "It wasn't at my apartment. I was with the man I'm seeing. At his house. Frank must've followed me there. And I don't know how he listened to what was being said, but what's on that Web site—" she covered her mouth for a moment as if the words were too hard to say— "is exactly what I said." A tear dripped down her cheek, desperation blowing through a cloud of what looked like shame. "And now I'm afraid."

"Afraid?"

"Of Frank. I'm afraid of what he might do. The conversation is about Frank."

"Let me assure you: Frank is not behind this Web site. But even if he was, why are you afraid? Frank would never hurt you in any way, besides possibly being a very big annoyance in your life. He's harmless."

"Sometimes harmless people who have been harmed become harmful." Something in her voice made Damien realize this wasn't an act. She was fearful.

"I'll talk to him," Damien said.

"He listens to you."

"Yeah. He listens. Rarely does he obey, though." Damien offered a conciliatory smile. "Don't worry, okay?"

"I'm not worried. I'm contacting my attorney. And if he does it again, any of it, I'm going to sue him. You can mention that if you want." Angela marched down the steps of the porch, all the way down the sidewalk and to her car, where she flung open the door, got in, and peeled out.

12

"ALL I'M SAYING is that you need to watch yourself around that woman. I know Frank can't see a thing wrong with her, but I'm telling you, she's no good." Kay furiously scrubbed a pan she held over the sink.

Damien had barely walked in the door. "With your history with Angela . . . I'm not sure you're the best person to judge the situation."

Kay shot him a harsh but agreeing look.

"Trust me. You have nothing to worry about. The day I smelled her was the day I became a hater of all things jasmine. Thanks for using personal scent self-control."

"What'd she want?"

Damien chose his words carefully. If Frank was involved with this, he didn't want things getting around. "Frank filed a missing person report. Turns out she was just over at her new boyfriend's."

"Shocking."

"I think I better go visit Frank tonight, though. You okay with that?"

"Oh, sure. Leave me alone with two kids that hate my guts."

Damien moved behind her, wrapping his arms around her waist. "They don't hate you. They just hate life right now."

"Why? They have a perfectly good life."

"Teenagers never think they have a perfectly good life. That is, until they get out on their own and nobody's making them pork chops and doing their laundry." He pecked her on the cheek. "Don't let it get you down. We knew this day was coming."

"If we can get through this year without Jenna beating somebody to a bloody pulp, I'll count that as a success. I thought boys were supposed to be the ones duking it out on the playground."

Damien walked upstairs to Hunter's room and gave a hearty knock without flinging the door open this time. His heart couldn't take another awkward moment.

"Come in."

Even with the invitation, he opened the door slowly. "Hey, buddy."

"Hey, Dad." He didn't look up from the computer. His fingers were flying over the keyboard.

"Listen, I know we were going to do some checking on that Web site together tonight, but something's come up. I've got to go talk with Frank."

Hunter's hands stopped and he turned. "About what?"

"Just grown-up stuff." Damien tried to read Hunter's expression. It was probably disappointment. That was the default expression these days. "But tomorrow night, let's sit down and we'll see what we can find out about the Web site and—"

"I already did." He turned the computer monitor to face Damien. "Whoever is doing this knows how to not get caught. Usually the IP information is easy to find, but it's locked out. Everything is locked out. See?" He pointed to the screen.

Damien moved closer. "Yeah. Looks, um, complicated."

"Whoever is doing this doesn't want to be found; that's for sure. There's no contact information anywhere on the site. And digging deeper, there are rabbit trails everywhere, leading to nowhere."

"Huh." Damien paused. He realized before he went to talk to Frank, he probably should have a good idea of what Angela was talking about. But should he bring Hunter into this? "Can you pull up the Web site again? I want to see something."

"Sure." A few fast keystrokes and they were at the site.

"You been following this?"

Hunter shrugged. "When I can."

"May I?" Damien said, gesturing to the chair. Hunter got up and Damien sat down. Using the mouse, he scrolled down, trying to read the various conversations. He found himself lingering on each one, wondering who said it, wondering about whom it was said. This was brutal and tantalizing, like a traffic accident you couldn't keep your eyes off of. He scrolled down some more. Damien stopped, reading a snippet of a conversation that seemed like it could be about Frank.

Hunter leaned over his shoulder and read out loud.

"I know! I can't believe it! He's such a moron. No . . . no! I mean it. Don't do anything . . . because, trust me, he's a maniac. He'll make your life miserable beyond comprehension. You'll pack up and move to Alaska. . . . No, I'm not overreacting! Listen to me. Just shut up and lay low. I'll handle this. Do not get involved."

"Wow," Hunter said.

Damien rolled the chair back and stood up. "I've got to go. I need to talk to Frank."

"About this?"

"I can't really discuss it right now."

Hunter cast him a wounded look. "I'm not a baby, you know."

Damien pressed his lips together and nodded. "I'm sorry. I know you're not. There's so much . . . It's just that life is complicated, and it's hard sometimes to explain why people do what they do . . . and why adults act like they do. That's even harder to explain, but—"

"Dad. I know."

Damien reached for Hunter's shoulder and squeezed it. "I

know you do, Son. Forgive your old man for being a buffoon sometimes."

"I practice forgiveness every day." Hunter smiled. "Now I guess you better go talk to Frank. If this is Angela," he said, pitching a thumb toward the computer screen, "and she's talking about Frank here, it can't be good."

Damien let out a laugh. "Okay, yes, obviously you're following the situation. Better than I am, I think. I'll see you tomorrow. Don't stay up too late. And make sure you hug your mom before you go to bed."

Downstairs, Damien kissed Kay good-bye and headed over to Frank's. He checked his watch. Normally Frank liked to go to bed early, but Damien figured he'd probably still be up. He shut off his lights as he pulled into the driveway. He should've called first, but Frank would've sensed something was off, because Frank was a cop and he could always smell bull.

Lights from the living room glowed. Everything else was dark, including his porch light. Among other things, Frank was a conserver of all things costly, and electricity was at the top of his list,. He'd been known to go through Damien's house turning off lights.

Damien pulled his coat around him and climbed the steps of the porch, tapping lightly on Frank's door. He tapped again, listening for movement. Maybe he was in the bathroom. Damien leaned to get a look into the small window by the door, but a lightweight panel revealed only vague shadows.

"Frank!" Damien knuckle-tapped the window. "Frank, hey! It's Damien. You in there?"

Silence.

Damien reached in his pocket for his cell phone only to find lint. In his rush to leave the house he must've forgotten it on the counter.

"Frank!" Damien pounded the door. Maybe he'd fallen asleep on the couch. His fist hit the door again, but this time the door popped open slightly. It was unlocked?

Slowly Damien pushed the door wider, looking for any signs of movement. "Frank, it's Damien. You here?"

The television was on, flickering through sports highlights on ESPN. Damien stepped in. His heart thumped erratically. It just seemed like something wasn't right, and that was what Frank always talked about . . . the gut instinct of a cop. He could drive the streets and sense when something was going wrong.

Damien swallowed, stepping lightly on the well-vacuumed carpet. He glanced back and forth, gauging whether danger was indeed nearby. Was Frank's truck in the garage? He should check that. But the garage door was accessible only through the kitchen, which was at the back of the house.

Damien stepped closer to the basement door. It was open, which wasn't unusual. But the lights were out, and it was pitch-black down there. "Frank?"

Nothing.

Should he go down and check anyway? or check around ground level first? Damien looked toward the hallway. No light came from that part of the house, not even a night-light. What if he'd had a heart attack?

Damien began flipping on any lights he could find. He headed to the back of the house, throwing open doors, calling Frank's name. Within seconds he'd flipped on every light in the back of the house and explored every room and closet, but there was no sign of Frank.

He should check the basement, but first he decided to check the garage, see if Frank's truck was here. There was certainly a chance that he'd left the front door unlocked accidentally. A slim chance but a chance.

Damien hurried down the hall and around the corner—

"Ahhh!" Damien clutched his chest.

Frank stood there, gun drawn, looking aggressive. When he saw Damien, his hands dropped to his side, but his expression was hard. "What are you doing here?"

"Looking for you!" Damien said. "Where have you been?"

"Why are you in my house?"

Damien drew in a deep breath, trying to slow his heart. "I knocked on your door and it swung open."

Frank turned and observed his door for a moment. "You didn't call."

"I had something I needed to talk to you about, and I thought I'd just come over."

"You never come over without calling first."

Exactly, Damien thought. Already Frank sensed something was askew. Damien sat on the couch and turned to

look at Frank, who still stood by the open door. Frank slowly
shut it, and Damien observed him studying the lock. Did he
think he picked it?

"Where have you been that you forgot to lock your
door?"

"I just left in a hurry," Frank said, walking into the living
room. He sat down in his recliner. "Quick errand. I ran up
to the QT for a two liter of Coke."

It was a strange moment, an invisible glint against the air
that held hesitation and caution and awkwardness. Damien
stared at Frank's hands because he was not holding a bottle
of Coke, and nowhere nearby was a bottle of Coke.

Frank blinked. Once. Then said, "They were out, so I
came home."

"Ah." Damien smiled, but it was uneasy.

Frank suddenly grinned as he got up and strolled toward
the kitchen. "You want something? I got a cold pizza in
here."

"No, I'm fine. Thanks. Kay cooked tonight."

Frank disappeared for a few moments. Sounds of silver-
ware and plates rattled into the living room.

Damien eased himself to the edge of the couch. This
didn't seem like the kind of conversation one should have
sitting casually with feet swung up on the coffee table.

Frank returned with a plate full of pizza. "So what's so
important that you had to come all the way over here to talk
to me?" His tone was playful, but there was something in his
eyes. Scrutiny.

It made Damien look at the carpet. "It's just that . . ."

Frank paused, midchew. "What?"

"Angela came by tonight. At my house. To talk to me." Damien finally looked up. "About you."

Frank sighed, slapping the pizza back onto his plate. "Let me guess. She's enraged about the missing person report."

"To say the least."

"She already complained at the station. It was a mistake," Frank said. "An honest mistake. That's all."

"That's what I told her."

"Thanks. It's good to know someone doesn't think I'm a raging lunatic."

"I didn't say that," Damien said. "I mean, you could push her over the edge. You know? She might do something crazy, like sue you."

"Whatever. Angela would never sue me." Frank crammed more pizza into his mouth.

Damien sat there, watching Frank watch him. He wondered if he should tell him that his ex-wife intended very much to sue him. That if Frank made another false move, things could get very nasty for him. Could Frank take it at this point?

Damien folded his hands together, placing his elbows on his knees. "I think she's really on edge right now. I'm just saying, be careful. She was mad enough to come over to my house, possibly run into Kay. The woman is angry."

"Yeah, yeah. I get it."

"You're not, like, spying on her or something, are you?"

Frank's face lit up. "Did that little zit of a rookie say something to you?"

"Your rookie? No. Why?"

"We're doing some investigating on this Web site thing," Frank said, looking irritated. "Seeing whether people's places are bugged. That Web site has already caused enough trouble. We need to get to the bottom of it."

"Okay." Damien smiled and stood.

"What? You're going already? I thought you came over to hang out."

"Gotta get back. Busy day tomorrow."

"All right, fine. I gotta get to bed myself." Frank rose, put his food on the coffee table, and embraced Damien, giving him a hearty pat on the shoulders. "Thanks for always watching my back."

"Sure thing. That's what friends are for. Talk to you tomorrow."

The cool air hit Damien as he left the house. He walked to his car in the drive, bypassing the sidewalk as he crossed the lawn. He got in his car, not bothering to let it warm up, and drove straight to the QT, where a huge stack of two liter Cokes was visible from the front window.

13

KAY WATCHED HER children gather their things for school, grabbing notebooks, jackets, backpacks. Years and years of hustling them out the door. Yelling at them to hurry up. Now she wanted them to linger.

Jenna stuffed her backpack and wrapped a scarf around her neck. Wasn't it just yesterday that Kay knelt down and tied the scarf around her, pulled on her favorite fuzzy Strawberry Shortcake hat, and embraced her? At what point, exactly, did she stop hugging her children? It was like it was there one day and gone the next. Should she try now?

Hunter glanced at her and Kay grinned but maybe not fast enough. She didn't think he saw it. He was struggling to zip his backpack.

"Here, let me help you with that."

"I got it," Hunter said, wiggling it until it suddenly zipped freely.

"Hunter, hurry up!" Jenna snapped from the front door.

"If you want a ride from me, you have to come now. I can't always be waiting for you."

Hunter rushed toward Jenna as she swung open the door.

Kay hurried to follow them out.

Jenna groaned. "Hunter, you stink! What'd you do, use the entire bottle of Axe?"

"Shut up!" Hunter barked.

It was freezing but Kay continued going outside without a coat. "Hey!" she called.

They both stopped and turned. Kay waved. They stared.

"Hey, have a good day. I love—"

But they'd both already hopped into Jenna's VW. Before Kay could wave again, Jenna had thrown it into reverse, backed out of the driveway, and they were gone.

The wind snapped, blowing her hair against her face and sending a chill through her sweater. She hurried inside. She had a showing in thirty minutes. Just enough time to go through Starbucks. Creamy, sugar-laden coffee never rejected her. She slid on her coat and grabbed her briefcase. She checked the oven and coffeepot and then headed to the front door, opening it so she could put out the trash before she left.

She gasped. "Jill?"

"I'm sorry. I was just about to knock. I didn't mean to startle you." Jill stared straight into Kay's eyes, a stare so intense that Kay took a step backward, which Jill apparently assumed was an invitation in. She walked forward, backing Kay up a few more steps.

Usually very juvenilely coifed and dressed, this morning Jill wore stained sweats and a baggy T-shirt. Her hair was pulled into an unruly ponytail. Her skin, normally as clear as porcelain, looked weathered and flaky. She appeared self-aware, with a hand covering one splotchy cheek and the other combing through the hair at her scalp. "I'm sorry to drop by unexpectedly."

"I was just on my way out."

"Yes, I see that. Do you have a few minutes, though? I won't take up much of your time."

Kay found herself completely indecisive, unable to even answer. She was shaking her head one instant and nodding the next, giving plenty of mixed signals. She was only going to Starbucks, after all. But did she want this woman in her home?

"I know we don't know each other well. But I don't really . . . It's just that I don't have anyone to talk to. Some bad things are happening . . . and I . . ." Jill bit her lip and searched Kay's eyes.

Kay's fingers drummed against her thigh as she tried to figure out what to do. Did she really want to be in the middle of Jill's drama? Plus, what would the other moms think?

Yet Jill seemed so desperate. For a woman with as much pride as Jill Toledo, she had to have a good reason for coming here looking like that. Was she drunk? This early?

Kay took a long look at her watch. "I've got a few minutes, I guess."

"Okay." Tears streamed down Jill's face. "I know we only

know each other from school, our girls knowing each other. This probably seems really odd."

Kay gave a polite smile. "What's on your mind?"

She took a tissue from the pocket of her coat. Tears now gushed down her face. She didn't appear to be trying to get ahold of her emotions.

Kay gestured to one of the entryway chairs that was mostly used to throw coats on. "Maybe you should sit down."

"That's kind. Thank you."

Kind? She was just trying to keep this woman from having a nervous breakdown in her entryway.

"My husband, Mike, is having an affair."

The words hung in the air. Kay had to glance away. What was she supposed to say? And was it true? She'd observed Jill being the flirtatious one, wearing tight-fitting clothes. "How do you know?"

"I saw him. With her."

"Aren't you two getting a divorce?"

"How did you know that?"

Kay couldn't even begin to backpedal on that one. "It's just something that's going around."

"We're trying to work through things," Jill said, frustration lacing her tone. "We've been going to counseling. I thought there was a chance we could save the marriage. But he's been acting very weird, very erratic. Sometimes he's . . . I just don't know what he's capable of."

Kay made an obvious glance at her watch. "I'm very sorry to hear that, but I don't see how I can help."

Jill, slouched in her chair and looking utterly pathetic, didn't respond at first. Her bottom lip quivered. Through the front windows on either side of the door, the normal traffic sounds of the neighborhood filled in the silence. "I don't guess anyone can," she said, patting her face with the tissue. "It's my problem, isn't it?" Suddenly her tone took on an edge of defensiveness.

Kay tried a soft smile. She was probably coming off rude. She wasn't trying to. Then again, she wasn't really trying to help either. But what could she do? "Have you talked to your marriage counselor?"

"It's three hundred dollars an hour. I'd sit there and spill my guts, and she'd just nod and tell me my feelings are normal. But honestly, this doesn't seem normal. None of this seems normal. My whole life is falling apart. And Natalie . . ." Her words trailed off.

"Does she know?"

"She knows we're having trouble. She's very distant. Won't talk to us much. I'm sure you can't relate. Jenna is such a nice girl. I'm glad the girls are friends."

Kay held back what seemed to be a natural response, that she could indeed relate to a daughter who had grown distant. But that might imply that she and Damien were having problems, and that was the last rumor she wanted to start.

"Kids are resilient" was all she could offer. "I'm sure she'll be fine." Another glance at her watch. Now Starbucks was out of the question. She loathed herself for even thinking it.

For the first time since she'd walked into the house, Jill seemed to be trying to compose herself. She avoided Kay's gaze, stood, and feigned a smile as she stuffed the tissue back into her coat pocket. She turned and opened the front door, then walked out.

It caught Kay off guard. She stood at the doorway, watching the woman go, unsure why she suddenly left.

No, that wasn't true. She knew.

She pulled her coat closed and rushed out the door. "Jill! Wait!"

Jill was unlocking her car door. She looked up.

"Please. Wait." The cold air filled her lungs, and her breath froze in front of her. "I'm sorry. I . . . I sometimes don't know what to say. You can ask my daughter." She punctuated that statement with a sad smile. "How about some tea? I can fix us some tea."

"Don't you have some place to be?"

"I can make a quick phone call. Put it off for thirty minutes or so."

For a moment, Jill looked indecisive, but then she walked toward the house. "I would appreciate it. Very much."

* * *

The problem was that Damien didn't have very many facts. The Web site provided no information about who was doing this. Besides what happened between the Caldwells and the Shaws, there was really nothing else there.

Edgar had twisted a paper clip—and his expression—out

of form. "Underwood, you know what you do when you don't have enough facts in a story? You go and get quotes from people who have strong opinions."

Which was why Damien was now entering the police station at a little after ten in the morning. He checked in at the front desk and waited to see if the captain would come to the front.

Ten minutes passed, but finally Captain Grayson came through the door, looking irritated. He noticed Damien in the waiting room. "I thought that's what the note said. Damien Underwood. Good to see you." He held out a hand for Damien to shake, then gestured for him to follow. "I'm glad you're here. Frank is out of control. Completely out of control. Can you talk some sense into him? Yeah, we all understood why the guy might've been crushed. High school's hard enough and then you grow up and your wife leaves you for the principal. . . . What I'm trying to say is that we, and by we, I mean the department, have been extremely tolerant."

"Well, the good news is he hasn't done anything crazy like this in, what, three years?"

"I've had it up to here. Here." He held a hand over his head as they rounded the corner into his bleak, white-walled office. "I'm assuming you heard he filed a missing person report on Angela?"

"Yes."

"Sometimes he disappears, Damien. Right in the middle of a shift. He's probably a closet smoker. I don't know. I've talked to him about it and sometimes it gets better, sometimes not."

"What about lately? Has he been disappearing lately?"

"Lately he's been making a rookie's life miserable just for the fun of it. So you see what I'm dealing with here." The captain plunged into his chair. "What can you do for me?" His expression filled with dread. "Or has Frank done something else? No, please. Please. Don't tell me he's done something else."

Damien took a seat that wasn't offered. The chair looked twenty years old, the vinyl ripped and repaired with duct tape. "I'm not here to talk about Frank."

"You're not?"

"No."

"Sorry." Grayson gave a vague smile. "It's just that last time you were in my office, what, four years ago or so, Frank was freaking out and you'd come to talk through some things with me. Get him grounded again."

"Please tell me Frank doesn't know about that."

"I never mentioned a word to him."

"Yes, well, I probably overreacted. You and I have known each other for a long time. Our sons played T-ball together. That first year after Frank's divorce, when he showed up on her doorstep on their anniversary, it startled me. Luckily he hasn't made that a yearly tradition." Damien grinned.

"So it hasn't struck you that he's acting strangely? I'm sensing some anger issues lately."

Damien tried not to pause. "When is Frank not strange?"

Captain Grayson snorted. "You got that right. Love the man, but could kill him too, you know?" He leaned forward, his elbows against a few folders spread across his desk. "So what's on your mind?"

"I wanted to talk to you about this Web site Listen to Yourself." Damien pulled out a pen and a notepad from his briefcase and set them on the desk, then froze as he noticed the captain's demeanor had shifted in less than a second. "What's wrong?"

"What's that for?"

"Oh, I can't figure out how to use the recorder on my phone."

"Put that away. Now."

Damien quickly slipped them back into his briefcase. "I'm sorry. I didn't mean to offend you."

"I'm not offended, but I don't talk to the press." Grayson studied him. "You're not the press, are you? I mean, I know you work at the paper, but you're not an actual reporter, right?"

"Believe it or not, I do fall under that category. Usually I do the editorial and opinion pieces."

"Usually?"

"I'm trying my hand at investigative reporting."

"Oh, brother," Grayson said, falling back in his chair, looking like the words put him into permanent exhaustion. "I would've never let you through had I known that."

"I only want to get a few quotes—"

"That's the problem. You reporters just want a few quotes, and then you take what I say totally out of context and use it against me, the department."

"Please give me the benefit of the doubt."

"My lieutenants handle these sorts of things. I can get you in touch with whoever is on call to talk to the media."

Damien tried an easy smile. "I just have a few simple questions. This Web site, I think it has the potential to cause a lot of trouble, and I'm wondering what the department is doing to investigate it."

"Nothing."

"Nothing?"

"We're off the record here, okay?"

Damien nodded.

"We don't have enough resources to chase down something like this. We don't have a cyber crime unit or anything of that nature here. It's Marlo, for crying out loud. If we started with this Web site, who knows what else would happen. We'd have to start chasing down people who pirate movies."

"But isn't it illegal? I mean, it's against the law to eavesdrop on people's private conversations."

"Yes, it is. Unless you're doing a wiretap or something like that."

"We've already seen what it's done to neighbors."

"That's one instance."

"I've heard of something else."

The captain threw his hands up. "I don't want to hear about it. Look, I think this is a perfect thing for you guys at the paper to go investigate. You like to stir up trouble and this is trouble. My preference would be to ignore it, and it'll probably go away. But that's just me. We've had no official complaints about the Web site, so I'm not pursuing any kind of investigation at this time."

Damien blinked. The conversation he had with Frank the night before blazed through his mind, that the department *was* investigating. "You're saying the department is *not* investigating it at all?"

"That's what I'm saying."

He had just caught Frank in lie number two.

* * *

Gavin stood next to Frank on the front porch of the Shaws' home, chewing a fingernail and staring at Frank.

"Stop looking at me," Frank whispered. "Just play this cool. Do you even have that mode? Cool, collected, calm? Any of that ringing a bell with you? We're the police. We're not the ones who are supposed to be nervous."

"We're not supposed to be here," Gavin said.

"Yes. Your expression is capturing that perfectly." Frank pushed the doorbell again. "Don't you have a pair of dark shades or something you can slide over those terrified eyeballs?"

"I don't want to get caught."

"Gavin, chill out. We're not stealing secret documents

here. We're only doing some minor investigative work. It's not sink or swim. It's more like an arm floaties kind of situation." Frank cut his gaze sideways to see if any of this was registering with the kid. Didn't look like it. "And you can be thankful we're not at Angela's house."

That seemed to bring fast relief. He smiled and nodded just as the door opened. Barely opened.

Peering through the tiny crack allowed by the chain lock, an eye blinked at them. "Yes?"

"Mrs. Shaw, Officer Merret here. I need to speak with you."

"Why?"

"It's about the incident." That was vague enough.

The wide-eyed stare vanished into the darkness, and soon enough the door opened wider. She stood in what looked like pajamas, grasping the side of the door, unwilling to do much more than show her face. A dark purplish-green bruise peeked from beneath her bangs. "Yes? What is it?"

Frank carefully chose his words. He was crossing the line. Just barely. But crossing nevertheless. He had to be careful to not say he was representing the department. "This Web site that your conversation was posted on, how did it get there?"

"I told you, like I told my husband, I don't know. I didn't put it there. Is that what you think? That I put it there?" Her voice crawled with panic.

"No, no. I think someone else is doing it," Frank said.

Gavin nodded.

Mrs. Shaw let go of the death grip she had on the door-frame. "I still don't know if Tim believes me."

"May we come in?"

She peered out a little and gave a long stare toward the Caldwells' house across the street. "Okay, fine."

Inside, the living room that was once very tidy looked messy. Mrs. Shaw quickly gathered up a few things so they had a place to sit. She dumped the pile into the corner. "I'm sorry for the mess. I'm still not feeling . . ." Her words trailed off.

"Is everything okay between you and your husband?"

"Yes. Thank you for asking." Her words and tone were proper. "So what can I do for you?"

"As you probably know, your conversation is not the only one that has been recorded. Dozens are on there. We're trying to figure out how this person is doing it. One theory is that he or she may have planted a listening device inside your home."

Mrs. Shaw looked startled. "You mean, like a bug?"

"Yes. They can be very small and virtually undetectable."

"But nobody's really been to our house except friends and family."

"No repair jobs? painting? Anybody like that?"

"No. Not that I can recall."

"Do you remember where the conversation took place? the one that ended up on the Web site?"

"Right in here. By that window. Tim was angry. He was staring out the window at the Caldwells'. Standing right there." Mrs. Shaw pointed to a spot near the center of the window.

"Gavin, get your flashlight, start looking under tables, lamps that sort of thing."

Gavin started with the coffee table.

Mrs. Shaw watched, disbelief in her eyes. She shifted her focus back to Frank. "Tim's a good man."

"I'm sure you love him very much."

"No, please, listen. That night . . . the night he said those things, he was angry. Do you understand that? He was saying those words to me. He was just venting. Nobody else was supposed to hear them. And when he found out they were on that Web site . . ."

"Yes, ma'am. I know. He lost his temper."

"He would never intentionally harm me. You have to believe that."

Frank gestured toward the TV. "Have you noticed any interference? any strange sounds coming from your electronic devices?"

"No," Mrs. Shaw said, watching Gavin check their phone.

"Or while you're on the phone, has it sounded funny?"

"No."

Gavin turned off his flashlight and returned to the couch. "I can't find anything out of the ordinary. I mean, besides this entire situation."

Frank shot him a look. He quickly sat back down.

Mrs. Shaw gazed out the window again. "Are we going to be charged? for the cat incident?"

"It's not up to us," Frank said. "The reports have been turned over to the DA. He'll make that decision."

She sniffled and fingered the material of her pants. "One day everything is normal, you know? Everything is fine. And then it's gone. Suddenly, like a blink of the eye, your life has changed forever."

Frank noticed Gavin staring at him. Mrs. Shaw looked at him with an unusual expression too.

Frank stood, blowing out a hard sigh, shaking off the heaviness that suddenly engulfed him. "I know, Mrs. Shaw. I know exactly what you mean."

14

"THIS IS STUPID! This is so stupid!" *Stomp, stomp, stomp.* "My father is a moron! You're a moron, Father!"

Damien sat at the kitchen table, sipping orange juice as he listened to chaos erupt one story up.

Even Kay joined in. "Damien," she hollered down the stairs, "what time is it? You didn't give us enough time!"

Damien checked the kitchen clock. "You're fine. You've got plenty of time."

"I hate you for this!" Jenna continued. At age five, the word *hate* got her a time-out, and this kind of tantrum at eight would've gotten her grounded. But these days, it was a hopeful sign that her emotions were all still intact.

Hunter descended the stairs first, his feet dragging down each step as if someone had poured lead in his shoes.

"Looking nice, dude," Damien said when he got to the bottom.

Hunter scowled, then went to the fridge to get the orange juice.

"Your sister and mother are taking it well," Damien quipped, adding a smirk.

Hunter smirked back. "Yeah. I think Jenna's going to light you on fire with her tongue. If she ever makes it down here."

"Oh, she's going to make it down here all right." Damien waited patiently, his resolve building with each minute that ticked by. Yes, this was a good move. Taking your family to church helped build a foundation, and that was what they needed right now. Some help out of the quicksand they'd found themselves sinking in.

A loud thumping, like roofers were up top, caused Damien to look up. Jenna stomped down the stairs, glaring harder with each step.

Damien smiled. "You look beautiful. Thanks for getting up early for this." She actually wore a dress that fluttered around her legs as if she were wrapped in a white butterfly.

"Save it," she said, throwing open the door to the fridge.

"More of that talk and we might have to make this a weekly tradition," Damien said, an eyebrow raised.

She peeked around the fridge door. "You wouldn't."

"I would."

"Ugh." She rolled her eyes.

"This is more for you than me," Hunter said, casting an evil grin her direction.

"Shut up. Please shut up about it. I've got a headache.

Probably because I had to wake up at the stroke of midnight."

"You're only eight hours off," Hunter said.

Damien snapped his fingers at him. This could go on for hours if he didn't run interference.

Jenna noticed the orange juice already on the table and grabbed a glass. She tossed herself into a chair. "You just don't get it. I'm exhausted. I don't need another day to wake up early."

"You can take a nap later," Damien said.

"Whatever." She scanned the orange juice carton. "Can anybody say 'pulp-free'? How hard is it?"

Kay hurried down the stairs, fingering her hair. "How do I look?"

"Really nice. Love the dress."

"This old thing? Ugh. But I wear suits all week. Didn't want to wear another."

"Why do we have to dress up anyway?" Jenna moaned.

"Because that's the proper way to dress," Kay said. "Your bra strap is showing, by the way."

"Just shoot me," she said, laying her head on the table.

"Let's save that for later," Damien said, standing and grabbing his suit jacket. He smiled. "Now, off to the torture chamber."

Otherwise known as church.

The two-mile drive was relatively quiet, except for an occasional grunt coming from the backseat. There was something different about Sunday mornings. The air sparkled with freshness. The noises all seemed subdued. People waved and walked their dogs. Maybe he should bring the Sunday morning drive back.

Better yet, write it as an op-ed piece! Perfect.

He remembered going to church with his parents. His father dressed in his best suit, an expensive fedora topping his head. It was the only time his dad wore a hat or showed his mother any affection. On Sundays they held hands and talked lightly.

The mood was quite different in his own car, but maybe it would change once they got there.

The church parking lot was crowded, and Damien hesitated, wondering if a two-year absence qualified him as a visitor.

"Right there," Jenna said. "It's wide open."

Damien pulled in and parked. Everyone except him was slow to get out. Damien led his family to the front entrance.

A greeter opened the door and smiled. "Welcome."

They stepped into the large sanctuary. A balcony loomed above them like an encroaching thunderstorm. Plenty of seats to choose from on the lower level. "Where do you want to sit?"

"Doesn't matter," Jenna muttered, her arms crossed.

"Fine. Let's just go down this aisle a few pews."

As Jenna led the way, Damien noticed she seemed particularly self-aware, messing with her hair and glancing around. Suddenly she stopped and turned. "Let's not. How about the other side? There are more seats over there."

"There are plenty of seats here. Look, just up ahead is an entire pew."

"No, I like the other side." She pushed between all of them. "Come on. I see the perfect spot."

"Oh, wait!" Kay said. "It's Shannon and Susan! Jenna, Zoey and Caydance are with them. Come on!" She hurried forward, waving and smiling.

Hunter shrugged and followed.

Damien glanced back at Jenna. "You okay?"

"Yeah."

"You're sure?" Damien caught the dread in the deepest part of her eyes. "You don't look okay."

Jenna's gaze drifted down the aisle, then to him.

Suddenly a hand was on his shoulder. Damien glanced behind him.

A man with a gigantic smile was offering his hand. "Hi. Pastor Caldwell. I didn't recognize you and your family. I just wanted to say hello and welcome."

Damien looked down the aisle. Jenna was making her way to her seat.

"What was your name?"

"Damien Underwood. My family is down there."

The pastor smiled, and Damien suddenly recognized him as the man whose cat was hung.

"I'm sorry to hear what happened in your neighborhood," Damien said.

The man nodded, his welcoming eyes turning sad. "I am sorry to hear what is happening to our town."

"Your friend Tim Shaw. Have you spoken to him?"

"Oh yes. Of course. He is ashamed of so much . . . what he was heard saying, what he did to his wife. I'm trying to help him deal with that guilt."

"So you don't think he did that to your cat?"

"No. I've known the man for a long time. My wife has had a hard time with what he said about me. It is a tough thing to hear a friend's words. I pray for her. For all of us. There is going to be a lot to forgive when this is over." His eyes turned cheerful again as he gently patted Damien on the arm. "I'm so glad you're with us today. I must get up front. It's almost time for the service."

Damien nodded and joined his family, sliding into the end seat just in time to hear Kay address Jenna. "Honey, say hi to the girls."

Jenna offered a half smile to the two girls sitting one row ahead. "Hi."

"Hi, Jenna," one of them said. Then the girls turned around and giggled.

Damien glanced at Jenna, who only stared forward, expressionless.

"I didn't know you came here," one of the women said to Kay.

"We haven't come in a while. But glad to be back. This is my husband, Damien. Damien, this is Shannon Branson and Susan Sanders."

Damien shook their hands. Shannon was overly made-up, as if she hoped that fresh-face youthful look would hold on, and when it didn't, she'd freaked out. Damien was glad Kay didn't overdo it. Susan's sharp eyes studied Damien. She was smiling, but it looked scrutinizing, like how rich people greet everyone who is less rich. Damien gave a short smile, and the woman finally turned back around. He noticed Jenna again. Her eyes had glazed over, and she blinked slowly. Damien leaned into her. "You're sure you're all right?"

Jenna nodded. But it was the kind of nod that didn't ring true.

Not surprisingly, the sermon was about gossip. Damien thought the pastor did a good job of not pointing fingers but rather showing the destruction of gossip and also the importance and power of truth in words.

Damien found himself uplifted. Even the family seemed in a better mood as the service ended. Jenna wrapped her arm around his waist as they left. Hunter saw a friend from school and hurried toward the foyer. Kay stayed and chatted with the cheerleading moms.

Damien held tight to his daughter as they walked. "Hey, what do you say we go eat at Chicken Annie's?"

"Fried chicken, are you kidding me?"

"When you were five years old, you used to eat four pieces. Your face was a mess of grease. You wanted to have your birthday party there!"

Jenna laughed. Giggled, actually. He hadn't heard her giggle in a long time. She sounded like a little girl again. "I guess one piece won't kill me."

"It might, but it'll be worth it. Go find your brother, will you? I'm starving."

Jenna nodded, and Damien watched the crowds for Kay. But soon his ears tuned into a conversation nearby. He couldn't help but listen. Their small words drowned the hundreds of nearby voices.

"I'm just saying, I wouldn't show my face the day after my divorce was settled."

"You know why he's here."

"And why she's wearing a short skirt."

Damien turned, trying to get away from it. He noticed Kay and waved at her. She held up a finger as she finished her conversation. That was when Damien noticed Zoey and Caydance. They both crossed their arms, glaring at someone across the room. Damien couldn't figure out who they were looking at.

"Let's go," Jenna said, coming up from behind with Hunter in tow.

"Jenna, who are those girls looking at?" Damien asked, pointing.

"Probably their own reflection. Let's go, okay?"

Kay joined them and they left, but Damien couldn't help but steal another glance. Whoever it was could be at the receiving end of a lot of unpleasantries.

* * *

After breaking up an impromptu scuffle in front of the Chinese restaurant, over a conversation off the Web site that may or may not have been about the tall guy's wife, Frank took lunch and heaped a giant serving of lo mein onto his plate, then pushed his tray down the long self-serve buffet line. He skipped the hot and sour soup but decided on a couple of egg rolls. He joined his rookie back at the table, eyeing the kid's steamed vegetables and rice. He watched him dash it all with a splash of soy sauce.

"Careful," Frank said, taking the soy sauce from him. "That sodium can kill you."

Gavin stared at Frank's heaping plate, then looked at Frank. He cracked a small, hesitant smile, unsure, Frank guessed, of whether or not Frank was kidding. For a cop, the kid was lacking some serious gut instincts.

"Chinese food is less healthy than it looks," Gavin said. He pointed his fork toward the egg roll. "Don't let the cabbage in there fool you."

"And don't let the smile on my face fool you."

Gavin stopped pointing and started eating. "You know," he said after a moment, "I've been thinking about this Web site. I read somewhere that there's a program that can be loaded onto cell phones, and then someone can listen to conversations wherever the cell phone goes. Even if the cell phone is turned off."

"Interesting idea."

"I went by one of the cell phone stores here, just asked some questions. Nobody seemed particularly nervous."

"That's what you're going on, whether people seemed nervous or not?"

"I figured if they'd done something, they wouldn't like me asking around."

"Yes, because criminals have a long history of not being able to hide under a facade." Frank tilted his head. "It's going to take more than that." Gavin looked wounded and Frank sighed. "But it's a good thought. It might explain some of this."

The wounds slid right off Gavin like Chinese noodles off a chopstick. His face was back to bright and cheery. "Also, there are some pretty powerful listening devices that use laser beams. But they're really expensive. And of course come with explicit instructions on how illegal it is to listen to private conversations."

"Yes, those types of warnings always discourage the bad guys."

Gavin leaned in. "You think this is a bad guy?"

Frank twirled his noodles. "He's breaking the law. It's up to someone else to decide whether he's bad or good."

A shadow passed over their plates, and Frank was just about to order another Diet Coke when he looked up. "Angela?"

"Hi, Frank." She had a hand on her hip and an attitude on her face. She glanced at Gavin, who sank back into his seat while staring at her as if she were a wild zoo exhibit. The idea that Gavin cowered to a harsh look from a female was not boding well with Frank. What was he going to do when a bullet stared him down? "Can we have a moment?"

Frank indicated Gavin should leave.

Gavin gathered his plate, water, and utensils and wandered off to find another table. Angela slid into his seat.

Frank kept eating. "I'm minding my own business here."

Her face softened. "I know, Frank. I know."

"How did you find me?"

"It's Sunday. You eat at this buffet every Sunday unless you're not working, in which case you order supreme pizza and stay at home."

"I might've changed my routine since we were together."

"You're here, aren't you?"

Frank finally set his fork down. He was rapidly losing his appetite. "Why are you here? To harass me some more?"

"Who is harassing whom?"

"I hate when you talk like that."

"Like what?"

"Like you ain't never met a piece of grammar that didn't turn you on."

"And I hate when you use *ain't*."

"I know." Frank smiled.

"And we wonder why we didn't make it." Angela stood. "Maybe this was a mistake."

Frank waved her back into her seat. "No, please. I'm sorry. Yeah, I'm kind of reeling from you reporting me to my supervisor. But I'll get over it." He started eating again. "You look nice."

"Frank, I don't have . . . I don't know who else to turn to."

Frank shoved his plate to the side. "What's wrong? I can tell something's wrong."

She nodded, tears brimming. "I've gotten . . ."

"Yes? What is it?" Frank reached across the table and took her hand. "Ang, you can tell me. You know that. What's going on?"

"I've gotten myself into a terrible mess."

"Talk to me."

"First of all, that awful Web site . . ."

"I know of it."

"One of my conversations is on there. I mean, I'm not named but I know it's me. I remember saying it. We'd gotten into a fight and—"

"We? You and I?"

She bowed her head. "No."

Frank sipped his drink, glancing away to try to hide the pain that was surely surfacing. He saw Gavin across the room staring at them.

"Things are getting very . . . complicated. I think I'm in way over my head."

Frank studied her. One shoulder slouched, a sign of perhaps a bigger imbalance in her life. "You're going to have to be more specific. You have to tell me what's going on. Is your life in danger?"

"I think so."

Frank's chest tightened and his ears burned, probably turning bright red. "All right, I'll handle this. What's his name?"

"It's not him. It's her."

Frank sat back. What was she trying to say here? That she was dating a—

"It's his wife." She clutched the napkin on the table. "Not my finest moment, I know. But they were in the middle of separating, and he swore it was over. But then she found out."

"How?"

"I'm not sure. I think maybe the Web site . . . She probably figured out it was Mike in that conversation." She looked at Frank now, her eyes begging for forgiveness, understanding. "She's very angry, threatening a lot of stuff."

"What kind of stuff?"

"You know . . . she's going to kill me."

"Does he think she's serious?"

Angela tore the edges off the napkin. "I don't know. I just don't know. He's acting weird too."

Frank tried a calming breath. This was a lot to take in. "Weird how?"

"He's very upset that the conversation is on that Web site. I don't blame him. I would be upset too. And . . . you're going to be upset also." The napkin was in shreds. Usually when she said he was going to be upset, she was right.

"What?"

It took three false starts, but finally Angela said, "The conversation on the Web site is about you." She opened her hands up, trying to explain. "I was angry with you. I didn't mean what I said. I was upset and I said some things. I never intended for anyone else to hear them."

"What exactly did you say?"

"Mike's scared of you, okay? It's no secret what you put Vincent MaLue through."

"Get to the point."

"We were having a fight, and he said he wasn't going to put up with you harassing him. Things were already getting weird. I was aggravated, and I said some things about you, all right?"

Frank felt his nostrils flare. That wasn't a good sign. "All right."

She reached for his hand. "I knew you'd understand."

"I don't understand why you're here."

Tears again, shiny and plump, balanced on her eyelashes. "I'm scared. I've made a huge mess here. His wife is furious, and I've heard a few things about her. I think she's unstable. And Mike . . . he's got a temper. He's never hit me or hurt me or anything like that, but he keeps getting more agitated, and when he's agitated, he doesn't seem to think clearly."

"What do you want?"

"I didn't mean all that stuff I said to Damien." Angela stared at the ceiling for a moment.

Frank's heart thumped heavily with dread.

"I would never sue you. And even though I saw you there, over the fence, I know deep down inside you're a good—"

"What are you talking about?"

They exchanged a tense stare, even as the waitress came and refilled Frank's Diet Coke.

"Don't act like you don't know," Angela said.

"Know what?"

"I'm trying to have an adult conversation with you. I came here, told you what's going on, even though really, you already knew, didn't you? Because you were spying on me." She took a deep breath. "I thought you were the one that put the conversation on the Internet. But when I went to look at the Web site, there are so many conversations. I don't know . . . I don't think you did it anymore."

"You thought *I* was the one doing this?"

"I saw you that day. You were behind the fence of Mike's house. You were walking away when I came out the back door."

"I don't know what you're talking about."

"You're telling me you weren't spying on me and Mike?"

"I don't know who Mike is. I didn't know you were seeing someone. If I did, I wouldn't have filed a missing person report. Because I would've known you'd probably moved in with him after the fourth date."

Angela's eyes widened with offense. "That was cruel."

"What do you want from me? Why are you here?"

She wadded up what little bit was left of the napkin and threw it on the table. "I don't know. You act like I'm the only person in your life, and then when I need your help, suddenly you're not interested?"

"You need my help to get yourself out of this tangled web you've created; is that it?"

Her voice reduced to a whisper. "I'm scared. I wouldn't be here if I didn't think that woman might do something crazy. I'm going to break it off with Mike, but I don't really know what he's going to do either. I just thought . . ." She bit her lip, smiled sweetly at him. It was that very smile on a

Sunday in May that had made Frank realize he would marry this woman. "I need your help. That's what I'm saying. I need your help to get out of this."

Frank's elbow went into his plate and came out with sweet and sour sauce dripping off it.

Angela grabbed his napkin, stood, leaned across the table, and dabbed. She was close to him, her hair swinging in front of his face, her perfume filling his nostrils.

He closed his eyes, trying to find clarity, but all he saw was their wedding day. Her dress, with a lovely, blissful train of white, flowing with life as she gracefully strolled down the aisle. The wispy veil, with tiny pink flowers dotted across it, fluttered against her face, giving him only glimpses into her eyes. The moment he lifted the veil and smoothed it over her beautiful hair, his heart had skipped a beat and caused a deep devotion that he couldn't explain to this day.

She stared at him as if there were nothing else in the room. "Frank?"

Frank fled the memory, snapping back into reality.

Angela sat across from him. A smile belied her unblinking eyes.

"Angela, you know that I've always loved you. And I always will."

Her smile spread into a grin. "I know."

"But I can't help you with this. I can't step into this situation. I can't. I won't."

Few things ever seemed to surprise Angela Owens Merret. Or at least she'd always had the ability to play it cool.

Not today. She stood, her chair falling backward and rattling against the floor. She dropped a few expletives on the table before she stomped out, leaving Frank with a plate full of cold food and a room full of people staring at him. Including Gavin.

Frank rose, throwing some money on the table.

Gavin hurried over, carrying his plate. "I'm not quite done here. We just—"

"Don't wet yourself, kid. I'll be back to get you."

"You're leaving me here? Again?"

"Eat your lunch. I'll be back."

There was someone he desperately needed to see. And nobody else would do but her.

15

DAMIEN STOOD IN Edgar's office, hands clasped behind his back, lips pressed together to hide any disappointment.

Unfortunately Edgar was not being as gracious. His gaze zipped back and forth, up and down, over the entire page. He slapped the paper down on his desk on top of the other piece of paper he'd already slapped down. "What is this?"

"It's my op-ed and my investigative piece on—"

"I know what it is," Edgar growled. "I also know what it isn't. It's terrific writing. Insightful. Poignant at moments. Humorous."

Damien smiled. "Thank you."

"It isn't the least bit interesting or relevant." Edgar's voice, baritone and full, sounded loud without much volume. "Why would you write a piece about church?"

"Well, I—"

"About your memories of your father and mother dressed up, all this nostalgia bull. Do you really think people care about this?"

"I don't understand. This isn't any different from what I've written in the past."

"Exactly. Except, if you haven't noticed, this town is in an uproar." Edgar looked out of breath. His eyes seemed unusually frantic. Edgar was a loud guy, but it was usually just for show. Something was different.

"The Web site."

"Yes! Yes, the Web site! It's all anyone's talking about! Two nights ago there was a conversation on there that I'd had with an old college buddy of mine. We were at a restaurant. Luckily it was innocuous, but can't you see what's on everyone's mind?"

"Well, sure. I figured a nice piece about the way things used to be—"

"It's now! It's in the moment! And this?" He held up the investigative piece. "This is all you've got?"

Damien fumbled his words. This investigative thing was harder than it looked. Lots of people wanted to talk, but it didn't tend to be the people with helpful information.

Edgar leaned across his desk, the wood creaking underneath his heavy arms. "I'm desperate to keep this newspaper going. It's been in my family for three generations, and it's not going down on my watch. Do you understand me?"

Damien nodded, holding his breath as he watched the veins in Edgar's neck pulsate.

Suddenly Edgar said, "Hush," just as the religion editor walked by the door.

"What?"

"You gotta be careful what you say and around whom you say it. Now, you get out there and get me some real news. And write me a piece that drives a stake through my heart. What is this Web site doing to our town? Is it a good or bad thing? Dig deep."

Damien's phone vibrated with a text message: *Harmon's Grocery.* He opened the office door. "I'm on it, boss."

Edgar smiled eagerly.

* * *

With flashing lights and wailing sirens, Frank and Gavin raced toward Harmon's Grocery on the corner of Twelfth and Medlane.

A small crowd had gathered in front of the store, with several baggers and clerks talking with customers. Frank pulled to the front curb, and they got out.

The store manager, the only one in a tie, greeted them with a handshake. "We tried to stop them. They're still going at it. Things are crashing in there. I removed everyone for safety."

"Any weapons?"

"Not that I saw."

Frank glanced around and noticed Pastor Caldwell standing in the crowd. He held a Bible and seemed to be praying.

Frank put his hand on his holster and walked in. Gavin followed close behind. A crash sounded, followed by raining glass.

The manager trailed them. "I think they're in aisle nine."

"Police!" Frank shouted. "Break it up!"

More glass shattered. Frank rushed to find the source. It was aisle ten, near the pickles. What he saw stopped him in his tracks. "Stand down!" Frank shouted.

The two men tangled on the floor were soaking wet from the contents of broken containers of vinegar. Bright red blood pooled and snaked through the vinegar and over the laminate floor like small rivers. The smell caused Frank to cough into his sleeve. Both men were hardly recognizable with cuts and bruises and bulging eyelids. Shards of broken glass caught the fluorescent light above, glimmering like diamonds.

Frank walked forward, his hand on his gun. "Move away from one another."

Both men groaned like that could hurt a lot. The man on the left had a long, dark line of blood from the top of his chest down to his belly. He clutched his shirt and moaned. The other man grabbed his own shoulder. Blood seeped through his fingers, but his attention was still on the other man, a glare frozen on his face.

Frank turned to Gavin. "Get two ambulances here."

The manager stepped around Gavin, inspecting the floor and then the two men. "There's a lot of blood," he whispered.

"I know. Get me some clean towels. A lot of towels. Hurry." Frank pointed to the man holding his shoulder. "Don't make a move. Stay right there." He stooped over the man who bled from the chest. "What's your name?"

"His name's Rob Tereau."

"Your name?" Frank asked.

"Randy Benjamen."

Rob's eyes turned glassy. Frank knelt next to him and grabbed his shoulders. He felt Rob's body go limp. He made certain there wasn't any glass behind him in case he fell backward. Frank's pants, right at the knee, began soaking up vinegar mixed with blood.

"Get a mop over here!" Frank yelled.

Gavin rushed up. "They're on the way."

"Take care of that guy," Frank said, nodding toward Randy.

The manager returned with some towels. Frank pulled up Rob's shirt. Two deep gashes, one over his sternum and the other above his navel, continued to gush. He grabbed a towel and pushed it against the top wound, then grabbed another one and pushed it on the bottom.

Ambulance sirens wailed through the skylight above them.

Gavin helped Randy up, checked him over, then took a towel and gave it to him.

Frank, still stooped over Rob, looked at Randy. "What happened here?"

"This man attacked my sister."

Rob mumbled. "No, I didn't."

"He did."

"Where is she?" Frank asked. "Is she hurt?"

"He called my sister a . . . I can't even say it. I won't say it."

Frank glanced down at Rob, whose eyes periodically

rolled back into his head. "I said . . . I didn't say it to him . . . or her. I said it at a . . . it was a party . . . I was in the back room . . ."

"The Web site? That's where you read it?"

Randy nodded. His glare turned to Rob again.

The EMTs scooted through the crowd that had come in from outside. Frank stood and backed away.

Both men looked like they'd been tossed into a meat grinder.

Gavin stepped beside him, pointing at his pants. "You're going to have to change."

Frank stared at the two men. His stomach turned at the sight.

"All this over a Web site?" Gavin asked, handing him a clean towel.

Frank tried wiping the blood off his hands, then handed Gavin the towel. "I'm going to need a minute."

"But—"

"A minute, Gavin. Take care of this mess."

* * *

Damien threw his briefcase onto the entryway chair and tossed his jacket on the armrest. He was too tired to hang it up now. The flavorful aroma of spaghetti and meatballs mingled with the smell of fresh basil from Kay's garden.

He walked to the kitchen.

"Hi." She hugged him with her elbows. "Sorry, have sauce on my hands."

"Smells good."

"You look exhausted."

"I am." He plopped himself on top of a barstool. "This town has gone insane."

"Bad day at work?"

"Depends on your perspective, I guess. Edgar hated my piece on how church used to be."

"Sorry, sweetie."

"He's obsessed with this Web site thing going on. And apparently so is the rest of the town. Two guys got in a fight over at Harmon's. Then an elderly lady got a threatening letter on her door. Dispatch said that today they actually had people calling 911 to report their conversations on the Web site. Tires are being slashed. Cars being keyed."

Kay had turned, giving him her full attention. "Let's make sure we park our cars in the garage."

"Let's make sure we don't say anything that would offend someone," Damien said.

"Time to eat!" Kay called.

"Yet should we censor ourselves in our own home?" Damien helped her carry the dishes to the table. Jenna arrived from upstairs, slumped and bored-looking. Damien sat down and engaged her. "What do you think?"

"About what?"

"Should we censor ourselves in our home because of the fear of what might be heard?"

"I dunno."

"It's a good question," Damien said. "Would make a good

op-ed piece. I mean, aren't we entitled to private conversations?"

"Of course we are," Kay said, joining them at the table. "Where's Hunter?"

The front door opened. Hunter came in, barely managing his skateboard and backpack.

"I thought you were upstairs," Kay said.

"Nah. Went down the street to skateboard a little." He set his backpack and skateboard down. "Yes! Meatballs!"

Damien passed them over as Hunter sat. "So the question is, Hunter, do we have a right to say whatever we want behind closed doors?"

"Sure. I guess."

"It's the old saying, if a tree falls in the forest and nobody's there to hear it, does it make a sound?"

Jenna sighed. "Dad, why does everything have to go deep for you? Why can't you just admire a tree and be done with it?"

"So you think this is admirable, this Web site? Be honest. I want your honest opinion about it."

Jenna sliced a meatball but looked like she was thinking it over. "I don't know. I guess it is. I think it's good."

"You do? Why?" Damien slid his plate aside, giving Jenna his full attention.

She glanced up, blinked like she was surprised. "Maybe people shouldn't say mean stuff. Like they don't think about what they're saying; they just say stuff and don't care what happens or how it makes people feel."

Damien leaned back, crossing his arms. "So you think this is calling attention to how we use our words?"

"It's right up your alley," Jenna said. "You know how you're really into the whole power of words thing."

"Yes, I was always more interested in the power of vocabulary, but it seems even simple words demand attention in this case—don't you think?"

"I don't know. Whatever. It's only a gossip site." Jenna gave a wry smile. "Or perhaps voyeurism in its most simple yet fatal design."

Damien jumped up and grabbed a pad of paper and a pencil out of the kitchen. "This is good stuff. So you think it's the voyeurism aspect that's captivating?"

"Yeah."

"What is it about verbal voyeurism that captivates?"

"Sorry. There's a limit to how much I can talk about voyeurism with my father, especially when he looks like he's going to quote me in the newspaper." Jenna's gaze dropped to the pad of paper.

"Sorry. I promise not to quote anybody. I'm just writing down some notes." Damien looked at Hunter. "What about you? What are your thoughts?"

"I don't know. I don't really have any."

"Oh, come on. This is fun. Be real with me. What are you really thinking about it? I promise not to quote you."

"Well," Kay said, "if I'm being real and honest, I have to say I'm totally addicted. To hear people's private conversations . . . it kind of lets you know who they really are. It's almost the only way to know who people really are. That's when their guard is down."

"So the question is, do the conversations we have privately define who we are, or are we who we are despite our private conversations?"

"It's like you are what you eat, which is why I want to finish eating these meatballs," Hunter said, stuffing one into his mouth.

"Did Frank say if they were getting closer to knowing who's doing it?" Jenna asked.

"No. They don't have any good leads. That's what he said." Damien set his pad down and started eating, trying to escape the thought that Frank might be behind it all. He'd pushed it out of his mind today, but it was back now. Frank had lied to him. Twice. And Frank was not one to lie about anything. But what would cause him to do it?

His thoughts were interrupted by the doorbell ringing.

"Probably the Mormons." Jenna sighed. "I'll get it. The boys can be cute."

Damien smiled. She did seem a little happier today, and if it took cute Mormon boys to make that happen, well, he'd take what he could get.

Damien heard a male voice, then Jenna say, "Dad, I think you better come here."

They all three got up from the table and went to the door. Standing on the porch was a Marlo police officer.

"Officer, what's wrong?" Damien asked.

The officer held up a picture. "We have a missing girl. Wondered if you know her or have seen her."

"A missing girl? In Marlo?" Kay gasped.

They all studied the photo; then Jenna said, "That's Gabby."

"Gabby?" Damien asked.

"Gabriella Caldwell. She's in my class."

Damien's heart stopped. The pastor's daughter?

"Yes, that's her name," the officer said. "Have you seen or heard from her?"

"No," Jenna said.

"Are you friends with her, Jenna?" Damien asked.

"No, not really. I kind of know her. She's quiet. Doesn't hang out much. She stays to herself mostly."

"Let us know if you hear from her or see her," the officer said.

Damien shut the door and turned. His family stared at him. Kay took his arm and squeezed against him.

"It's going to be fine," Damien said. "I'm sure they'll find her. She's probably out with friends or something."

"She doesn't have any friends," Jenna said. "I mean, not really."

"Maybe she ran away," Hunter said.

"Maybe," Damien said. "You guys finish dinner. I'm going to have to cover this."

When Damien had decided he wanted to be an investigative reporter, he never imagined he'd be investigating the quick unraveling of his beloved town.

16

Frank zipped his coat all the way to the chin and pulled on his heaviest leather gloves. The wind snapped and howled. The moon, nearly full, provided decent light at 2:30 in the morning. The quietness was undone by the distant sound of dogs barking and people shouting Gabriella's name.

"Come on. Get something hot to drink," Frank said, urging the volunteer team into the parking lot. They'd searched the large park in the center of Marlo but came up empty and dejected.

Captain Grayson handed Frank a cup of hot cider. "Nothing?"

"Nothing."

Nearby, Reverend Caldwell huddled with his wife, his gaze darting to every sound. He clutched a Bible to his chest.

"We've issued the Amber Alert, and we've got the FBI coming in with more dogs." Grayson laid a map down on his car. "When we get light, we'll start here. There's a lot of country out there, lots of trees and shrubs."

"Light? We can't wait that long."

"And then there's the river."

"I know."

Lou leaned against the car, sipping the cider. "Her parents are sure she didn't run away. They said she's very responsible, very reliable. They said she's been upset since the cat incident, but she wasn't upset with them, just with the circumstance. She left her money, her coat. Her car is still in the driveway, and the keys are at home. She takes medication that was left."

Frank scanned the hillside, listening to the volunteers call her name, watching the lights bounce through the darkness. "She didn't run away. Call it a gut instinct." He tossed his cider. "I'm assuming we've interviewed Tim and Darla Shaw?"

"Yeah. Murray tracked them down. They have solid alibis."

"Which means there's a good chance they had nothing to do with the cat either. Because it seems to me these two things could be connected."

"Maybe."

Frank looked out over the crowd of people. Their faces, cold and chapped, told the whole story. They were losing their town. Innocence was fading. Nothing like this had ever happened before. Fear shone in their eyes, haunting and hollow.

"You okay?" Grayson asked.

Frank swallowed hard, trying to shove memories aside. But today they wouldn't budge. Not even a little. "You know how many calls we covered yesterday? I saw two men, bathed in blood, on the floor of a grocery store. All because one man said something about another man's sister."

"Well, we all know what that leads to."

"Except he didn't say it to him—he said it to his wife at a party in a back room. And now it's on the Internet for everyone to read. The Web site is showing eight thousand hits a day. People are devouring this stuff."

"I know. I started reading it myself."

"You still think we shouldn't investigate?" Frank knew his tone was heavy and intense, but that was the best he could do under the circumstances.

Grayson let out a hard sigh. "We don't have the resources. I think I can get Sampson to pull a detective off Robbery to monitor it, and we may be able to gain a lead if they slip and make a mistake, but we need some computer experts in here. We can ask state, but you know that'll take weeks to process."

"People are growing paranoid. They're not trusting their friends, their neighbors. Relationships are being permanently ruined."

"My hands are tied."

"What's it going to take for you to see how bad this is going to get?"

"Frank—"

Frank slapped the map. "I'm going to the alley off Gordon Street."

"Wait. Let me get some volunteers together to—"

But Frank didn't wait. He couldn't. He had to find this girl if it was the last thing he did. Ever.

* * *

Damien's entire body shivered as he made his way inside his home. The heated air enveloped him when he shook off his coat. Unwinding the scarf from his neck, he took his first deep breath since he'd left the house hours ago.

He still trembled but from the inside out. Even as he sought to reassure anyone he could, dread seized every word. Nobody was reassured. Not even him.

Quietly, he turned the light on above the stairwell and tiptoed toward the top, hoping not to wake anyone. He'd left to cover the story and ended up joining a team searching for Gabriella. They marched through a field high with weeds, calling out her name, flashlight beams bouncing around like pinballs. It felt haunting, frantic, but slow and methodical. At one point, he'd stooped down, catching a glimpse of a shoe. Turned out it was an old farmer's boot. But his emotions swelled, and it was all he could do not to show them.

He topped the stairs and stood looking at the closed doors of his children's rooms. Both said Keep Out. But he longed to check on them, make sure they were okay. He grabbed the doorknob to Hunter's room. His door always squeaked.

He gently pushed his body against it and it popped open. Hunter stirred in his bed but didn't wake.

He used to check on the kids several times a night. When they were first born, he'd stand over their cribs, watching them breathe. When they were toddlers, he'd stand over their beds and pray. Then one day, they didn't want night-time stories read anymore, and they didn't come downstairs for good-night kisses. The routine vanished, and now they all simply slept and didn't think about one another until the morning.

Damien tried to shut the door quietly, then felt someone grab his arm. He jerked around to find Kay in her pajamas, tears streaming down her face. "I can't sleep."

Damien wrapped an arm around her and led her to their bedroom. "Have you been crying all this time?"

She nodded, wiping the tears. "I kind of freaked out earlier, after we got home from handing out flyers, and told the kids they weren't walking by themselves in the neighborhood. And I told Jenna she couldn't drive by herself. Then I made some stupid remark about her skirt. . . . They're both mad at me."

"They'll get over it."

They sat at the edge of the bed. Kay put her head on his shoulder, blotting her face with her hands. "I just can't believe this is happening. What terrible thing has happened to this poor girl?"

"I don't know. I'm trying not to think about it. They sent us home tonight and said we'd resume in the morning.

Maybe if you came with me, it would help you feel like you were doing something. Rather than sitting here worrying."

"Yes, that's a good idea. I want to help."

"Let's get you to bed." He pulled down the covers.

Kay scooted back and lay down, her body sinking into the sheets. She suddenly started crying harder.

Damien turned, rubbing her shoulder. "Sweetie . . ."

"They called me a slut."

"What? Who?" Damien sat straight up. "On the Web site?"

Kay turned over to face him, her hands tucked between her cheek and the pillow. "In high school. It was painted on my locker one day after school. I couldn't scrub it off." She broke down, burying her face in the pillow.

Damien didn't know what to say. Kay had never mentioned anything like this.

"I used to wear these really short skirts. They were kind of the style. But then these rumors started going around about me. They weren't true but . . ."

"Why haven't you ever told me this?" Damien said, taking her into his arms.

"I was so embarrassed. It hurt me so much. My friends stopped talking to me. I was totally alone. I had nobody. All because of a stupid rumor. And now I see our daughter . . ." Kay clutched his chest. "Don't you see that string around her wrist? Don't you know what that means? And those blouses she wears? I feel like I'm living a nightmare with her. In her."

"Sweetheart, I am so sorry. I had no idea."

"I just don't want her to end up like me. I don't want—" she covered her mouth for a moment—"anyone to ever call her a . . ."

She cried for a long time. Damien held her until she finally fell asleep. He put her gently on her pillow.

In the darkness, he sat on the edge of the bed and listened to her breathe until each breath was slow and deep and he was sure she was in a deep sleep.

He rose, walked to the bathroom, shut the door, and kept the light off. He slid to the floor and stared into the darkness.

17

FRANK WALKED ALONE, shining his light up and down, side to side, hoping to see something other than an alley cat. His hands tingled from numbness and his nose dripped.

This was his town. His town to serve. His town to protect. He wasn't losing a girl to a crime like this. As innocent as Marlo was—or once was—he knew there were shadows, cast long and harsh against its streets. Long and harsh and old. The curse was not new. Just forgotten.

He called the girl's name. It echoed against the buildings in the town square area. The crisp night air did nothing to stifle the rotten odors that fumed from the Dumpsters.

"Come on, Gabby. Where are you?" Frank whispered. He stood at the end of the last alleyway. Maybe he would go to the river tonight on his own and search.

Suddenly his phone vibrated against his hip. It was his personal cell. Who would be calling him in the middle of the night? He quickly snatched it up and looked at the caller ID. It wasn't a number he recognized. "Frank Merret."

"It's Jenna."

"What's wrong?"

"I need to meet with you."

"Now?"

"Yes, now."

"Are you okay?"

"I'm fine. I just need to talk to you."

"Where are you?"

"Meet me at the park on the north side, where the bell is."

The phone went dead. Frank checked his watch—3:45 a.m. What in the world was Jenna doing out at this hour? Did Damien know? He started to dial Damien's cell, then stopped. He should meet Jenna first, see what was wrong. She called him for a reason.

Frank got in his car and hurried to Marlo Park, the only park in town. It reminded him of a perfectly groomed woman—manicured, brushed, coddled, coifed. Large silver maples boasted their color in the fall. Bright tulips spelled out *Marlo* in the center of the park in the spring.

Frank pulled into one of several small parking places and got out. His mind flashed back fourteen years to a warm Sunday afternoon. He and Angela strolled through the west side of the park, where five weeping willows marked a path that led to a small, man-made waterfall. There was nothing out of the ordinary that day.

Except that day, near the sound of the rushing water, with

the birds singing their songs in the trees, he had knelt down and opened a small, black box. Inside, a tiny ring with a tiny diamond that had cost him an arm and a leg barely glimmered. It was small, but it didn't seem to matter to her. She adored it as if it were of great value.

It seemed like yesterday.

Frank had yet to get warm. He stuffed his hands deep into his pockets and searched through the darkness, trying to find Jenna. There, on a bench.

She watched as he walked toward her. She looked cold and tired. And scared.

He sat down, his body aching and weary. He turned to her. "You're okay?"

She nodded. In the dim moonlight, her eyes glistened with tears. "I have to tell you something."

"You know you can always tell me anything."

"It's about Gabby."

Frank tried not to look startled. "What about her?"

"It's just . . . It's . . ."

"Take your time."

Jenna took in a deep breath. "It's hard."

"Do you know what happened to Gabby?"

"No. Not exactly. But there are some girls at the school . . ." She took another breath as if each word sucked every bit of air out of her. "One girl especially, who hates Gabby." She glanced at Frank. "I've heard her talk about Gabby. In mean ways. In really mean ways."

"You think she might've done something?"

Jenna's words came in short, anxious bursts. "I don't know. I mean, sometimes I think maybe I'm overreacting, that it's just girl stuff. But they . . . Nobody would believe me. Everyone thinks they're nice girls. They say stuff, though. And do stuff. Under the radar so nobody suspects them."

"What's the name of the girl you think might be involved?"

Jenna's gloved hands were at her mouth, her fingers curled against her lips.

"It's okay. You can tell me."

"That's what nobody understands," she whispered. "There are consequences."

*   *   *

Frank got out of his car just as Lou Grayson pulled up.

Grayson looked around at the abandoned rest stop as he shut the door on his car. "Hey, Frank. You happen to stop for coffee?"

"No."

Grayson nodded like he wasn't expecting that he did. The two men joined each other on the sidewalk. Lou put his hands on his hips. "You got a tip, huh?"

"Yeah. Anybody else coming?"

"No. Left them there, didn't want to try to relocate everyone yet. This place isn't too terribly big. We can at least go in and look, see what we see. Maybe come back at daybreak with more people."

"All right. You got your flashlight?"

"Yeah."

"Beyond this rest stop there is supposedly a clearing."

They turned on their lights and walked forward. To their right was a small, covered eating area, rotting picnic benches the only reminder that people used to use this place. Closed-up bathrooms hid underneath the shadows of a large group of trees.

Frank checked the doors. Both were chained shut. "Gabby? You in there?" He pounded on a door.

Silence.

Grayson yelled from behind the bathroom building, "Windows are sealed up. Let's keep moving. We'll double-check this in a little bit."

They headed toward a line of trees, where it became dense. Limbs and vines, splashed with the blue light of the moon, tangled like lovers.

"On the other side," Frank said, motioning with his flashlight, "is that small clearing where the girls supposedly hang out." He pushed forward, hacking at vines, aiming his light ahead. "Gabby? You out here? Gabby?"

A sharp thorn caught Frank's pants at the shin, ripping them and his flesh. He grabbed his leg and felt the blood ooze into his hand. There was no end in sight to these thorny weeds.

Grayson came up beside him. "There are cockleburs everywhere. This is like walking through tiny sharp spikes. We're going to have to get some tools to clear these out before we can go forward."

Frank grabbed Grayson's arm. "You hear that?"

They stopped. Both men steadied themselves, and Frank drew his gun. Ahead, a sound that Frank couldn't identify competed with the wind. Maybe a small animal?

"What is that?" Lou whispered.

"I'm going in."

"Frank! Wait! You can't go through those—"

"Gabby?" Frank tore through the weeds, hacking at them with his gun. Each cut stung worse than the one before, but he couldn't stop. This was the only way. Blood soaked his pants and dribbled down each arm.

As he neared the clearing on the other side, Frank's light hit a large tree. He stopped to listen. Moaning? Was that what he heard?

Then he saw her.

Frank fought through, breaking the remaining vines and branches. "Gabby!"

As he made his way into the clearing, the entire sight startled him to a near standstill. Her eyes, hollow and vacant, stared, unblinking. Was she dead?

"No!" Frank scrambled forward, stumbling toward her. "Gabby!"

Her hands were tied behind her, and she was gagged. She sat at the base of the tree, four ropes tying her body to it. She'd been stripped of all her clothes except a tank top and boxer shorts. She didn't seem to be responding to the light or her name being called.

"Lou!" Frank shouted. "I found her! Get some medical attention!"

He heard Grayson radioing in the call as he threw off his coat. He approached her slowly, cautiously laying his coat over her. Her hand was ice-cold. He pulled the gag off her mouth and gently patted her cheek. "Can you hear me?"

Her gaze suddenly shifted to the left. She stared directly at him, through him, still unblinking. Her lips, a deep purple, moved slightly as if she was trying to speak.

Relief flooded Frank so fast and hard, tears stung his eyes. "We're here. You're going to be all right. Just stay with me, okay? I'm going to cut the rope." He hurried to the other side of the tree. His hands were so cold he had a hard time sawing.

Frank rushed back to the girl. He took her hands and rubbed them and her arms as fast as he could. Her skin, already fair, looked ghostly white against the moonlight. A dark blue half circle hung under each eye.

Her lips moved again. Breath froze right in front of her face.

"Gabby, it's okay. I'm here. My name is Frank."

"Help me . . . ," she whispered.

In the distance, the siren's scream grew louder.

"Help is on the way. Hang in there."

Her eyes closed. Her mouth gaped open.

"No, Gabby, no! You've got to stay with me! Stay awake!"

He heard Grayson hacking his way through the shrubs. Soon he was at the tree with a blanket from his car. "They're on their way," Grayson said.

Frank covered her with the blanket and pulled her next to him to try to get more heat to her. Her limp body leaned against his, her head resting against his collarbone. "Hang in there. You can't die. Open your eyes. Meredith, look at me."

Grayson stepped forward. "Her name is Gabby."

Frank looked up, a startle electrocuting his heart. What had he said?

Grayson eyed him for a moment, then pulled out his phone and took a piece of paper out of his pocket.

Frank continued to rub her arms and hands. Color was starting to return to her skin. Her teeth chattered. Frank stroked her hair.

Grayson dialed a number. "Mr. Caldwell, Captain Grayson here. . . . We've found Gabby. . . . Yes, sir. She's alive but in need of medical attention. . . . I think so, but we need to get her to the hospital. . . . The ambulance is here now. I'll give you more details at the hospital."

The quiet night air was undone by sirens and commotion. Within minutes, a dozen police officers, firefighters, and EMTs had arrived on scene.

"We can't get the gurney through here," one of the EMTs said, as he wrapped a silver thermal blanket around Gabby.

"I'll carry her out," Frank said. "See if you can get the firefighters to chop through some of those vines and branches."

Gabby's cheeks suddenly flushed, and her lips turned pink. Her wide eyes dimmed a little, but she looked peaceful. She gripped Frank's arm. "Thank you."

Frank shoved his arms under her and stood, lifting her off the ground. She was lightweight. She buried her face in his chest as the lights shone on her. Frank made his way through the shrubbery, holding her tight. The warmth of the blanket helped his body warm up too. He could finally feel his hands again.

Once he made it through the trees, a stretcher was there waiting. He carefully laid her on it and brushed her hair out of her face. For the first time, he noticed what a beautiful, innocent-looking young woman she was. Big brown eyes blinked at him. "I was praying and praying. I thought I was dead. You're my answer. You got here just in time."

Frank only stared. He couldn't say anything. He felt tears trickling down his cheeks.

"You're going to be fine," Grayson said, stepping up to her as he glanced at Frank, giving him an odd look.

"Let's get an IV started," one of the EMTs said.

Frank moved away and let them tend to her. Within two minutes, they had her loaded into the back of the ambulance. The sirens wailed into the night. Officers wound crime scene tape around the trees.

Grayson slid up next to him. "This could've ended much, much worse."

Frank nodded, trying to get himself under control.

"You okay?"

"I meant to say Gabby, not Meredith."

Grayson gestured at his legs and arms. "I meant those cuts all over you."

"I'm fine."

"Who's Meredith?"

An EMT offered to inspect Frank's legs but he waved him off. "This kind of thing doesn't happen in our town, Lou."

"You got a lead off that tip?"

"Let's go."

*   *   *

Restlessness, inky black and suffocating, turned Kay over and over in her bed. She kept her eyes closed, trying to force sleep upon herself. But it came in short spurts, and then her body would jolt awake, her heart pounding as if it were twice its size, like she'd been running from something she couldn't see.

She opened one eye. The clock glared at her. Five thirty in the morning and she'd barely slept. Then something caught her attention. A white note sat perched against her lamp. By the glow of her digital clock, she read it: *They found her alive. Be back later. D.*

Kay propped herself up on one elbow, emotion filling the emptiness that was there just moments before. Tears dripped down her cheek, and she fell back into her pillow. It cradled her. Moments before, it had tormented her. She turned over, hoping for another hour's sleep.

But gasped.

She scrambled to a sitting position, reaching behind herself and yanking at the lamp cord. Jenna? She grabbed her shoulder. "Jenna? Are you okay?"

Jenna moaned and rolled over. "I'm fine. Go back to sleep."

Kay sat there, her hand on her chest, staring at her daughter. The last time she'd crawled into bed with her was when she was six years old. Kay studied her face, still dainty and innocent, especially without the makeup and the attitude. Kay stroked her hair, combing it out of her face. She turned off the lamp, then slowly, quietly, slid back under the covers. She wrapped her arms around her baby girl and fell into a deep sleep.

* * *

Frank stood with Grayson outside Gabriella Caldwell's hospital room. Nurses shuffled in and out for thirty minutes. Then the doctor stepped out.

"How is she?" Frank asked.

"Stable. She's lucky she was found when she was. It took us a while to get her body temperature back up. She should make a full recovery."

"Can we talk to her now?" Grayson asked.

The doctor nodded. "But make it short. She seems . . . traumatized. I know you guys want to catch this person, but take it easy on her, okay?"

Frank and Grayson opened the door and entered the room. A woman sitting by the bed stood when she saw Grayson. "I'm Beth Caldwell. This is my husband, Ted." They all shook hands.

"I'm Captain Grayson. And you know Sergeant Frank Merret."

Frank moved closer to Gabby's bed. "She looks good. Color back in her face."

"Thank you so much for all you did. I can't imagine—" Beth's voice cracked—"what she's been through. Who would do this?"

"That's what we want to find out. Can we ask her a few questions?"

Reverend Caldwell walked to the bedside. "Gabby?"

Gabby opened her eyes, blinked slowly.

"Gabby, can you talk to the police?"

Her eyes widened as she spotted them. "I don't want to."

The reverend looked confused. "What? We've got to find who did this to you."

"I didn't see anything." She shook her head. "I don't know anything."

Frank fingered the railing of the bed, trying to find the right approach. He pulled up the stool the doctors normally sat on. As he sat down, he patted her arm. He could tell she recognized him. "Remember me?"

She nodded.

"Do you remember my name?"

"Frank."

"That's right." He smiled. "How are you feeling?"

"Fine."

"Warm, I bet."

"Yeah. Warm."

"Gabby, do you know how we found you tonight?"

She shook her head.

"Somebody came forward, told us that they suspected someone from your class did this to you."

Gabby gazed out the window on the other side of the room. The sun, plump and dark orange, had lifted just above the horizon.

"Maybe this is too much," her mother said, stepping next to Frank.

Frank held up a gentle finger. "The person that came forward risked a lot to tell us where you might be and who might be responsible for this. I know this is scary. You feel threatened. But we can't let them get away with this."

Ted stepped to the other side of the bed. "He's right. What this person did is horrible. You could've died." He took her hand. "We're here for you. Nothing is going to happen, I promise."

Gabby remained expressionless, seemingly staring straight through her father. "I don't know what happened. I didn't see anything. I don't know anything."

18

DAMIEN STOOD AT the printer, his fingers tapping against its white, plastic top. The paper couldn't come out any slower. It had already jammed twice.

"Come on," he muttered.

He took a deep breath and turned away from it for a moment. The large east window showed the glory of morning. Soft-hued light spread over the horizon, melting into the dark sky like watercolor.

Damien walked to the window, pressing his hands against the glass, looking over the town from the eighth floor of the tallest—and newest—building in Marlo. It seemed cradled, trees and rivers swaddling it on all sides. Safe. Pure. Beautiful.

"Hey."

Damien turned. Bruce stood behind him, a grim look on his face.

"Hey, Bruce. You're in early."

"Yeah."

"I'm about to drop dead."

Bruce stared at him, his face strangely absent of emotion. "Is there something you want to say to me?"

"Say to you?"

"Yeah. Say to me."

"No, what's on your mind?"

"I just believe that if there's something you want to say to someone, you should say it to them."

"I believe that also," Damien said, starting to bristle.

"Are you sure there's nothing you need to say to me?"

"I'm positive. What's this about?"

Bruce glanced away as if he needed a moment to settle himself down. "I read something on that Web site. Someone doesn't like how I write my articles. Doesn't like my use of vocabulary."

Damien groaned. "It wasn't me, okay? I mean, is my name mentioned?"

"No. Neither is mine." His gaze fixed on Damien. "But sometimes you gotta read between the lines."

"And sometimes you have to trust that a friendship is more powerful than a few words you read on a Web site."

Bruce looked caught between relief and indignation. So he just turned and left.

Damien took a moment to compose himself. After the night he'd had, this was what he had to deal with?

Damien returned to the printer, grabbed the pages, and walked to Edgar's office.

What he didn't expect to see was Edgar's startled face as he pushed himself away from the computer and leaned in to quickly punch a button. His face, red and flustered, remained expressionless as he looked at Damien. "Yeah?"

"Here's our headline," Damien said, holding up the pages.

"'Found Alive.' Perfect." Edgar stood and stretched his back. "Do you know the last time we put out a special evening edition was when that bank was robbed? Nothing bad ever happens here, which makes for a great place to live and a horrible place to be a newspaperman. The only controversy around was those op-ed pieces you wrote when you were in a bad mood." He took a breath as he skimmed over Damien's paper. "Did you hear?"

"What?"

"The police department is offering a reward."

"For the person who did this to Gabby?"

"No, for the person who's running the Web site."

"Really? I thought they weren't investigating it."

Edgar grinned. "I guess we changed their mind." He sat down, folding his chubby hands together as his chair creaked to hold his weight. "All right, I want something good ready to roll tonight. This investigative piece is great. I won't lie; you're becoming a dandy reporter. But I also want something from the heart. What's on your mind with this kidnapping and near murder of this girl? I want a symphony, got it?"

"Yeah. Sure." Damien started to leave. "Hey, who told you about the reward from the police department?"

Something flickered across Edgar's expression, then disappeared into another grin. "Maybe I read it on the Web site."

Damien returned to his desk. Only adrenaline had caused him to go strong for the last few hours. Now all he wanted was a bed. But Edgar was right. There had never been anything like this before in Marlo. And if he could make any difference at all with what he had to say, then there was no time to waste.

Except something seemed wrong. With everything. With everyone. Like he was living inside the movie *Invasion of the Body Snatchers.*

He glanced around the room. Everyone was hunched over his or her keyboard, drawn into some other world.

Damien's hands hovered over his own keyboard. Thoughts numbered like random words on page after page. He had to organize them, make them concise, put them to use without a heavy hand. Nobody wanted to be preached to. What did they want?

Truth.

Hope.

Well-being.

But what they once had was no longer. Damien typed his headline: "What Lies Beneath."

* * *

"Where's Jenna?" Hunter asked as he cut up his Eggo.

"Upstairs. I'm letting her sleep in. This whole thing with Gabby really upset her."

"I'm glad Gabby's okay," Hunter said quietly.

Kay came over and hugged him from behind. He always had such a tender heart. "I know. These things often don't turn out well." She stepped to the side and touched his face. "Are you all right?"

"I'm good. I better get going though."

Kay walked back to the table. "It's kind of early. And remember, I said that you can't ride your bike to school. Not until this person is caught. Hold on. I'll drive you. Let me run upstairs and throw on some sweats."

Hunter sighed. "Look, I realize you're freaked out and I'll allow you some freak-out time. Just don't go overboard. That's all I'm saying."

"Like insist that you embed a GPS tracking device under your skin?" Kay smiled.

Hunter laughed. "Exactly. I'll be in the car."

Upstairs, Kay jumped into a cozy sweat suit and slid on old sneakers. As she started back across the room, Jenna stirred.

Kay sat on the edge of the bed and clicked the lamp on. "I let you sleep in a little, but you better get up and get to school. I'm going to run Hunter in and I'll be back. I'll write you a note to be excused."

Jenna peeled open her eyelids. "Mom?"

"Yeah?"

"Don't make me go."

"What?"

"Please. Can I stay home today?"

Kay smoothed the hair out of Jenna's face and touched the back of her hand to her cheek. "You're feeling bad?"

"No. I just don't . . . I want to stay home."

Kay nodded. She couldn't imagine how traumatizing this must've been for her. "Sure. You can stay home. Get some more sleep and I'll fix you some breakfast in about an hour."

Jenna rolled over and Kay turned off the lamp. As she stood in the doorway looking at Jenna, she thanked God that her daughter wasn't involved.

* * *

Frank got out of Detective Murray's car, and both men stood on the curb for a moment, observing the house. A small sign near the mailbox boasted lawn service. The sidewalk leading to the house was swept clean enough to belong on the inside. Bushes lined the porch, and a grotesquely large Christmas wreath hung on the red front door. Two luxury SUVs were parked in the driveway.

"Somebody's home," Murray said, running his thumbs along the inside waistband of his pants before hiking them up a notch. "Let's go."

Frank tapped on the front door and stepped back to provide a clear view from the peephole.

A few seconds later the front door opened. A middle-aged woman with crunchy-looking blonde hair pinned back with diamond-studded barrettes blinked at them. "Yes?" she asked, shading her face from a sun that had barely made its entrance into the sky.

"I'm Detective Dean Murray. This is Officer Frank Merret. Are you the mother of Caydance Sanders?"

"Yes. Susan. What's the matter?"

"Is your daughter home?"

"She's upstairs getting ready for school."

"We'd like to speak with her for a few moments."

Susan clutched the side of her door. "About what?"

"You heard about the girl who was found last night?"

"Yes, of course. We were so thankful she was found alive."

"We have reason to believe your daughter might know something about what happened," Detective Murray said.

"We're interested in talking with several of her classmates," Frank added.

Susan looked confused but nodded and opened the door wider. She gestured toward a sitting room off to the side. "Wait here. I'll go get her."

Frank stepped in, observing the giant floral patterns that engulfed the tiny room. It smelled as if the carpet were made of potpourri. Or that eighty scented candles were burning all at the same time.

Murray put his forearm up against his nose. "Good grief," he choked out.

"No kidding," Frank said. He dropped his weight onto a couch that was less comfortable than it appeared. He lowered his voice. "Should we bring up the cat incident, see if it's connected here?"

"Not yet. I want to keep it to this thing first, see what, if anything, we can get out of the girl."

They both heard footsteps above them, some muddled conversation, and then the padding sound of feet coming downstairs. Susan entered, her daughter behind her, hands on her hips and attitude worn like an expensive accessory. "Caydance, this is Detective Murray and Officer Merret."

"Am I going to be late for school?" she asked her mother.

"Just sit down, please. These men need to talk to you."

She eyed them suspiciously, her arms now tightly folded across her chest. She plopped down in a floral chair and tucked her feet underneath her.

Murray said, "You're Caydance Sanders?"

"Yeah."

"Do you know Gabriella Caldwell?"

"Yeah, she goes to my school. She was found last night, right?" Her eyes grew round at her own words.

"That's right." Murray took out his notepad. "Did you see Gabby at school yesterday?"

"I don't know. Might've. We don't hang out."

"So you're not friends?"

"She's not a cheerleader, so no. We're not friends."

"Are you enemies?"

Caydance looked put out. "I don't think about her. She's not on my radar. Do you get what I'm saying?"

Susan stood beside her daughter. "Caydance, just answer the questions."

"I am," she said, rolling her eyes up toward her mom.

Frank watched Caydance's every movement. Her face

looked at ease, but her hands were telling a different story as they wound and unwound a piece of thread hanging from her tight-fitting jeans.

Murray scooted forward on the love seat a few inches, giving his full attention to the girl. "We have reason to believe you might know something about what happened to Gabby."

Susan gasped. "What? What are you talking about?"

Murray kept his focus on Caydance. "If you know something, you need to tell us. It's a serious offense to lie to the police or to withhold information you know would help in an investigation."

"Do we need a lawyer?" Susan asked Frank.

"I don't know, ma'am. That's not up to us to decide. We're just here to ask your daughter what she knows that could help us in the investigation."

Caydance stared at Frank. Frank stared back at her. The kid was brash, as if the word *authority* had no meaning to her. She tucked her hair behind her ears and examined her cuticles.

"Caydance, do you know anything about what happened to Gabby?" Murray's tone was kind, familiar, as if he were a favorite uncle chatting about holiday traditions. The intent was to lower her guard, though she didn't seem bothered by anything other than being inconvenienced.

They watched the young woman; several seconds ticked by. Frank expected her to deny it, but instead she grew very still, her eyes fixed on the carpet. Her mother seemed not to know what to do. Her hand slid onto her daughter's shoulder, and she looked back and forth between Frank and Murray.

"Look," Caydance finally said, "it's Zoey's fault. She screwed it all up."

Susan knelt next to Caydance. "What are you talking about?"

"It wasn't supposed to be a big deal. It was just a little revenge for what she said."

"What she said?" Frank asked.

"On that Web site. About cheerleaders." Caydance sighed heavily. "I tied her up, and Zoey was supposed to go untie her in like ten minutes."

"I think you better stop right there," Susan said, nearly out of breath. "We need to call a lawyer."

"Mother, please. It's not a big deal. If anyone should get in trouble, it's Zoey. She didn't do what she was supposed to do. She's the one that left Gabby out there. And I even told Zoey that we didn't know for sure if Gabby said that stuff anyway."

Frank tried not to react in any way, but inside it was all he could do to suppress what wanted to come out. How could she be so flippant? Frank glanced at Murray, who played it cool, keeping an even expression. "I see. So Zoey was supposed to go untie her but didn't do it?"

"I guess. I haven't talked to Zoey. She was supposed to call and she didn't, so I just assumed it all went down. I tried to call her and she didn't answer her phone."

Murray jotted on his notepad, keeping his tone easy. "So tell me exactly how it was supposed to take place."

"Caydance, stop. Just stop. Don't say anything else."

Murray's calm eyes turned toward Susan. "With all due respect, I don't think this is the time to look out for your best interest. A young woman almost died last night, and if Caydance can help us piece together what happened, I think you should let her. But if you'd like, we can finish this up at the police station."

Susan stared at her daughter, tears making her eyes shiny. "Caydance, you realize what you've done, don't you?"

Caydance's attitude seemed to have suddenly sobered up. Her hands dropped to her lap, and she studied her mother's face without scorn. "I don't know. I mean, we didn't think this would happen. It wasn't supposed to happen like this."

"Tell me how it was supposed to happen."

"Gabby's just very . . . Sometimes she wanted to be one of us, you know? She's nice and all that, but it wasn't going to happen. But she kept trying to buddy up to Zoey, act like they had a lot in common. It was really getting on Zoey's nerves. And then there was this thing on the Web site about how stupid cheerleaders are. So Zoey kind of pretended like they could be friends, and it was supposed to be a practical joke."

Tears streamed down Susan's face. She stood and backed away from the chair, shaking her head.

Caydance watched her mom for a moment, then looked at Murray.

"How did you get Gabby to go along with this?" Murray asked.

"Zoey asked her if she wanted to go to a party with us. Gabby snuck out of her house, and I picked her up a block away. I took her to the back room—"

"The back room?"

"That's the rest area. That's what we call it. I took her there and told her we were playing a little initiation game. I left, texted Zoey, and came home. That's it."

"You mean you left after you stripped her down and tied her to a tree?"

Susan stepped forward, wiping her damp face. She stood straighter and her eyes stirred with harshness. "All right, that's enough. Is Caydance going to be in trouble? She told you everything. I think it was very courageous how she told the truth."

Frank got up. "Yes, ma'am. Your daughter has nobility written all over her."

Susan scowled. "What's going to happen?"

"You're not to leave this town," Murray said. "The DA will decide whether or not to press charges. At this moment we are not going to take you in because you cooperated. We'll be in touch. You need to make yourself available."

"Is Zoey going to be in trouble?" Caydance asked.

Susan glared at her. "I think Zoey is the least of your concerns right now."

"What your mother means," Frank said as they began walking out of the room, "is that she is sure your first concern is for Gabby and her well-being and recovery."

Susan opened the door for them as she speed-dialed someone on her cell. As the door closed, they could hear her ranting into the phone.

Murray and Frank walked toward the car.

"You're going to make sure this girl goes down, aren't you?" Frank asked.

"In a big, bad way." Murray smiled. "And now, let's go meet the Princess of Darkness."

19

Kay didn't have a showing until later in the morning, thank goodness. Something told her Jenna needed her. In fact, she would cancel the showing if need be. Maybe she should anyway. Maybe they could spend the day together talking.

Kay sifted through the pantry, deciding what to fix for breakfast. Just spend the day talking? Like that was going to work. But maybe spending any time together at all would be proactive in restoring their relationship.

She stood at the refrigerator door and looked at all the pictures held there by magnets. She studied the picture of Jenna at seven, dressed up for Halloween as a cheerleader. Times had been really good and uncomplicated back then. She knew the transition into adulthood would have its rocky times, but she never suspected it would be like climbing the Alps. Cold and harsh with little oxygen.

Kay opened the fridge and decided on an omelet. She paused and listened for any movement upstairs. All was quiet. Checking her watch, she realized she had time for a quick Starbucks run. She'd bring Jenna some green tea.

On her way, she tried not to think about how badly last night could've turned out, but her mind kept running over the scenarios. And she couldn't help but insert herself into the scene. What would she do if Jenna went missing like that?

She shook off the dark thoughts and whipped into the Starbucks parking lot. A north wind snapped around the building as she tugged the door open. Once inside, she stood for a moment, trying to warm and compose herself.

She reminded herself that everything was fine. Yet fear nagged at her, and she wondered if Jenna was safe at the house. She'd locked all the doors, checked all the windows, turned on the alarm.

But still . . .

"Help you, ma'am?"

Kay blinked, focusing on the young man with shaggy hair, who kept swinging his head to the side, trying to get his bangs out of his eyes. Kay almost felt compelled to dig in her purse for a bobby pin. "Um, yes. Sorry. A venti green tea and a venti nonfat mocha."

"Kay?"

Kay turned around. Shannon, Zoey's mom, stood behind her, grinning.

"Hi, Shannon. Didn't even see you in here." Kay handed the barista her credit card and stepped to the side.

Shannon shuffled up, sporting a velour sweat suit. "I'm exhausted. Didn't sleep well last night."

"I know. Wasn't that horrible about Gabby?" Kay asked, grabbing a napkin and stirrer.

"Yeah. And Zoey was being a beast to top it all off. We had to ground her and then she totally wigged out, yelling and crying. It was ridiculous. She was just headed to eat pizza with the girls. You'd think the world had imploded."

The barista handed Kay her card and took Shannon's order. Kay waited for her by the cream and sugar.

A minute later, Shannon joined her, running her fingers through her long, shiny hair. "Anyway, it was nuts. Is Jenna acting this way, all superdramatic and whiny and stuff?"

Kay hesitated. She wanted to relate with Shannon, but at the same time, she wanted to protect her daughter in every sense. "You know how teenagers are. Hormones can get the best of them."

"I guess," Shannon muttered. "I swear I thought I was going to pack up and leave for Hawaii last night. It was constant screaming for two hours. Finally she fell asleep on her bed and put us all out of our misery."

Kay nodded, studying Shannon. The woman had always seemed so pulled together, so happy and energetic. It was like she was the eleventh member of the cheer squad. Today, though, Kay saw the familiar lines of regret, guilt, and worry on Shannon that Kay had seen many times in her own reflection. Maybe she wasn't such a supermom after all. And maybe Jenna's behavior lately, while baffling, was better than what Shannon was dealing with.

"Green tea and mocha for Kay!" the barista called.

"You drink both?"

"No. One's for Jenna. I'm letting her stay home from school today. Last night really shook her up."

"It did? What, is she friends with this Gabby girl? Zoey said Gabby's kind of weird, a loner." Shannon's phone came to life, blaring out the *Sex and the City* theme. "It's Zoey. She's supposed to be on her way to school right now." She flipped it open. "What is it?"

Kay turned and walked to the counter to pick up her beverages. She started to wave bye to Shannon but stopped.

Shannon grew pale right in front of her. She snapped her phone closed.

"Is everything okay?"

She shook her head, her eyes wide. "That was Zoey. She told me to get home. The police are at the house."

* * *

About the time he usually arrived at work, Damien felt the need to get out of the office. It had become all at once stuffy and suffocating.

In one sense, it was exhilarating. The news was a driving force, and everyone was a willing passenger. But even though he was a newsman, he was also a guy with a lot of ideals. As much as he didn't want to admit it to the people around him who were doing their jobs, what had happened last night shook him to the core.

This was Marlo. He'd grown up here and decided to plant his family here. It once was a place where dreams flourished and happiness bloomed. Now it had the stench of death.

By nine thirty, he'd made his way to a solitary bench in the middle of Marlo Park. In the spring, ten thousand dollars would be spent planting flowers and grooming the grounds. He'd once written an editorial about its importance after there was an uproar by some people aggravated that so much money was to be spent on a park.

But Damien had swayed their opinion. He'd pointed out that this was the heart of the city, and the roads were the arteries leading to the rest of the body. If the core of the city was not taken care of, what would be next? The schools? The retirement home? The churches?

The editorial had been so popular that the town created Grounds Day on April 1, and three hundred people showed up to work, saving the city five thousand dollars.

Even in its dormant state in the winter, the park held a certain majesty and pride. People still walked the sidewalks, kids still rode their bikes, and on a good snow day, on the south end of the park, a small hill provided hours of sledding entertainment.

But now, in the middle of the pristine park with its vibrant evergreens and neatly swept sidewalks, Damien felt betrayed, as if Marlo were a living, breathing person that had just slapped him in the face and blackmailed him to boot.

Maybe it had always been this way and Marlo was just now giving up its bag of secrets. Or maybe they hadn't watched over the town carefully enough, and slowly but surely a dry, putrid rot had set in.

He was weighed down like tree limbs burdened under heavy snow. He should've done more to protect Marlo. Pushed harder to not let complacency win at the end of the day. In a sense, the residents had decided that their pristine and tidy little town was incapable of foolishness and treachery. But still there was the question: had complacency been here all along or had it slipped in as an unexpected guest?

Damien considered the slow-drifting wispy clouds. That was the Marlo he knew and loved, pure and innocent, floating high above messy humanity. But when he closed his eyes, all he saw was a terrified young girl, shivering in the cold, calling out for help. Swirling from the harsh north wind were the angry words of this town, words jumbled with other words, whispers, indecencies. Behind the walls of every home and around every dark corner, gossip waited for its cue; its mad dogs were on the hunt for prey.

He had to stop this craziness. But how? Who was behind all this? And did it have anything to do with Gabby? Had the person hiding in the darkness of cyberspace come out in the blackness of night to strike in a new and evil way?

His phone vibrated in his pocket, indicating he had a text message. It was from Edgar: *Get back now. Breaking news.*

*   *   *

Frank and Murray sat on an enormous leather couch that dominated an already-impressive living room. Zoey Branson stood nearby, her arms crossed, doing something with her bright pink phone. Her hair was swept high in a ponytail, and her makeup sparkled like she was headed to a disco.

Frank found himself staring at the sixty-two-inch TV. He felt like throwing himself sideways on the couch, grabbing the remote, and counting their cable channels. Instead, he looked at the nine-foot Christmas tree weighed down by festive bling.

Marlo had always had a decent number of upper middle-class citizens. If they weren't really rich, nobody knew. There was a certain kind of house you wanted to keep, a certain kind of lifestyle you had to live. It never seemed dangerous or excessive. It wasn't by any means Frank's cup of tea. He lived in a small, two-bedroom wood frame house that was built in 1942. But he never minded the people with more wealth. He was not bothered by having less. He had responsibilities, and those were his priorities that he would never, ever give up.

Yet now, sitting in this room, he couldn't help but feel engulfed by status. Genuine oil paintings hung on three out of the four walls. Besides the enormous television set that could rival the local movie theater, there were the leather furniture, the Persian rug, the enormous chandelier. For a house this size, it seemed cram-packed with overstated luxury.

From the back door, a Chihuahua whined and scratched.

"Shut up!" Zoey barked, sounding like she might be one gene off from the breed.

The front door suddenly flew open, ushering in, presumably, the mother. Her eyes widened as she saw Frank and Murray sitting on the sofa.

Frank stood, offering a hand. "Officer Merret. This is Detective Murray."

She shook hands limply, then rushed to her daughter, patting the girl's cheek as if she had a fever. "What's wrong?"

"Get off me!" Zoey said, backing away and straightening her outfit. "I don't know what's going on. I just thought I should call you. This seems like the kind of thing a parent should be aware of." Her sulky eyes seemed to drown in their own burden.

"Your name, ma'am?" Murray asked.

"Shannon Branson."

"You're Zoey's mother?"

"Yes. Tell me what's going on."

"We'd like to ask Zoey some questions about what happened to Gabby Caldwell last night."

"Why would she know anything about that?"

Frank heard someone else come through the front door. He assumed it was the father, but when he turned, he was taken by surprise. "Kay? What are you doing here?"

"I was with Shannon when Zoey called. She asked me to come over. Is everything okay?"

"No," Shannon said. "No, everything is not okay. This is ridiculous. My daughter doesn't know a thing about what happened to that girl."

"Gabby Caldwell," Frank said. Maybe repeating her

name would help Zoey find her humanity. "That's her name. Gabby."

"I know who she is," Shannon said, her eyes narrowing. "That's not the point."

Murray said, "Let's all sit down and discuss this."

Shannon and Zoey sat on the small sofa. "Why didn't you tell them you don't know what happened?" Shannon said.

Zoey stared at the carpet.

"Zoey?" her mother said. "Don't be rude."

"Look," Murray said, "we'll tell you what we do know, all right? Gabby thought she was being invited to a party. She snuck out of her house, joined up with a girl named Caydance Sanders. You know Caydance, correct?"

"Of course she knows Caydance. They're best friends."

"But Gabby wasn't being invited to a party, was she, Zoey? Caydance took her out to the rest stop, tied her to a tree, and left her there."

"We know Caydance Sanders! She would never do something like that!"

"Ma'am, she admitted that to us forty minutes ago. She told us the entire plan."

"Plan?" Shannon's gaze wandered from person to person in the room.

"Zoey, tell us how you were involved in all of this," Murray said.

"She was not involved in this!" Shannon's pitch was rivaling that of the frantic Chihuahua out back. "She was home all night! She was grounded, as a matter of fact, from leaving the house and from using the phone or computer."

Frank looked at Murray, then closed his eyes and shook his head. "Wow."

"What?" Shannon asked.

"That's why you didn't go untie her, right, Zoey?" Frank asked.

Even Shannon turned to her daughter, who sat on the couch, bound up with her own seeming indifference.

"Zoey?" Frank asked again.

Shannon leaned forward, touching her daughter's knee and trying to get an angle to look at her whole face. "What happened? You were going to go save this girl? untie her?"

"Not quite," Murray said. "The plan was to leave her out there for ten minutes, right, Zoey? Caydance took her out there, tied her up, and you were supposed to come untie her. What then? Were you going to leave her out there in her skivvies to hitchhike back home?"

"This is ridiculous! Ridiculous!" Shannon breathed.

Finally Zoey unwrapped her arms and stared at Frank. "It's not my fault. I tried to explain to my parents I had some-where important to be, and they didn't care. They grounded me, and I couldn't even call. It's not my fault!" Her glare turned to her mother, then back down to the carpet.

Shannon sat still. The entire room quieted except for the barking and clawing at the back door. Frank glanced at Kay, trying to read her.

Shannon suddenly started babbling. "I . . . Yes, she tried

to say something. . . . I didn't understand. . . . I thought she, um . . . There was no way for us to know—"

Frank cut her off. "Did Zoey tell you that someone's life was in danger or indicate in any way that she needed to go help Gabby?"

Shannon's hands were moving everywhere as she attempted to sort out her words. "It's just . . . There was a lot of yelling. She mentioned something, but I didn't understand what she meant. I thought she was talking about hanging out with friends."

"Did she ever mention Gabby specifically?"

Shannon shook her head slightly as if guessing what the right answer should be.

"And you knew your daughter was home all night?"

"Yes, of course. I checked on her at about eleven and she was asleep." At the word *asleep*, Shannon stopped as if the entire thing had crashed down right in front of her.

Frank tried not to react, but they all knew how cold this was coming across.

"I think we need a lawyer," Shannon said quietly, standing, fretting as she tried to find her cell phone in her purse.

Zoey watched her mom, then looked at Frank. "So Caydance told you all this, huh? The little rat."

"Caydance admitted to it but didn't come to us. Someone else gave us a tip that led us to save Gabby. If that wouldn't have happened, Gabby would be dead right now."

"Whatever." Zoey sighed.

"Shut up!" Shannon screamed, leaning down to her

daughter's face. "Don't say anything else!" She clutched the girl's chin in her trembling hand.

Frank got up, not sure what was about to happen next. "Ma'am, please. Just calm down. Yelling is not going to solve anything."

"Weird," Zoey quipped. "That's what she's always saying."

Shannon stood upright, put her hand over her mouth, shook her head. Then she said, "You've got it all wrong. This is just circumstantial evidence."

"Not anymore, ma'am. Your daughter confessed."

Frank turned to find Kay in this madness, but the front door was wide open and she was gone.

20

Kay swerved into her driveway, her tires peeling rubber against the concrete. She grabbed the keys out of the ignition and threw the door open. She didn't bother closing it as she ran to the front door, the quickest way into the house. It was locked. Her hands shook as she tried to insert the key. Four attempts later, it slid in and she swung the door open. Punching in the alarm code, she hurried to the kitchen.

Kay dropped the keys on the counter, trying to catch her breath.

Jenna sat at the kitchen bar, slouched over a bowl of cereal. She glanced up as Kay practically dived through the room. "Mom? You look scared. I got your note. I knew where you were. It's okay; calm down. Omelets just didn't sound good."

Kay shook her head, but no words would come out. She tried to compose herself, taking deep breaths.

Jenna watched her, a spoonful of cereal hovering over her bowl. "Mom?"

Kay took one final deep breath. Her hands were still shaking, but she couldn't help that at the moment. She tried a calm, motherly smile as she slid onto the barstool next to her daughter. "Honey . . ." Her eyes stung with tears, and she knew Jenna hated seeing her cry.

"Gabby's safe, remember? Everything's okay."

"No, everything is not okay. I need to tell you that . . . I'm sorry."

"For what?" Jenna kept staring at her but shoved some cereal in her mouth.

"I understand now."

"Understand?"

"Caydance, Zoey . . . they are horrible, horrible girls."

What had earlier been an uninterested expression vanished. A bundle of new expressions flashed over Jenna's face. Kay knew she'd struck a chord.

"I sat there and told you that you should try to be friends with these girls. You tried to tell me, and I didn't listen to you. I didn't. All I could see was what I wanted for you." Kay wiped the tears that had dripped down her own cheeks. She looked directly into Jenna's eyes and held her gaze. "Can you ever forgive me?"

Jenna stared for a moment, every feature on her face frozen. Kay started to say something else, but the next thing she knew, Jenna grabbed her around the neck and cried. Hard. Almost wailing.

Kay gripped her as tightly as she could, held her, wishing she could swaddle her and rock her and sing to her like she used to. Instead, she stroked the back of her head over and over, rocking her body back and forth just a little. Jenna laid her head on Kay's shoulder and didn't budge.

* * *

Frank spotted him immediately and trekked through the middle of the park until he reached the bench that his friend sat on. Damien didn't even look over as Frank plopped himself down, his belt and all its contents rattling against the cold wood.

"Hey," Damien said. He looked like he was staring at clouds.

"Hey."

Damien sighed and finally glanced at him. "Busy morning?"

"We caught the suspects in the kidnapping."

"I figured," Damien said, holding his phone up and inspecting it. "Edgar has now texted me eight times and called five. Breaking news."

"Ah. Probably got tipped off from the department. Nobody can keep their mouth shut around there." Frank adjusted his belt to sit more comfortably around his waist. "Two high school girls did it." He faced Damien, who continued to stare upward. "Did you hear me?"

Damien nodded as if it were too much effort to speak.

Frank studied his friend for a moment. Damien looked forlorn, withdrawn, way too interested in the clouds.

A moment of silence passed; then Damien said, "I think

I'm having . . ." His voice trailed off as if he couldn't find the right words.

"Leg cramps?"

"No."

"A gallbladder attack?"

"Huh-uh."

"A nervous breakdown?"

"That's it."

Frank grabbed Damien's shoulder. "Did you buy some expensive item you can't afford?"

"No."

"Are you cheating on Kay?"

"Of course not."

"Have you been thinking about how to fake your own death?"

"No," Damien said.

Frank smiled. "Then you're fine."

"I'm not fine. I can't get off this bench. I can't get myself to go back to work."

"Talk to me."

"I don't know. This town, what's happening. I'm a second-generation Marlo citizen. I always relished the quietness of this town. But it wasn't quiet, was it? It was just hidden."

Frank sat. Listening. That's all he could do.

Damien turned to him, his gaze hard and unmoving. "It's not you, is it?"

"What?"

"You're not the one listening to everyone's conversations, are you?"

Did Frank hear that right? "Me? Why would you think it's me?"

"Just answer the question."

"Of course it's not me!" Frank stood, backing away from the bench. "How could you even think that?"

Damien shook his head, motioned for Frank to sit back down, which he did. "Sorry. Of course it's not you. See what's happening to me?"

"We're all stressed. It's normal. And people handle stress differently." Not usually by accusing their friends, but he should let this pass. Obviously Damien wasn't in his right mind.

"You seem on edge lately. Just kind of acting weird." Damien stared at the clouds again.

Frank swallowed back a few words that wanted to escape . . . a confession he had told only one other soul.

But then Damien said, "The thing is, everyone's acting weird. You should see Edgar. With every bad piece of news, he's popping champagne corks. Kay's becoming ultraobsessed with every piece of clothing our daughter wears. My coworkers make paranoia look like a new trend. It's getting ridiculous."

"This kind of thing, what's happening here, it's what gets me up in the morning. It's my job. I fight crime."

"I'm in the news business. It should be what gets me up in the morning too." Damien gazed at the open expanse of the park. "Marlo Park. Lame name. We should've come up with something different." He faced Frank. "I don't know how to say this, so I'm just going to say it."

"What?"

"It's not just about the incident last night. There are other things on my mind." Damien pressed his lips together as if he were holding in a mouthful of words. "If Hunter comes and talks to you, that's cool, okay? I think he's into some things— some things he shouldn't be into, some things he can't talk to me about. You're like an uncle to the kids, and that's good. I wish Hunter could talk to me, but if he can't, I want him to talk to you. I didn't want you to feel weird about it." His phone vibrated and lit up. He read the screen, then stood. "Got to go to work."

"What'd the message say?"

Damien turned his phone for Frank to read. *Get here or you're fired.* Then he walked to his car.

Frank sat there for a moment, contemplating, when he noticed a man standing by a distant tree, seemingly watching him. He thought the man would eventually look away. Instead, he began walking toward Frank.

When he was a few yards away, Frank recognized him as Gabriella's father, Reverend Caldwell.

Frank rose as he approached. "What are you doing out here?"

"Praying."

"You have a lot to be thankful for."

"And a lot to be worried about. Bad things are happening in this town, Officer Merret. You see, don't you?"

"Yes. Of course. And let me assure you that we're doing everything—"

"Nothing can stop it."

"Stop it?"

"In one breath it praises our Lord God Almighty. In another it curses the very thing made in His image."

Frank nodded, feeling the reality of Caldwell's heavy, somber words. The two men stood for a moment. Then Frank patted him on the back. There was nothing more to say. They understood each other and understood far more than that.

*　*　*

"Merret! Wake up!"

Frank wiggled awake with a startle.

"You were asleep," Grayson said, leaning against the doorway. "I know it's been a rough twenty-four hours."

"Sorry," Frank said, rubbing his eyes and then adjusting the paperwork on his desk. He must've dozed off while filling out the police report. One side of his face felt wet.

"How's it coming?" Grayson asked.

"Good. We'll have plenty for the DA."

Grayson stepped farther into the room, shutting the door. "Gavin came to talk to me this morning. Requested to be assigned to a different training officer."

Frank rolled his eyes. "Fine. Whatever."

"Said you talk down to him, won't answer his questions, and dump him off somewhere for an hour while you disappear."

"I get it. It's okay—"

Grayson smiled. "Are you kidding me? The kid needs to suck it up. I told him if he can handle you, the criminals won't be a problem."

Frank laughed. Finally they were on the same page.

"But," Grayson said, "I do want you to follow up on an idea Gavin had. About the cell phone being used as a spy device."

Frank sighed. "Okay. Sure. I'll go this afternoon."

"Finish that up and take a couple hours to rest first, all right? We've got to stay on top of this Web site deal. We've had double the number of calls this morning. People are losing their minds."

Frank nodded. Yeah, he kind of predicted that. Grayson left, and Frank started back on the paperwork but couldn't continue. He threw down the pen. Trying to concentrate was useless. Maybe he needed more coffee.

No.

It wasn't coffee.

Frank sighed heavily, twirling his pen through his fingers. The sounds of the police station echoed down the hall.

What nobody knew was that Frank already suspected someone of the Web site fiasco and was pretty close to proving it.

But he wasn't sure he wanted to.

21

KAY ROSE FROM the computer, straining to see clearly for a moment. She rubbed her eyes and stretched. How long had she been sitting here, reading all that?

She checked on Jenna. Still watching TV. She climbed the stairs, deciding laundry was calling her name. She grabbed the basket in the hallway and went to her bedroom, intending on hanging the clean clothes. But something caught her eye in the far corner. She set the basket down and walked toward the freestanding mirror.

The bedroom lights dazzled in the background of the long mirror and the reflection it held. She was thinking of changing into something a little nicer than sweats. She didn't want to feel grungy.

Except as she stood there, it wasn't the outside that was bothering her. It was something deep, internal, voiceless.

Kay covered her mouth, trying not to acknowledge it, trying to hold back the tears. But there it was, right in front of her. Not what she wore. Or how her hair looked. But something nobody else could see.

Why was it rearing its ugly head now? Why wouldn't it go away?

Kay was unable to look at herself. A deep, heavy cry was unwillingly forced out. It was maddening too, and she slammed her hand against the mirror. It tipped backward and crashed into the wall.

"Mom?"

Kay gasped, scrambling to pick up the heavy mirror. "Jenna?"

"What are you doing?"

Kay swiped at her face. "Nothing . . . I just . . ." How could she hide this? Gauging Jenna's expression, she'd been standing there long enough. She opened her mouth, intending to falsely confess this was about Gabby. But as she stared into her daughter's eyes, she knew that wouldn't do. It wasn't fair. To anybody.

Kay sat on the edge of her bed and motioned for Jenna to join her. Her daughter sat next to her, crossing and recrossing her legs. Stale air and awkward silence wedged between them, but Kay wasn't going to be deterred.

"I want to tell you something. About myself. I was about your age, in high school like you and all that. But I wanted to fit in better. I had a few friends, but not the kind that I felt I wanted. So I went against my parents' rules and started dressing . . . loose."

"Loose? You mean, like, baggy clothes?"

Kay smiled a little. "No. Actually really tight clothes. Low cut. Supershort shorts. Miniskirts galore. I'd sneak them out of the house under other clothes, then change at school. And you know what? It worked. I was noticed."

Kay's shaky hands stroked the silky comforter on the bed. "One day I was coming out of chemistry. I rounded the corner, and there was spray paint all over my locker." She paused, but not even a deep breath could stop the tears from rolling. She looked away from Jenna. She didn't want to see her face when she told the next part. "Spray-painted all over my locker were the words *slut* and *whore*."

Kay finally glanced over, afraid of the shame her daughter would feel toward her. But instead, to Kay's surprise, the hard and steady glare that had disappeared overnight had returned. Jenna's eyes sank underneath her furrowed brows as if they were backing slowly into a deep and dark cave.

Kay quickly added, "I'm just telling you this because it was so painful. It was the worst day of my life. Still is. I'll never get over standing there staring at those words." She reached for her daughter's hand, but Jenna pulled away. Jumped to her feet as if something had grabbed her underneath the bed. "Jenna? What?"

Jenna didn't look her in the eye. "Nothing. I get it, okay? It's a long-winded way of saying it, but I get it."

"Get what?"

"Please. Don't sit there and act like that was an innocent little story you wanted to tell to get off your chest."

Kay swiped at more tears that began to fall. "You're right.

But, honey, a mother's hope is that she can prevent her children from making the—"

"Same mistake. Yeah, I get it. Except I don't have to have my mistake painted across a locker. I've got you writing it all over me every day, don't I?" Jenna turned and rushed out of the room.

Kay fell backward on the bed, too exhausted and emotional to do anything but lie there and stare at the ceiling.

So they were now back to square one. Thanks to Kay opening her big mouth. She knew there was a reason she had kept it secret all these years. She curled into a little ball and willed herself to sleep.

* * *

There was a disproportionate number of cell phone stores to the number of residents in Marlo, but Frank decided on the popular one that offered rollover minutes, free phones, unlimited texting, and every other useless but endlessly fun thing on the planet.

He tried to stop smiling to himself, but he couldn't help reveling in Squirmy over there in the passenger's seat. He'd driven through Starbucks in silence, letting the kid believe whatever he wanted to about Frank's mood. He didn't help matters when he refused to let Gavin order.

Frank glanced over while taking a sip of coffee.

As if he had superpowered peripheral vision, Gavin turned and offered a tentative smile.

"So," Frank said, lowering his voice to sound the slightest

bit irritated, "you don't like working with me." He had to sip more coffee to keep from smiling.

Sweat burst onto Gavin's forehead. "I didn't mean anything by it. It's not personal; it's really not. You're a great cop, the way you found that girl and everything last night. I have the utmost respect for you in every way. But sometimes personalities clash and that can't be helped—"

"What's wrong with my personality?" Good grief, he was having so much fun.

"No, no. Nothing. There's nothing wrong with you. I mean, not you. Your personality. And you. There's nothing wrong at all." The kid looked like he was about to hyperventilate.

"Calm down. Let me let you in on a little secret: don't be a tattletale. You learned that in kindergarten, right? Guess what. It applies to the police force too. I'd risk my life trying to save you. Right here, right now. And you're going to go in and complain that I'm not easy to work with? Doesn't bode well, my friend." Frank was pretty sure he'd already discussed this before, but maybe it didn't stick.

"I wasn't . . . I wasn't tattling. I didn't say anything bad about you. I just felt like I could possibly learn a little more from someone who wanted a rookie."

"Nobody wants a rookie, Rookie. I'm glad you're eager to learn. There's nothing wrong with that. But as important as police work is, what's more important is camaraderie. You gotta trust the guys you're working with. Okay?"

Gavin grinned. "Now you're teaching me something."

"Oh, brother. Don't go all sentimental on me. So tell me, how'd you get this idea about cell phone spying?"

"I saw it on the Internet once."

"Just stumbled upon it while searching the World Wide Web?"

Gavin shifted. "I had an ex-girlfriend. Thought she was stalking me. Seemed to know where I'd be. Someone told me she could've loaded this thing on my, you know, phone."

Frank pulled to a stop at the light, looked at Gavin, who didn't seem to want to make eye contact.

"All right, fine." Gavin sighed, a finger tracing the dashboard. "Yeah, okay, I looked into it. I was a freshman in college. I'd been serious with this chick since high school. She went to college and swore we'd stay together, but then she didn't have time to see me. I got suspicious."

"You do it?"

"No. I just looked into it. Had heard in the frat house that it could be done but nobody really knew how."

Frank pulled into the parking lot of Cell Buy, with its tacky storefront promising deals of the century that were apparently not profitable enough to help them afford anything more than neon cardboard for the grand announcements. "This the store you went to?"

"No. The one on the other side of town."

"Let's go." Frank got out and walked in, Gavin trailing.

One guy stood behind a half-circle counter, cradling a phone in his shoulder and talking fast. Without glancing up, he continued typing on the computer and carrying on the conversation. "Yeah, that's right. Two years . . . Uh-huh. Then you can get the BlackBerry upgrade. . . . Sure, come on in. We'll get you signed up." He dropped the phone into his hand, then snatched a cell phone off the counter. "Sorry, dude. . . . No, I'm not busy." He suddenly noticed both of them. "Let me call you back." He snapped his phone shut. "Help you?" His name tag read Dave.

"We're needing some information."

"Looking for a new plan that can save you money?" He seemed to suddenly remember the smile that was supposed to go with that pitch.

"No." Frank approached the counter, put his hands flat on top of it. "I'm looking for a way to spy on someone."

"We're a cell phone store."

"With a cell phone."

Dave blinked. "Let me get Pat. Pat knows everything."

A few seconds later, Dave returned, followed by Pat. In every world, including the techno-geek crowd, there is the revered. Apparently Pat was that person. Dave offered him a front-row spot at the counter, pulled up a stool for him, decided he needed to do introductions. "This is Pat, our store manager. I've never seen him unable to answer a question."

"Officer Merret. Officer Jenkins," Frank said, studying Pat. He had a certain self-assurance you normally didn't find among pale-skinned, superskinny, hairless males with a Bluetooth sticking out of unusually large ears.

He didn't make eye contact as he said, "What can I do for

you?" Instead, he typed on the computer, his full attention on the screen.

"First, you can give me some outstanding customer service," Frank said.

Pat swiveled so he faced Frank. He didn't say anything and his expression remained neutral.

"They want to know how to spy on someone using a cell phone."

Pat, his expression unmoved, said, "We of course don't sell anything like that here."

Frank leaned in. "Of course. But let's say we wanted to do this. Hypothetically, how would one go about doing it?"

Pat tilted his head to the side, a superiority-complex kind of smile nibbling at his lips. "It's easy."

"Tell me."

"It's a program you load onto the cell phone."

"What does it allow you to do?"

"Pretty much whatever you want. You can listen in on phone calls. You can retrieve call logs. Any data or pictures."

"You can even listen to conversations when the phone is off," Dave added, then cleared his throat. "That's what I've heard."

"You're telling me," Frank said, "that this program allows someone to listen in on whatever is going on in a room, even if the phone is off?"

"That's right," Pat said. "The only way it doesn't work is if the battery is taken out."

"Is this kind of thing readily available?"

"Sure. It's all over the Web."

"How do you get it on the phone?"

"You have to have the phone in your possession to download the software."

"So if it's a girlfriend or someone you want to spy on, you have to snatch the phone, download it, and give it back."

"That's right."

"Or you could have the software already on a phone you were selling."

Pat started to nod, then stopped and glanced between Frank and Gavin. "What?"

"Hypothetically."

"What are you saying?"

"Let's say you wanted to listen to an entire town's conversations. You load up these phones with some software, send them out, something like that?"

Pat's otherwise colorless skin suddenly flushed pink. "In theory."

"You guys doing that here? maybe thought it'd be a fun kind of prank? maybe got a little addictive, thought you'd take it a little further?"

"No. I can prove it. Pick any phone you like in the store. I'll show you the programs on it. Or take my phone. You won't find anything like that on there." Pat slid his phone toward Frank, crossed his arms, and waited.

Frank slid it back. "No, thanks. That's all the information I needed."

Pat leaped to his feet. "Wait a minute. What are you saying? You think we're behind this mess? we're bugging people's phones?"

"No, man. Just trying to figure some stuff out." Frank held out a hand to shake.

Pat stared at it for an awkwardly long time before shaking it.

"Thanks for your time. Next visit I'll look into that text-messaging package." Frank winked, then turned and left the store, Gavin right behind him.

As soon as the door closed, Gavin rushed to Frank's side. "See? See! It could work. I mean, here these guys are, selling phones that are going out to all the residents. How easy would it be for them to download that program onto these phones and—"

"No, it's not them."

Gavin stopped on the sidewalk, watching as Frank opened his car door. "What do you mean?"

"They're not doing it."

Gavin dragged his feet and got into the car, closing the door. "How do you know that? You're a mind reader or something?"

Frank tried to give the poor kid a break. "You're just going to have to trust me on this. It's not going down like you think."

Gavin slid down in his seat and stared out the window of the cruiser.

Frank glanced at him. "I'm taking a break. Where do you want me to drop you?"

* * *

Damien stood in his boss's office for a solid ten minutes listening to Edgar blow off steam. He yelled questions but didn't leave time for responses before going on, so Damien just took it. There was no point in arguing. He couldn't explain any of this anyway.

"Now get out there and get me what I want!" Edgar commanded, jabbing his finger toward the door.

But Damien didn't budge. He stayed there and stared his boss down. "What is going on with you?"

"Excuse me?"

"We've known each other a long time. You're acting strangely. You're yelling at me like I'm some sort of idiot. Is there something on your mind? something you need to tell me?"

Edgar stood still, huffing, glaring, a vein on his forehead throbbing.

Damien crossed his arms. "It's the site, isn't it? You've been reading it. From the look of your bloodshot eyes, reading it nonstop."

Edgar sat down in his chair, pushing a few papers around. "Just leave me alone."

"But we're frie—"

"Go."

Damien turned and went to his desk, where his early-morning coffee was now cold. Cream circles floated at the top. He stirred it with the little red stirrer anyway as he tried to process the idea that evil had not arrived in their town with horns and a pitchfork. In fact, he thought, with much disgust for thinking it, that this kidnapping of Gabby Caldwell might've been easier to handle had it been a convict on the prowl in the quaint town of Marlo.

But no, it was not evil from the outside. It was evil from within. Evil that had disguised itself so brilliantly that no one ever suspected it.

Damien heard footsteps on the carpet and looked up.

Reginald Boren, the staff photographer, hurried up to Damien's desk, out of breath. "Sorry," he said, putting his hands on his knees and breathing heavily. "I took the stairs. Elevator's too slow." He yanked the camera strap off his neck and pulled a cord out of the small satchel at his waist. "You gotta see these."

He knelt beside Damien's computer, plugged something into the computer. Within seconds, a picture popped up on his computer.

"Look at this!" Reginald said. "Can you believe it?"

Damien made himself look. "This is Caydance?" She was trying to cover her face with a jacket as she left her house in an SUV.

"Yes. Caydance is the blonde. Zoey is the brunette." He pushed a key. The brunette was on the screen, with a hand extended as she faced what was sure to be a lawn full of people with cameras. Both men stared for a moment. "They look so normal, don't they?"

"They're friends of my daughter's," Damien said, then

punched off the computer screen. "How am I going to tell her this?"

Reginald unplugged his camera and leaned against the edge of the desk. "Yeah. This is whacked-out. I'll let you know when I've got them downloaded."

Damien nodded and Reginald left. Damien reached to turn on his computer screen again, but someone else was already standing over him.

The mail clerk greeted Damien and tossed a bundled stack of letters on his desk.

"Thanks," Damien said.

Then he handed Damien another stack. "And give this to Sheryl. We're not speaking."

Damien didn't stop him. It was just another day in the office these days . . . a night of reading on the Internet, a day of cold silence toward former friends.

He pushed both stacks aside, determined to get this article written. How could he even start? What could he possibly say to make sense out of any of this?

Cold. Hard. Facts.

Yeah, this was as cold and hard as it came.

Something caught Damien's eye from the stack of mail. It was the letter on top. In bright red ink next to his address were the words *Open immediately* underlined twice. There was no return address. A small, greasy stain bled into the corner of the envelope.

Damien lifted the rubber band and pulled it out of the pile. He slid his letter opener underneath the flap, tearing it neatly. He held his breath, not in anticipation but rather from fear the thing was laced with anthrax. Was it so far-fetched these days?

He carefully pulled out the folded piece of paper. Didn't seem to be any powdery substance involved. He let out the air he was holding in and opened the paper.

A crossword puzzle.

And an amateur one at that. Just a handful of words to solve? Please.

He threw it down and stared at his screen. He had to get comments from the police department. Or at least call Frank, who'd be willing to be an unnamed source for a good friend. He needed to try to get quotes from the families, knowing full well they would have nothing to say.

Leaning back in his chair, he grabbed his favorite cross-word pen and decided to do the little crossword puzzle. Puzzles always relieved stress. Besides, this one was curious. Simple. And with no key, which always accompanied a sub-mission. The theme read *Listen*.

One down. Guaranteed, like taxes.

Easy. *Death*. He jotted it down, but the word felt heavy, morbid.

Five across. Also, always spelled wrong.

Too.

Four down. Steering, made easy.

Power.

Damien hurried through the puzzle.

Life. And. Of. Now. Stop. Tongue. Can't. Stake. Much. Are. In. Is. At.

What was this? Tiny words?

And then he saw it. He held the paper up to read so his eyes would adjust properly. The words popped as he followed the first line from top to bottom: *I can't stop now.*

The second line, from left to right, jagging toward the bottom, read *Too much is at stake.*

The last one caused his breath to catch: *Life and death are in the power of the tongue.* Someone was sending him a message? Why him? He put the paper down, looked hard at it, tried to calm himself.

Whoever was behind this Web site knew him? knew he worked at the newspaper?

Damien grabbed the paper and barreled down the hallway toward Edgar's office. He paused outside. Was Edgar the right person to talk to? With this sudden influx of paranoia and flat-out anger? The door was shut, but he could hear Edgar on the phone. He peeked in the window. Whatever Edgar was discussing, it seemed important, judging by the deep line down the middle of his forehead.

He barely heard a few words. Something about the newspaper lifting out of despair.

Damien backed away from the door and studied the puzzle. *I can't stop now. Too much is at stake. Life and death are in the power of the tongue.*

What did this mean?

Suddenly Edgar's door flew open, and he almost knocked Damien over. Damien stumbled backward.

"You need something?" Edgar asked, pausing his swift step.

"Um . . ."

"What?"

"No, nothing. It can wait."

"Fine. Get me that article!"

Damien returned to his desk, where he laid open the letter. He could not stop staring at the words. His mind raced through the million possibilities linked to this.

His fingers brushed the tops of the keys on his keyboard. He should write the investigative piece.

But his heart said there was more to say than facts. The facts didn't do justice to what Marlo had become, at its own hand, no less.

He glanced back at the paper. Disclosing this to Edgar was the obvious and only choice.

Except . . .

The author had reached out to him. Had sent him the message. Was communicating this to him. If he kept it private, he might have more of a chance of discovering who was behind all of this. Did anyone else receive a letter?

He grabbed the paper, carefully slid it into his briefcase, and hurried down the flights of concrete stairs. At ground level, he burst through the door, gasping for breath. He leaned against the brick in the alleyway, breathing. Thinking. Worrying.

This was too much.

His daughter had been friends with girls like this.

His son and the things he'd chosen to do behind closed doors. The way he couldn't talk to him anymore.

His town, rotting from the inside out.

Damien closed his eyes, willing himself not to break down. The world felt heavy now, but there had to be a solution. Some way to stop this madness.

He took in the cold air, hardly fresh thanks to nearby smokers. He fingered the loose threads of his sleeve.

He should tell.

But he wouldn't. He'd wait and see.

And maybe send a message of his own.

"Mr. Underwood?"

Damien looked up to find Reverend Caldwell approaching him, his hand outstretched just like on Sunday morning.

"Reverend," he said, shaking it. "What are you doing here?"

"I came to see you, actually."

"How is Gabby?"

Pain flashed across the reverend's eyes. "She's hanging in there. I don't know if she'll ever be the same."

"I am so sorry this has happened to your family."

"I wanted to tell you that Gabby is starting to talk a little about what's going on."

Damien wished he had a pen and a pad of paper.

"She mentioned your daughter."

"What?"

"Jenna apparently hit a girl recently? Gabby said that Jenna was defending her." The reverend's eyes filled with tears. "I can't tell you what it means to us, to our family, that someone would stand up for her. I wanted to personally thank you and ask that you would thank Jenna on our behalf."

Damien felt himself choking up. Pride swelled through his whole body. "I will. Thank you for letting us know."

The reverend started to walk off, then turned back to Damien. "You have a chance."

"A chance?"

"I've always enjoyed all the columns you've written over the years. There's a war raging now, and you have the right weapon."

22

FRANK GOT OUT of his cruiser, shut the door, and stretched and groaned, trying to shake the achy feeling in his muscles.

On the other side, Gavin did the same. "This must be how cops feel in Los Angeles."

"I've never taken so many calls in one day." Frank twisted his lower back, hoping to relieve the pain.

They walked toward the station.

"The women at the hair salon?" Gavin said, shaking his head. "Assault with a hot iron? over a dress size? And another fight at the post office. When is this going to stop?"

Frank nodded.

"Last night," Gavin continued, "I was having a conversation with my girlfriend and I stopped, you know? I was like, man, I don't want everybody to know this."

They walked a few steps and then Gavin said, "Frank, where do you go?"

Frank glanced at him.

"I know it's none of my business, but sometimes you just kind of disappear."

He slapped Gavin on the back. Tried a warm smile. "Nothing for you to worry about. You ask a lot of questions. Maybe you should consider a detective spot later, huh? Go get some rest. Good work today."

"Thanks." Gavin turned toward the locker room.

Frank went for the coffeepot.

"Frank!" Grayson was flagging him down. "Get to my office, will you?"

Frank poured himself a tall Styrofoam cup full of the cheap stuff and headed toward the captain's office.

"Come on in."

In the corner of the room a man with broad shoulders and a shaved head stepped forward, offering a hand. "Gary Blanco."

"State police sent him in to help with the investigation," Grayson said. "He does a lot of work in child porn cases."

"Good to meet you," Frank said as Grayson gestured for them all to sit.

"Frank, it's been crazy out there, hasn't it?"

Frank nodded, glancing at Blanco. "People are losing their sense of self-control and reasoning."

"Gary was just explaining to me what he's turned up so far."

Gary sat comfortably in his chair, glancing over some notes he'd grabbed out of his briefcase. "Usually these things are pretty easy to crack. The first line of defense is the use of the registrar's privacy service. This normally comes with a fee, but it protects your identity if someone wants to go searching for who the Web site belongs to. Hackers usually can get past this anyway, and a subpoena works pretty fast for the host to cough up the information.

"And a lot of times these guys will put in fake names and addresses or what have you, but normally we can trace back to the computer being used and find them in their house."

"Normally?" Frank said. "I take that to mean this isn't normal."

"Yeah," Blanco said. "Sometimes they'll slip up and host the site on an IPS with other sites they own. A lot of times they'll try for a PO box or some such. But again, those just cause delays. They're hurdles we can jump over." He checked his notes. "The name on the account and the address are fake. Looks like he paid a year in advance, possibly with a Visa prepaid money card, which is untraceable when purchased with cash. We're still working on that. He's apparently using a CMS, allowing him to add content from anywhere, and is most likely using public terminals to access the site."

"And," Grayson said, "there's no e-mail on this Web site."

"Right. Sometimes these guys will use disposable, untraceable e-mail accounts, where they keep rotating and dumping. A lot of times we can get them on that if they slip up in any of the steps getting those, but there is nothing on the Web site. Whoever this is, they don't want anyone contacting them."

"So where are we at?" Frank asked.

"Well, first we thought the guy, or perhaps lady, was

running a Freenet node. Won't go into all that, but basically that's where you'll find a lot of these child porn guys going. We're still confirming, but it looks like what he's done is selected a registrar and host that is out of our jurisdiction."

"Meaning," Grayson said, "he's gone to a foreign country."

"That's right. Possibly China. My international contacts tell me that China's hot for these kinds of things right now. Someone has gone to a lot of trouble to bury his or her identity."

"So what do we do now?"

"We'll keep monitoring it, see if this guy makes a mistake. If this were a terrorist group, the CIA would get involved, send agents overseas, and hunt this provider down. Unfortunately, in this case, our hands are tied. This guy hasn't sent any notes or threats, has he? to the paper or here at the station?"

"No," Grayson said.

"Too bad. That's usually where we can get someone like this." Blanco got up. "I'll keep an eye on this from my end, contact you if anything develops or we see a possible crack we can climb in. You might contact the National White Collar Crime Center. They might be able to help you with the international angle."

The captain stood, prompting Frank to. "Well, Gary, thanks for your time. We appreciate the state stepping in to help."

"Sure," Blanco said. Frank offered his hand. "Best of luck to you guys. This is a little crazy. Never seen anything like it."

*   *   *

Kay heard the back door open as she slid the chicken potpie casserole out of the oven. She'd spent the rest of the day taking her frustrations out by baking like a madwoman. Cakes. Cookies. Scones. And a casserole. She set it on the counter and turned just as Damien walked into the kitchen. She immediately noticed his somber body language. "Babe, you okay?"

"Huh?"

"You all right? What's wrong?"

"Oh, nothing, really," he said, taking off his jacket. He pecked her on the cheek, then sat at the breakfast bar. "Just made Edgar mad today. Twice, actually."

"Not 'you're fired' mad?"

"No, nothing like that. He wanted me to write a piece on the kidnapping, and I did, but not the piece he wanted. I did it as an op-ed."

"Well, you are the op-ed writer."

"I felt like my words would serve a better purpose writing about the Web site. Trying to convince whoever is doing it to stop. I wrote a letter directly to the person."

"I know. I'm hearing that all kinds of terrible things are happening. Fights. Tires being slashed. Windows broken out. It's like we're on the verge of a riot. And then with this kidnapping . . ." Tears stung her eyes for the fortieth time that day.

Damien hopped up and wrapped his arms around her. "You seem . . . sad."

"I'm just in disbelief that those girls were involved in taking Gabby. And I'm horrified at myself that I didn't see the signs."

"How could you have known?" Damien asked, turning her around to face him.

"It's a mother's instinct. Jenna kept trying to tell me she didn't want to hang out . . ." More tears. Damien swiped them and pulled her close. "And I tried to . . . Anyway, I think we're back to not speaking." Kay wanted to pour out her heart, but she wasn't sure how. She never dreamed of telling Damien about her past. She'd not even told him why she and Angela stopped being friends. She couldn't get herself to.

"How is she doing?"

"She doesn't want to go to school tomorrow either, but I told her she had to. She's doing okay, I guess. We had a good morning together, anyway. Talked a lot." Kay smiled at the thought. "Kind of like old times."

"Nothing like tragedy to bring people together."

"I just keep picturing . . . I see Jenna out there, tied to that tree . . ."

Damien stroked her cheek. "Look, we're all here. Everyone's here, right? Hunter too?"

Kay nodded.

"We're all here and safe and together." He pointed to the casserole. "And chicken potpie casserole? You haven't made that in a long time."

"It's Jenna's favorite."

"Where is she?"

"Her cell phone rang. She answered it and went upstairs. Can you grab the butter out of the fridge?"

He opened the door, digging beyond the yogurt and milk.

"Oh, and Frank's coming over. He just called. Wanted to have dinner here."

Damien emerged from the fridge with the butter as Kay poured the green beans into a bowl. "We've got to get Frank dating again."

"Good luck with that," Kay said. She walked to the bottom of the stairs. "Time to eat!"

The doorbell rang. Damien smiled. "Must be Frank, right on time."

Kay poured the water into glasses as she listened to the kids hurry down the stairs. She hadn't heard that kind of enthusiasm for dinner in a while.

Hunter arrived first, followed closely by Jenna. "Potpie casserole?" She grinned. "My favorite!"

"Ugh. Did you put peas in it?" Hunter asked Kay.

"Just a few."

Kay couldn't keep her eyes off Jenna, who looked up again and offered another smile. Softer. As if there were a lot of good words behind those lips. Kay smiled back and continued serving while holding back a few tears that wanted to escape out of sheer relief her daughter didn't hate her.

Damien rounded the corner, followed by Frank.

"Hey, Uncle Frank!" Hunter stood to give him a sideways hug.

"Hey, gang," Frank said, plopping down in his usual chair. "Thanks for feeding me."

Kay set a plate in front of him. "You look exhausted."

"Yeah. Long day."

Hunter asked, "Have they arrested the girls?"

Kay started the casserole around. "Let's not talk about that tonight."

"It's okay," Jenna said, grabbing a roll. "Not talking about it doesn't make it go away. A wise uncle told me that." She smiled at Frank.

Kay nodded. "You're right. I'm sorry."

"No charges have been filed yet. But they're coming. The DA has to put the case together, but we've got more than enough evidence."

Frank served himself the casserole, but Kay noticed he wasn't eating. Normally he just started digging in.

"Frank? Not hungry?" Kay passed him the green beans.

"Well," Frank said, "there is another reason I'm here."

Kay followed his gaze. He was staring at Jenna. Kay set down her fork. An uneasiness swirled in her stomach.

"With Jenna's permission, I'd like to tell you something," Frank said, his voice way softer than normal.

Jenna and Frank exchanged a glance.

Kay looked at Damien, whose mouth had frozen mid-chew. Their eyes met, and Kay read fear. She knew that fear. It was coursing through her own body. What was Frank talking about? Was Jenna involved in the kidnapping somehow? She glanced at Jenna, who just stared at her plate.

"What is it?" Kay asked, trying to keep her voice steady and calm.

Frank held out a hand. "Relax. It's nothing bad. In fact, it's the opposite."

Kay sat up straighter, tried to prepare herself for whatever she was about to hear.

"You know we found Gabby last night. The reason we found her in time is because a very brave person tipped off police. And that brave person was your daughter."

A small whimper of relief escaped Kay.

Jenna glanced up, her eyes searching everybody for a reaction.

Damien reached for Jenna's hand and looked at Frank. "Jenna?"

"Jenna knew something was going down. She didn't have details, but her gut told her that those girls were involved. She alerted me to what was going on, where she thought Gabby might be. Turned out she was right."

"But Jenna was upstairs in her room asleep that night," Kay said.

Jenna smiled weakly. "I kind of snuck out to meet Frank. Sorry."

Kay took a deep breath as she sorted through it all in her head.

"Sweetie," Damien said, "why haven't you told us any of this?"

"I didn't think . . ." Jenna shook her head and looked down. "I didn't think you'd believe me."

Damien started to say something, but Kay held up her hand. "She's right. We haven't been listening, have we, Jenna?"

"It's okay. It's just what I needed to do."

"She's a hero," Frank said. "She saved Gabby's life."

Hunter reached over and patted her on the back. "Way to go, Sis."

"Thanks." She smiled at her brother like she used to when they were young.

"Jenna," Frank said, "why don't you tell your parents the rest?"

"The rest?" Kay asked.

Jenna pressed her lips together and took several seconds before she said, "Once the girls are charged, I might be called as a witness." She glanced back and forth between Kay and Damien. "I want to do it. I'm not scared."

"Scared of what?" Damien asked Frank.

"There could be some retribution at school. But we'll keep Jenna's name out of it as long as possible. In fact, this thing probably won't even go to trial until next year. A lot of emotion will have passed by then, so I don't anticipate any problems. The DA and the department understand the sensitivity of the situation."

"A lot of people are upset; that's all," Jenna said. "I mean, this is hard to take."

Kay kept nodding with each statement, trying her best to understand that Jenna's heroic move would not be viewed as heroic by everyone. What had this world come to? She saved a life and now feared for her own?

"There's a chance the DA might not need her testimony at all. We have confessions from both girls, so they'll probably enter guilty pleas and be turned over to the court to decide what to do with them."

"Okay. Sure. We understand," Damien said, but Kay could see it in his eyes. He was unsure.

Still, to look at their daughter, to know what goodness dwelled deep inside her . . . it sort of wiped out all the apprehension.

"The state brought in an investigator," Frank continued. "He's making some headway into figuring out who is doing the Web site. As long as it's up, he's fairly sure he can get who is doing this."

"That's good," Damien said, beginning to eat. "The sooner, the better."

"You haven't received anything at the paper, have you? any letters to the editor from this guy? any threats?"

"No," Damien answered.

The conversation continued throughout dinner. Damien mentioned that Reverend Caldwell had stopped by to commend Jenna for sticking up for Gabby. Then talk turned to lighter topics. It seemed like old times, if just for a little while. Frank even agreed to stay for ice cream and a game of Monopoly.

But Frank came into the kitchen as Kay was clearing the dishes and Damien was getting down bowls. "I'm sorry, but I'm going to have to pass on ice cream and Monopoly tonight."

"You do?"

"Sorry to back out. There's just something I need to do."

Kay studied Frank. The lines on his face sank deeper than normal, like how they looked after his divorce. Kay touched his arm. "Everything all right?"

"Yeah, fine. Just tired." Frank gave Damien a quick hug and a hearty slap on the back. "Thank you, my friend. You got a fine family here," Frank said, winking at Jenna as she and Hunter came into the kitchen.

"You're leaving?" Jenna said.

"Yeah, sorry, guys. Maybe next time. Hey, Hunter, I've got something for you in my truck. Want to walk me out?"

"Sure," Hunter said.

"Kay, thanks for dinner," Frank said. "Damien, see you soon."

Kay and Damien watched from the window as Frank stood for a few minutes talking with Hunter.

"What do you think they're talking about?" Kay asked. "Looks like a lively conversation."

"I don't know," Damien said. "But that right there is a good thing. And a good man."

* * *

Frank pulled into the small circular parking lot and checked his watch. Ten minutes before visiting hours were over. He got out and lumbered toward the front doors, his back aching from stress.

The glass doors swooshed open, creating a short breeze against his face. Lisa Yaris, now Lisa Hall since getting married two weeks ago, was working the desk tonight, and she always had a smile for him. "Hi, Frank." She checked her watch. "Cutting it close tonight."

"Just throw me in a wheelchair and toss me out when you're ready for me to go."

Lisa laughed, stretching over the desk to pat his hand. "You know we love you."

Frank signed in and walked toward the third hallway, room 412. He knew she'd be done with dinner, done with her bath, and would have her nightgown on.

The door was open and he walked in. She sat in her specially equipped wheelchair, strapped tightly in, with her back to the door. A silent, flickering television played an old variety show in black and white. The tiny Christmas tree he'd brought two weeks ago, with its miniature ornaments, still looked in its place and untouched.

He came around to face her, pecking her on the cheek, then sat down on her bed, eyeing the room to make sure it was well kept and everything was in its place. For a while her gowns kept disappearing, but that seemed to have stopped.

"Hey, kiddo."

Like always, there was no response. Her contorted face didn't move. Her eyes blinked every ten seconds. Her mouth gaped open as if it were in the middle of a bloodcurdling scream. Her neck stretched and strained to the right, causing her cheek to almost rest against her shoulder, which lifted up slightly by an arm that was permanently twisted against her chest. Her hands were frozen, clawlike.

Frank took the brush off the bedside table and moved closer to her. Her hair, still long and shiny but gray now, gently waved against her cheeks. He carefully brushed it. The scar around her neck was still there, deep purple, after all these years. He lifted her hair and touched it.

"I'm trying to save this little town," he began, continuing to brush. "I'm not sure it wants saving. I'm not sure it can bear to know the truth." He pulled the hair away from her face so he could see her eyes . . . once a deep and sparkly brown. "Kind of like you. If you could, I know you'd tell me how much you hate me for saving you that day. That you wouldn't want to live like this—" Frank cut off his words and set down the brush. He took her hand. It was cold like usual. "I just wish you had known your worth. That's all I wish. That you hadn't believed all the lies other people said about you. I wish this town could learn . . . would listen to one another instead of talking so much."

Willie stepped in with a mop. "Oh, hi, Frank. Didn't know you were here. Didn't I see you this morning?"

Frank nodded. "Needing to see her a little more these days. Will you give me a couple of minutes?"

"Sure thing. I know Miss Meredith wouldn't have it any other way."

Frank smiled and watched Willie exit, then looked at Meredith, then at the floor. Every single day, guilt was like the choking rope he'd found around his sister's neck. It was always there, squeezing the life out of him. He knew Meredith would not have wanted to live endless years like this, but this was how it all turned out. If he'd come home just two minutes sooner, it might've turned out differently. Two minutes later and he'd have buried her. If he hadn't changed shifts at work, he wouldn't have come home for another four hours.

Frank folded his hands together and slumped. "I wish you could tell me how to get over Angela. She's moved on. Like it was no big deal. And yet I can't ever seem to get her out of my heart. I can't imagine being with anyone else. She's the only one I ever wanted." He wiped his nose. "I know you'd have good advice for me."

He sat there for a moment. Sometimes he'd imagine that they were having a conversation.

Frank unbuckled her from the five-point harness that kept her upright in her wheelchair. Sliding a gentle hand underneath her back and careful to not knock her feeding tube, he lifted her. She seemed to be weightless, just like when she was twenty. Probably barely ninety pounds.

He laid her in the bed and pulled the covers up to her chest, turning her slightly and putting a pillow against the small of her back.

Frank stared out the window for a minute, into the black, cold night, then leaned over and, like he'd done every day for two and a half decades, whispered in her ear.

*   *   *

From a deep sleep, Frank sat straight up, trying to catch his breath, staring wide-eyed into total blackness. He clutched his chest, gulping down air, wondering if he was having a heart attack. Slowly, like moving shadows, the dark contents of the room came into focus. But the walls closed in like a groaning, hulking beast.

He threw back damp sheets and stood for a moment, trying to get a grip. The clock read 4:02 a.m. What had he dreamed?

In the bathroom he splashed water on his face, pressed a towel to his eyes, and leaned against the sink, his head propped against the mirror.

Something stirred inside him. Some sort of warning. Something unsettling.

But he had been sleeping. Was it just a nightmare? It seemed to have already retreated to the recesses of his mind.

He finished wiping his face, throwing the towel onto the counter. He intended to go back to bed but was fairly certain he wouldn't be able to get back to sleep. He pushed his feet into his old, ratty slippers and trudged to the kitchen.

As he opened the fridge, staring at the small selection of snack foods while letting the cold air hit his face, he again tried to remember what had caused him to awaken.

Maybe it was the stress. Angela had told him once that he didn't handle it well. He thought he handled it fine. No, he didn't break down and cry. He didn't talk about it with people who didn't care. He just handled it. He moved on. What point was there to keeping it around?

But this time, there was no denying it. A lot was happening. And it was very personal, getting more personal by the day.

He poured himself a large glass of milk and mixed some strawberry Nesquik in, then went to the living room and turned on QVC. He settled in for an hour-long infomercial about exercise equipment he swore he'd buy come January.

Noticing his cell phone on the table, he decided he should send Damien a text. He'd read it in the morning, then scold Frank for not having the courtesy to pick up the phone, regardless of the hour. Frank smiled at the thought as his fat thumbs struggled with the tiny keys. He finally got it all typed out: *good talk w/ hunt-man. he didn't admit it, but i think i sent him a clear msg w/out accusing him since we don't know 4 sure. will try again next wk.*

He'd just gulped the last of his milk when he gasped, which pulled the milk down the windpipe, throwing him into a fit of coughing that took him to his knees. As he coughed and hacked, struggling for breath, everything became clear. The fuzzy thoughts he'd been trying to capture came into focus.

He remembered. He remembered what had startled him out of sleep!

Still choking through every breath, he managed to get to his feet. He hurried to the basement door, scurrying down the cold concrete steps.

He sat down at his computer and shuffled the mouse, bringing the screen to life. Frank's fingers flew across the keyboard. He typed in the address to Listen to Yourself.

Thanks to the early morning hour and the awful exhaustion he still felt, the words blurred for several seconds. Finally he was able to read. And reread. And read again.

"Oh no . . . ," he breathed. "Oh no. No. No."

He flung himself out of the chair, taking two steps up the stairs at a time. Without turning on the light, he yanked open the drawer in his bedroom and grabbed his gun.

23

DAMIEN FIGURED HE fell asleep about 3 a.m. He'd tried not to watch the clock, but the other alternative was to continue to play the recent events over and over in his head. And somehow everything came out much worse when he did that. The scenarios took dark twists . . . the "almosts" became reality.

At midnight he'd even heard his neighbors arguing outside on their lawn.

Finally, though, his mind tired of it all and he was able to catch a few hours' sleep. The blaring alarm clock reminded him it had, indeed, been just a few hours.

When the alarm suddenly shut off, Damien opened his eyes. Kay's hand was now on his shoulder as she stood above him. "Out of bed, sleepyhead."

He managed to keep one eye open. "You're already dressed? How late am I?"

"Not late. I'm just early. Hurry and get ready. I've got breakfast cooking."

He knew he smelled something good.

He sat up, put his feet on the floor, and tried to get moti-
vated to stand. He noticed his cell phone light blinking. He'd
missed a call? He flipped it open. Not a call but a text from
Frank. Didn't he have the decency to call?

He looked at the log. It had arrived at 4:32 a.m. *Glad
he had the decency not to call,* Damien thought. He held the
phone close to his face, trying to decipher the strange word
codes that texting seemed to bring out in people.

He breathed a sigh of relief as he finished reading. The
message about Hunter couldn't have come at a better time.
Much of his night had been consumed dwelling over the
state of his two children, wondering how badly he'd screwed
them both up. Frank's message said Hunter was fine. Had a
good talk.

Glancing at the time, he hurried to get dressed, then
went downstairs. Everyone was already at the table, enjoying
French toast.

"This is a first. Everyone beat you downstairs." Kay took
his plate and loaded it with three pieces.

Jenna handed him the syrup.

"You doing okay?" Damien asked.

"I'm fine. Seriously. You guys are going to drive me insane
about this, aren't you?"

"No more than we'd drive ourselves insane," Damien said,
winking at Kay. "Just remember, like Frank said, nobody
knows you made the call, so you're going to be fine."

"I'm not worried," Jenna said. "I just hope there isn't all
this big drama at school."

"Please." Hunter laughed. "There's big drama about zits. This thing is going to skyrocket with drama."

"True," Damien said.

She rolled her eyes.

They finished eating and Jenna grabbed her backpack off the counter. "Hey, Hunter, I'll drop you off if you want."

"Really? Yeah, that'd be great!" Hunter jumped up and threw on his coat.

Kay caught Damien's attention and smiled. He returned it. Sibling love being shared? "Take a picture," Kay whispered.

Damien laughed.

He finished his breakfast and tried to gear himself up for the day. Edgar had called late last night, told him though he hated him for not following orders, the op-ed piece was brilliant. In it, Damien had written to the people talking. He'd raised the question that he could not shake himself: What harm was done when words were spoken in private? Who could be hurt by words they never heard?

And what now? Should we stop speaking? Should we be afraid of every word that leaves our mouths?

And most importantly, do the words we speak have any power over us, whether heard or not, by someone else?

He wasn't sure what kind of reaction would be coming in. Probably lots of e-mails. A few phone calls. He was pretty certain he was still not off the hook with Edgar. But who knew. Edgar was acting so strangely that it was hard to predict what was going on with him.

Today he knew what he had to do. He had to create a new

puzzle. And in it, a message to the person wreaking havoc on their town. It was almost expected, wasn't it? That the message should be returned in the same way it was received?

A hand touched his shoulder. "You're in deep thought." Kay turned him toward her and put a hand on each cheek. "And looking very tired. Maybe you should stay home, get some rest."

"I can't," he said, taking her hand in his. "I'll rest later. There's always later, right?"

His phone beeped and vibrated in his pocket. Things were getting started awfully early. He pulled it out and sighed.

"What?" Kay asked.

"Another text from Frank. I think he's doing it just to annoy me. He knows how much I hate it." He flipped open his phone and read. "See? I can't even make sense of this. I don't know what all these abbreviations are."

Kay took the phone and read. "Something about . . . I don't know. These aren't abbreviations. It's like he's typing while he's jumping up and down."

Damien took the phone back, holding it close to see every letter. *Hpp meee. At Angas hou.* Was Frank drunk or something? "HPP?"

"Nothing that I know of." Kay shrugged.

"Sort of sounds like help. Help me?" Damien looked up at Kay. "Is that what this says?"

Kay put her finger on the screen to underline the text. "Help me. At Angas?"

"Do you think he was trying to spell Angela?"

Kay nodded. "Yes. Look. *Hou.* Like he was trying to say house."

"Help me. At Angela's house."

Kay crossed her arms. "Now what is he up to?"

Damien stared at the screen.

"Honey?" Kay's quizzical face was in front of his again.

"Yeah, sorry. Angela's place is just a few streets over. I'll run by. Check it out."

"Don't let him pull you into any crazy ideas, okay?"

"Who, Frank?" Damien smiled. "That guy would never do anything insane."

"Yeah, right," she said, tossing him his briefcase.

* * *

Damien turned in to the apartment complex, still trying to rub the sleep out of his eyes. The morning was unusually cold, and his car kept lurching forward, trying to warm up. He patted the steering wheel. "Come on, baby. Relax."

He didn't know exactly which apartment Angela lived in, but as he drove toward the back of the complex, he saw Frank's truck parked crooked across two spaces.

Damien parked nearby and got out, pulling his gloves on and scrunching his neck down to keep his ears warm. He looked around, trying to figure out which apartment was hers. A few had some distinctions, like plastic flowers in a pot or a Christmas wreath hanging on the door. Other than that, they all looked alike.

He strolled along the sidewalk, glancing left and right. "Frank?" he hollered.

No answer.

He walked a few more paces, until he noticed an apartment with the door wide open. Maybe they'd know Angela. He stepped toward it and stood in the doorway. He knocked loudly on the doorframe and moved back, hoping not to startle someone.

Standing still, with his hands clasped in front of him, he regarded the apartment. Very homey, a bit rustic, nice and tidy. "Hello?"

No answer.

He stepped forward again and knocked. "Hello?"

Then something on the floor grabbed his attention. Two feet nearly hidden by the sofa. Damien walked in, quickly making his way toward the feet near the television set. "Hello? Hey?"

As Damien rounded the corner of the sofa, he saw his face, one side flat against the beige carpet. Eyes closed.

"Frank!"

Damien dropped to his knees. Frank was in uniform, his head twisted to the side, an arm grotesquely squeezed underneath him. The apartment was mostly dark. The sun hadn't risen high enough to provide much light. But in what little light he had, he could see a small bloody circle on Frank's back near his backbone. Damien reached for his shoulder, shaking him. "Frank! Frank!"

No response.

Damien took the other shoulder and tried to turn him over. It took three tries, but he finally rolled him. A cell phone dropped to the carpet. It had been in his hand. Damien picked it up. On the screen it said *911*. Damien grabbed the phone and put it to his ear. "Officer down! Please send help!"

"Sir, we have help on the way. He called us but went unconscious. What is his condition now?"

"It's Frank Merret." The name sounded like he was saying it in slow motion. Blood seeped out of Frank's chest. "He's been shot!" Damien threw off his jacket. He put a gloved hand over the wound.

"Is he breathing?"

He put an ear to Frank's mouth. "I don't know! I can't tell! He's still unconscious!"

"We're on the way. Stay on the line with me."

Suddenly Frank moaned and opened his eyes. His pupils looked very big, and his eyes rolled back in his head over and over.

"Frank, Frank! It's me. I'm here. Hang in there, buddy, please. Okay? Help is on the way."

Frank's dim eyes focused on Damien. He opened his mouth, and Damien heard a gurgling sound.

"Don't talk. Just . . . just stay calm." Damien shook so badly he could barely hold his hand in place on the wound or the phone up to his ear. "He's been shot," he said again into the phone.

Distantly, the first sirens approached. The 911 operator's

voice faded in and out. Something about putting pressure on the wound.

Frank stared up at him, his skin pale, almost gray. He whispered something. Damien couldn't hear, so he bent down, putting his ear to Frank's mouth.

"I can't move . . . can't feel any . . ." More gurgling.

"Okay, buddy. You're not in pain?"

"No," he whispered. Then he mumbled something again. Damien put his ear back to Frank's lips. "She's worth fighting for. . . ."

Damien looked at him again. In the midst of frail, glossy eyes, life sparkled and flickered like a struggling flame.

"Angela? Okay, yes. Hang in there. You've got way more hang-ups to overcome."

"Don't give up. . . . She's worth it. . . . Fight for her. . . . She has worth. . . ." Frank's eyes rolled back in his head again, and his body convulsed.

"Not me, Frank!" Damien shouted, tapping his face. "Not me, you! You have to fight. Don't give up!" Damien pressed the cell phone to his ear. "Where are they? I'm losing him! I'm losing him!"

He knew where they were. He could hear the haunting wail of the sirens just outside the door and the abrupt end to them as they parked. Voices outside.

"Hurry!" Damien shouted. He grabbed Frank by the shoulders. "Frank! Don't do this, man! Don't leave me! Hang in there! Who did this to you?"

Frank's eyes closed. "Take care of—"

Footsteps behind him, then heavy hands, standing him up and backing him away. EMTs and firefighters swarmed around Frank to the point that Damien could only see his fingers twitching against the carpet.

Damien moved, trying to see what was happening. "He's been shot! He can't move his legs or his arms!"

A small gap gave Damien a glimpse of Frank. Two EMTs were sliding an orange board underneath him. Another was squeezing a bag off the mask they'd put over his mouth. Within seconds, Frank was on the stretcher and they pulled it to waist height. An EMT crawled on top of Frank, pressing his palms against his chest.

The stretcher was whisked out. Damien hurried after it, watching them load Frank into the ambulance. Three police cars circled the street. Damien rushed toward the back doors of the ambulance, intending to climb in, but the doors were slammed shut and the ambulance rolled forward, its sirens blaring against the brick walls of the complex.

Damien stood there, staring at his bloody right hand. The phone was still in his other hand. He tried to dial Kay's number, but the phone fell and the battery popped out and onto the sidewalk next to his foot.

Nearby Captain Grayson got out of a dark sedan, frantically motioning for Damien to get in the car.

24

"DAMIEN, WHAT DID you see?"

"Nothing. I got there; Frank was on the floor."

"Nobody else?"

"No one but me."

"And you received the text from Frank this morning."

"Yes. It was very jumbled, but we read it as *Help me. Angela's house.*"

"So you went right over?"

"Yes. I didn't think anything was really wrong. I didn't know where Angela's apartment was exactly. I saw the truck, then saw the apartment door open. I knocked and saw him."

"I need to tell you something."

"What?"

"We've been internally investigating Frank for about four days now."

"Why?"

"The Web site."

"What about it?"

"We came across some information that led us to suspect that Frank might be involved."

"That's ridiculous."

"I know this is hard to hear."

"It's not hard to hear. It's ridiculous."

"Did you know that Frank has a sister?"

"Frank doesn't have any family. His parents died years ago, and he has no siblings."

"He does have a sibling. Her name is Meredith. She's in an adult home a few miles from here in Camden, where they grew up."

"I don't understand what you're saying."

"We're just now putting the pieces together, having just learned it ourselves. But apparently she tried to commit suicide when she was twenty. Frank walked into the garage and found her and cut her down. She was alive, but her brain lacked oxygen for too long, and she's been in a vegetative state all these years."

"I don't understand what this has to do with anything."

"Meredith attempted suicide after she overheard a conversation. Two friends went into a room at her house, said some horrible stuff about her, not knowing there was a baby monitor in the room. She heard all of it. Three days later she hung herself."

"How do you know this?"

"His ex-wife told us."

Damien pushed the conversation from the night before out of his head and walked without breaking pace down the softly lit hallway, took a right, and found himself in a small, black room carpeted from floor to ceiling. Against the back wall was the casket, gaping open like a mouth.

He wished he could stop playing the conversation in his head, but it was relentless, like a fly darting around his face that he couldn't ever quite shoo away. He focused on the elevator music in the background. For once it was actually welcomed.

Frank looked peaceful. Damien stepped closer, within a few inches of the casket. At first he studied the plump, fragrant flowers set on the floor on either side of the casket. But then slowly, he made himself look.

Frank in a suit made him smile. Damien had made the decision, mostly because Frank was always uncomfortable in his uniform. Called it "ill-fitting." But he was equally uncomfortable in a suit. Said they never looked right on him. But Kay had convinced him that if Frank had to choose, he'd choose the suit. He had only one in his closet, so that made it easy.

His badge stuck out of his pocket. And beside him was his cell phone. Damien smiled again, but this time the smile couldn't stop the tears, and he found himself laughing and crying all at once.

That guy loved his iPhone.

A few other medals were put into the casket too. Frank didn't have much hair to fix, but what he did have was slicked down like he would never wear it. Also, his cheeks were kind of pink, and Frank never had a hint of pink on any part of him.

Still, he looked like he was resting, as if he'd fallen asleep during a Sunday afternoon football game. His hands were folded over his belly as if he'd just eaten a big bowl of chili.

Damien touched the casket, running his fingers along its rim, grazing the silk lining.

Captain Grayson's words whispered in the corridors of his mind again, and their conversation at the hospital started to replay. He blinked, trying to kick it out again.

"Why didn't you tell me about Meredith?" Damien said to Frank, wiping the tears from his eyes. "How could I not know that? I know everything about you." He never told anyone except Angela. Not even his closest friend. What kept him quiet all these years? Was it guilt? shame?

He took a few steps back and felt a hand on his shoulder. He knew it was Kay.

"The kids are here," she said quietly.

Damien nodded and turned. Jenna rounded the corner first, followed closely by Hunter. Jenna's dress glided around her knees as she walked. Hunter fidgeted with his collar. Damien held out his arms, and they each buried their face in a shoulder.

"You know," Damien said, still blocking their view, "you don't have to see Frank like this. It's all right to remember him how he was."

"It's okay, Dad," Jenna said, her gaze drifting toward the casket. "Frank was family. We should be here for him, even like this."

Damien took them each by the shoulder and turned.

Hunter trembled beneath his hand. Jenna leaned into him. Kay came up beside them and they stood silently for a while, just looking.

"I hope you two find as good a friend as Frank was to me." Damien wanted to say more, but his voice quivered and he hated his kids seeing him like this.

Then Jenna lightly laughed. "Is that his cell phone?"

Damien grinned through his tears. "Yeah. Figured Frank wouldn't want to go through eternity without his technology. The police finished their investigation of it and gave it back."

Hunter looked at him. "Is the lid going to be open during the funeral?"

"No. This is called a viewing. We'll close it before the funeral starts."

"Good," Hunter said. "Frank would not want to be seen in a suit."

Damien laughed. "Exactly, buddy."

"He's in heaven," Jenna said. "I know it. I remember when we were little, Frank would always talk to us about heaven and God and Jesus. He always said he wasn't getting there by his merits, which he thought was funny because of his last name."

Damien smiled. Sounded like a Frank joke.

"Jenna, you got your cell phone?" Hunter asked.

"Yeah. Why?"

"Let me see it."

She dug in her purse and handed it over. Hunter's thumbs flew over the number keys.

"Son," Damien said, "now's not a good time to be texting—"

Suddenly Frank's cell phone lit up and vibrated. Hunter smiled.

Damien leaned in to read it: *We luv u Frank. Rest well.*

With another smile came another swelling of emotion. Tears dripped down Damien's face faster than he could wipe them. Kay brought him into a hug, then let go, nodding that he should look behind him.

He turned.

Angela.

"Honey," Damien said, "why don't you take the kids out. I'll be there in a minute. It's almost time for the funeral to start. We need to get over to the church."

Kay gathered them by the shoulders and ushered them out, disregarding Angela as she walked by her.

Angela gave a short, polite smile, clinging tightly to her black clutch. She was dressed from head to toe like a mourning widow.

Damien drew in a deep breath, careful to keep his emotions—and tongue—under control.

Without saying anything, Angela came up beside him, her eyes fixed on Frank. She blotted her face every which way with a tattered tissue. "Oh, baby . . ."

Damien stepped back and rolled his eyes. He couldn't watch this. In fact, he couldn't be near this woman. He started to leave.

"I know what you think of me," she said.

Damien stopped, willing himself not to turn around.

"But I didn't have anything to do with this."

Damien faced Angela. "He was at your apartment when he was killed. You had something to do with it."

"Like I told the police, I wasn't there. I was at work, which has already been confirmed." Angela glanced at Frank. "I went in early because I'd skipped some days and was behind on my work. I have no idea why he was there."

"I imagine that he was there because he still loves you." Damien looked down. "Loved you, I mean. After everything you did to that man, he never stopped loving you."

"You probably don't believe this, but I never stopped loving him either. Frank was not an easy man to live with, but that didn't mean I didn't still love him."

"Sure. You loved him enough to keep calling him from time to time, giving him hope."

"That's not true."

Damien sighed. "I don't want to get into it. Not here. Not now, over Frank's . . ." He shook his head and turned to leave.

"I'm a suspect. They haven't officially said it, but I know it. They keep returning, looking through my stuff, asking me questions."

Damien turned around one more time. "Why didn't he tell me about Meredith?"

Angela shook her head. "He made me swear to never tell. I never visited her myself. He wouldn't allow it. But he told me once that every time he went, he would whisper in her ear."

"Whisper what?"

"All the good things about her. All the things she couldn't believe about herself."

Damien kept walking. He couldn't take any more of Angela. Maybe she was worth fighting for in Frank's world, but she wasn't worth dying for.

The police chaplain greeted Damien as he left the hallway and entered the foyer of the funeral home. Walking behind him was Reverend Caldwell.

"Chaplain, good to see you," Damien said, shaking his hand. Captain Grayson stood beside him and shook Damien's hand too. "Hi, Lou. Reverend Caldwell, thanks for coming."

"Sure," Reverend Caldwell said, holding his hand with a tight, knowing grip. "Have any questions about how or when you'll be speaking?"

"No, I'm good. Thanks," Damien said.

"We better get to the church," the chaplain said. "They'll bring Frank over in about ten minutes. I'll see you both there."

Damien nodded, then turned to Lou. A tense moment of silence passed between them. Damien couldn't hold it in any longer. "I know Frank wasn't behind this Web site. I heard you found nothing on his computer linking him to it."

"We're still investigating. There's the possibility that he used a remote computer not tied to him."

"I would hope that you'd be investigating his murder."

"They may be all connected."

"How so?"

"When we went to Frank's apartment, his computer was on. He'd been checking the Web site."

"So? Everyone is checking it."

"We can tell that he viewed it early in the morning, before he went to Angela's."

Damien folded his arms and stared at the carpet.

"Also, there hasn't been an updated post on the Web site since Frank died." Lou put a hand on Damien's shoulder. "I'm sorry. "

"It's not true. Frank wouldn't do this. I know him. You need to look elsewhere. And you need to figure out who killed Frank."

"We're looking into all the angles, including whether or not Frank knew Angela was seeing someone."

"Just find out who killed him, okay?"

25

As MUCH AS he splashed cold water on his face, Damien still couldn't shake the fatigue he continued to feel every morning. His sleep was fitful at best, and even if he managed a good night's sleep, he never felt rested. And when he had the time, he didn't want to rest. He wanted to find out what happened to Frank.

As he trudged downstairs, his mind reeled with the facts he knew. Ballistics confirmed the gun type that was used to kill Frank, but no weapon had been found yet. He was shot from behind, most likely as he stepped into the apartment. The apartment was unlocked because there was no forced entry and no key was found on Frank that matched the lock at Angela's apartment.

There were no witnesses to the crime, but one resident confirmed hearing what sounded like a firecracker at 6:55 a.m., and several others reported seeing the apartment door open.

Angela had been cleared as a suspect, at least as directly involved in the murder. Damien suspected she could be involved in another way, like hiring a hit man.

He tried to shrug off the thoughts as he joined his family at the table. "Good morning," he said.

"Hey, Dad," Jenna said.

Damien noticed she looked better. Her eyes had life in them again. He sat down and Kay served him eggs. "Thanks." He studied Jenna some more. She even looked like she'd put on some weight, which she desperately needed. "Jenna, how's everything at school? With what happened with Frank, I've been a little distracted. I'm sorry."

"Everything's fine."

"Really?"

She actually grinned. "Yeah. Really. Everything's like, totally normal again."

Damien believed it. She looked really healthy.

"Dad?" Hunter asked.

"Yeah, buddy?"

"Did Frank die because of the Web site?"

"What makes you say that? Are people talking at school? blaming Frank?"

Hunter shrugged, playing with his toast.

"Don't believe everything you hear. Frank was killed by a coward who shot him in the back. I know what people are saying. Don't believe it."

"Kids, you need to get going if you don't want to be late," Kay said.

They got up and grabbed their coats and backpacks. A minute later they were out the door.

Damien was still hunched over his uneaten plate of eggs.

Kay slid into the chair next to him, wrapping an arm around his shoulder. "You're struggling."

"Yeah."

She put her head on his shoulder. "I know you miss Frank. You haven't grieved him, though. You have to let yourself grieve."

"As soon as we catch who did this, I—" Damien stopped.

Kay sat up. "What? What's wrong?"

Damien held up a finger, trying to retrieve the thought that had just passed through his mind. He turned to Kay. "I think . . ."

"What?"

"Is the computer on?"

"I think so. Why?"

Damien hurried into the study, dropping into the chair while reaching for the keyboard. He quickly typed *www.listentoyourself.net*.

"What are you doing?"

"Hold on," Damien said, using the mouse to scroll down until he found the last conversation recorded. "Read this."

Kay leaned in.

"Hey, yeah, give me another."
 "You're a bourbon and Coke man?"
 "I am these days. Might even drop the Coke."

"Bad day?"

"Bad week. Month. Life."

"Me too. Lost my job."

"About to lose my mind."

"Then there must be a woman involved."

"Do they make anything stronger than bourbon that I can stand to drink?"

"Trouble in paradise?"

"Yeah, I guess. I was seeing a woman. She sort of freaked on me. Threatened to . . ."

"What? Hey, slow down there. Drink it too fast and you'll puke or pass out or both."

"Gimme another."

"So, your woman freaked?"

"My woman threatened to tell my other woman."

"Oh. Ouch."

"Yeah. And see, that can't happen. It won't happen."

Kay stood upright. "Okay, what? I'm not following."

"This is the last conversation on the Web site, the one Frank was supposedly reading."

"Uh-huh."

"Maybe this conversation is about Angela. The woman, one of them, might be Angela."

"So you think Angela was seeing someone and he was cheating on her?"

Damien peered at the screen. "Or Angela was the woman whom this guy was cheating with."

Kay studied the words again. "The woman that was going to tell the other woman."

Damien pointed. "'It won't happen.'"

"Sounds like he's desperate."

Damien clicked Print.

* * *

Damien waited near the interrogation room, watching a small, very fuzzy closed-circuit television. Angela sat in a small chair and fidgeted with her blouse. The camera angle made her look small and insignificant.

Detective Murray entered, dropping his jacket onto the corner of the table, which was no bigger than a card table. "We wanted to talk to you about Frank's murder."

"I didn't do it," Angela said, sniffling.

"We have reason to believe you are not being totally forthright with us."

"I don't know what you're talking about."

"You told us that you weren't seeing anyone."

A drawn-out pause. Her fidgeting could even be seen on the small screen.

Damien glanced at the captain, who nodded. "We got her."

Angela spoke. "I was seeing someone."

"Why didn't you tell us this before?"

She looked down. "Because I was embarrassed."

"About?"

"He's married. We didn't . . . we didn't want anyone to know."

"Did Frank know you were seeing someone?"

"I talked to Frank one day about it, because this man . . . he started acting strangely and I was afraid."

"Strangely how?"

"His temper was out of control. He was always yelling at me. I told him I thought the stress of the affair was too much, but he said he could handle it. I didn't think so. I wanted to break off the relationship, but he wouldn't let me."

"What does that mean?"

"It means he said that wasn't going to happen. Then I told him that if he didn't back off, I was going to tell his wife. I had to threaten him because he wouldn't . . ." She broke down in tears.

Detective Murray waited patiently, without sympathy. "So," he said after a moment, "you told Frank about this guy."

"Yes. I don't think Frank . . . I mean, I think he was fed up with me. And for good reason. He didn't see how he could help."

"What happened after you told this man you wanted to break it off?"

"I didn't hear from him."

"How long ago was this?"

"Four days before Frank was killed. You don't think . . . ?"

"What is this man's name?"

Angela shook her head.

Damien glared at the television. "How could she not tell us this before?"

"Ma'am, we need this man's name. We have good reason to believe he could be involved."

"What? No, no. You've got that wrong. He's a moody guy, but he's not a murderer."

"We believe he had intentions to harm you."

Angela's stunned expression was clear even through the grainy television.

"The Web site that's wreaking havoc on Marlo recorded a conversation that could be linked to you." Detective Murray pushed a piece of paper across the table to Angela. "This page was up on Frank's computer the morning he came to your apartment. We believe that Frank may have believed this conversation was about you."

Angela picked up the paper, read it, and slowly put it back down. "Are you saying Frank came to my apartment looking for me? because he thought I was in danger?"

"We can't say for sure, but it looks as if Frank walked in, startled this guy, who was there intending to harm you." Detective Murray leaned forward. "We need that name. Now."

26

DAMIEN RODE WITH Captain Grayson to Mike Toledo's residence. His wife said that he was at work. They arrived at his work a little after noon, and his supervisor said that he was on lunch break but was planning to do some Christmas shopping at the town square, specifically at RadioShack.

The captain parked his car in an empty space near RadioShack. Three patrol cars accompanied him, pulling to nearby curbs.

Grayson gathered them on the sidewalk across the street from the store. "Murray, I want you to go in easy. Let's not spook this guy. Tell him we just want to bring him in and talk to him about what he knows. Guys, let's stand by, out of line of sight."

Murray pointed. "That's his car, right? The red one?"

"Yeah. Looks like our boy is in there. All right, let's go in. Damien, wait by the car."

Damien nodded and got comfortable leaning against the door, trying to ease the adrenaline that was pulsing through him. He watched Murray and Grayson cross the street toward the store, which was lit up with signs declaring all kinds of Christmas sales.

He loved the little town square with its tower clock and its swept streets. Every store glowed with holiday lights and festive decorations. Shoppers traveled from store to store, managing their shopping bags.

A heavy thought hit him. Frank's Christmas gift. He'd gotten it online a month ago. It was some gadget that projected movies from a tiny device onto any surface. The guy at the store said it was the hot new gadget for the holidays.

Frank spent every Christmas with them, bringing over loads of presents for the kids and thoughtful ones for him and Kay. What was Christmas going to be like without Frank there?

He blew out the sorrow and watched the men approach RadioShack. The front door opened, and a man fitting the description of Toledo came out, zipping up a lightweight navy coat.

He glanced up, noticing Grayson first, then Murray. Damien took a couple steps forward, hoping to hear at least part of the exchange.

Grayson waved at the man. "You Mike Toledo?"

Suddenly the man bolted, dropping his bags and racing the opposite direction.

Damien couldn't help himself. He took off in a run as Grayson called for backup and Murray chased Toledo. Barely dodging an oncoming car, Damien made his way across the street, about ten yards behind Murray.

Toledo knocked against shoppers as he raced toward an alley. More shouting from the police and Grayson. Damien rounded the corner after Murray.

Toledo had hit a fence and was scrambling up the chain link when Murray caught the bottom of his pants and dragged him off. Toledo fell against the concrete with a thud and rolled over, groaning. Murray accosted him, followed shortly by Grayson, who drilled a knee into his backbone. Within seconds, he was cuffed.

"Something you want to run from?" Grayson growled, yanking him to his feet.

* * *

Edgar laughed heartily, slapping his hands against his desk. "Whew! It just doesn't get any better than this."

Damien crossed his arms, trying to keep his hands from fidgeting.

"An eyewitness account," Edgar continued, smiling. "This is stellar. The way you put in these details, it's like I'm right there. Any new information since the story broke?"

"No. They're pretty quiet over there right now. They let me stay for the interrogation of Angela because I brought the conversation to their attention. I'm assuming they're interrogating Mr. Toledo and probably getting a warrant to search his premises." Damien sighed. "Frank was always my inside guy there, so I don't know anything more than that."

"That's okay. This is good for now." Edgar's smile faded. "Listen, um, why don't you shut the door for a sec."

Damien hesitated, then shut it. "What's going on?"

"First of all, I know this has been a hard few days for you. Frank's death was an incredible tragedy for this town but most especially for you."

Damien agreed.

"But this is a newspaper, and we've got to run with the story."

"I understand. Of course we've got to cover this. I'm glad you let me write it."

"There's another side to this story, Damien."

Damien searched Edgar's face. "What do you mean?"

"You know what I mean." Edgar waited. "That Frank might've been the person behind the Web site."

Damien slammed his fists against the chair he stood behind. "What are you talking about? It's only a rumor! Frank is not behind it."

"The story presents it as an angle, just like the police are doing."

"You wrote it?"

"I assigned it to Bruce."

"There is no evidence pointing to Frank."

"You're his friend, so I understand that you're not seeing this clearly."

"There is nothing to see except speculation."

"He had motive."

"Edgar—"

"Hear me out," Edgar said, his voice rising. "He had motive. It was no secret he was never able to let his wife go. He wanted to keep up with what Angela was doing. And now a source at the police department says there was a sister who attempted sui—"

"Don't you think it's a little elaborate to have this entire Web site full of people's conversations just so he can listen in on Angela's life?"

"I don't know. Maybe he was more desperate than anyone knows."

"Circumstantial. That's all it is."

"His rookie shed some light on his state of mind."

"Meaning what?"

"We have him quoted as saying that he believes Frank could've been a part of it, that he disappeared sometimes for no reason, with no explanation of where he'd been."

"What a guy. Really knows how to wear that uniform."

"The posts have stopped. There hasn't been one since Frank died."

"There is also no evidence on Frank's computer that he was involved."

"There are theories attached to why that is."

Damien walked to the door and opened it. "I'm sure there are."

"I know this is difficult. And believe me when I say that

we're not presenting it as fact. It's not proven yet. But it is a story that Marlo has a great interest in."

"Marlo? Or you? Because as far as I can see, this isn't hurting you any, is it?"

Edgar flinched but seemed dismissive of the accusation. "If it was Frank, it would solve a very big mystery."

"Or cause harm to a man's reputation, a man who can't in any way defend himself."

Damien tried to read Edgar's expression, while filtering it through the utter disgust he felt. But Edgar didn't say anything else. He only stared at his desk.

Damien walked out, slamming the door behind him.

* * *

Kay barely heard the phone ringing over the vacuum. She shut it off and hurried to the wall phone. She grabbed it on the fifth ring. "Hello?"

"Mom?"

Kay's heart skipped a beat. The voice sounded urgent. "Jenna? What's the matter?"

"Mom, I just . . . I wanted to call."

"You sound frantic."

"No, I'm okay. I had a break between classes. What are you doing?"

"Vacuuming. You don't sound okay."

"I'm. . . you know, it's a lot to . . . It's just one of those days. Maybe it's all hitting me."

"Do you want to come home? I'll come get you."

"No. It's fine, really. Listen, that's the bell. I gotta go. See you after school. Let's get a movie tonight, okay? Pizza?"

Kay smiled. "Of course." The line went dead and Kay hung up the phone. She unplugged the vacuum and was wrapping the cord up when the doorbell rang. Hunter had been expecting a box from Amazon.

But it wasn't a box on her front porch. "Jill?"

Sobbing, Jill collapsed to her knees. Her wail echoed off the concrete porch. Kay hurried outside, kneeling in front of her and grabbing Jill's wrists. "Jill? Is it Natalie?"

Jill shook her head. "It's Mike. They've arrested him. For that police officer's murder."

* * *

Damien fled to his desk, not knowing what to do with the anger he felt. Part of him needed to leave, take a walk, maybe a vacation. Just get out.

But no. Not with all this hanging over Frank. He knew his best friend, and he knew he wasn't behind this. Frank would never knowingly cause chaos in this town. And what would be the point of listening in on people's conversations?

He rolled his fingers around on his temple, then dialed Lou Grayson's cell phone.

"Grayson."

"It's Damien."

"I need to call you back. We've got—"

"No. Listen to me. Your rookie is talking to the press.

The Gavin kid." Damien could hear Lou breathing. "Giving theories about Frank's involvement with the Web site."

The captain cursed. "They probably ambushed him at home. Doesn't he know there's protocol for this sort of thing?"

"I guess Frank hadn't gotten to that yet," Damien said flatly. "I want to know something. What is your investigation finding in regard to how these conversations are being recorded?"

A pause. "Off the record?"

"Yeah. Okay. Off the record."

"We're looking into the possibility that someone is using a laser listening device. They sell for hundreds, sometimes thousands, of dollars but ironically can be built fairly cheaply."

"Built? What do you mean?"

"I gotta go. Google it, and you'll see what I mean."

The line went dead. Damien googled "build a laser listening device." Within seconds, he was reading step-by-step instructions on how to do it.

He scrolled down, trying to figure out how it worked. He learned they didn't use a microphone. Instead, a change in light was measured by the way it reflected off a surface, usually a window. Wading through the scientific jargon, Damien read that basically the laser light reflected off the glass toward the operator would be shifted, continuously changing. By detecting this shift, the vibrations returned to the operator as sound.

Or something like that.

But what Damien found particularly interesting was that these types of devices could record conversations from a long distance without access to the space. All that was needed was a window. Because infrared laser light was invisible, detecting the device would be almost impossible.

Damien tried to think back to the conversations he read on the Web site. It seemed most of them would be conversations one would have indoors. It was impossible to prove, but the scenario was playing out better than anything else.

He continued to search, finding instructions on how to make a homemade device. It was mostly over his head, but anyone with even the slightest bit of interest in electronics or technology could probably pull it off.

Damien sat back in his chair, pondering it all. He'd considered bugs in phones and in homes but never a device like this.

But for Damien, the more important question was why. What was the purpose of this madness?

He slid the mysterious crossword from his briefcase. He reread the messages hidden there. Whoever was doing this knew Damien or at least knew of him. Knew that he constructed crossword puzzles.

And was still out there, no matter what anybody said.

The question was, why did he or she stop?

Damien withdrew from his file drawer the heavyweight paper he used to construct crosswords. The paper already had the lightly penciled boxes ready. He just had to color in the black spaces and make his puzzle.

Except this puzzle would hopefully solve another puzzle.

It was time to send a message in return.

27

DAMIEN ARRIVED HOME a little before 9 p.m. Kay, Hunter, and Jenna sat crowded on the couch in front of the big screen. Movie credits rolled.

Damien kissed the top of Kay's head and clapped his kids on their shoulders. "What are you doing?"

"Just a little movie and hang time." Kay stood and turned to him. "We saved you some pizza."

"Nice of you." He grinned. He looked at Jenna, who was still seated, staring at the TV. "You okay?"

She rose, taking her plate off the coffee table. "Just tired. I'm going to shower and go to bed, okay, Mom?"

Kay took her plate and embraced her. "Sure, baby. Whatever you want."

"I gotta do my homework," Hunter said, leaving his plate and bounding upstairs.

Damien retrieved the plate off the coffee table and

followed Kay to the kitchen. "When is that kid going to learn to put his dishes up?"

Kay smiled as she rinsed Jenna's in the sink. She glanced up the stairs, then turned off the water and faced Damien. "Reverend Caldwell wanted to see how we were doing."

"Did he show up?"

"Show up? No, he called. Why?"

"Nothing."

"What's the latest on Mike Toledo?"

"Wanted a lawyer, wouldn't talk. They're getting a warrant to search his house. That's the last I heard. Lou called me and said they're confident this is their guy. Now they just have to prove it."

Kay sighed, fiddling with the edge of the dishcloth. "Does Jenna seem all right to you?"

"Why?"

"She seems sad to me."

"She's been through a lot."

"Yeah, but she bounced back, was doing great. Lately she seems very mellow."

"Have you talked to her about it?"

"I've dropped a few hints, but she always says she's fine." Kay threw the dishcloth on the counter. "Will you try?"

"You know me. I never know what to say—"

"Just try. Please. I want her to know she can talk to us."

"All right. I'll see what I can do."

Kay hugged him, pressing her cheek against his. "How are you?"

"I'm okay. If it turns out to be Mike Toledo, I don't know what I'm going to do."

Kay stepped back. "It will mean justice, and that's what Frank would've wanted. He would also want you to continue living your life."

Damien couldn't stop the tears.

Kay wiped them with her hands. "I know how much you miss him," she whispered.

Damien pressed his wrists to each eye. "Yeah. I do." He took a deep breath. "I'll go upstairs, talk to her."

"Thank you."

Damien headed up the stairs and turned toward the kids' rooms. He was just about to knock on Jenna's door when he heard the shower running in the bathroom. He forgot. With every year that went by, ten minutes was added to the shower time. She was up to an hour now. It could be a while.

He decided to chat with Hunter while waiting. He tapped on the door and turned the knob.

As it cracked open, he saw a familiar sight . . . Hunter scrambling toward his desk, nearly knocking over his chair, practically diving for the mouse. Within seconds, he stood upright, working hard at mustering up a casual expression. "Hey, um, Dad."

Damien felt flustered, yet deep inside there was some resolve building, something that told him it was time to confront the situation. Frank was no more, and even with Frank's assurances that he'd talked to Hunter, Damien realized in that instant that there was nobody who could talk to

Hunter except him. He was the father, and no matter how uncomfortable it got, he had to do it. He should do it.

Damien held his son's gaze, which soon dropped to the carpet and one untied sneaker. "What's going on?"

"What do you mean?"

Damien's courage quavered. He took a moment to compose himself. "There's something on that computer you don't want me to see, isn't there?"

"No . . ." Hunter's attention shifted to his computer. He stepped forward as if he were guarding a small animal.

"Look, I'm not mad. Disappointed, yes. But not mad. The truth is that I should've talked to you about this myself. Much earlier. I was afraid I wouldn't know what to say. How to handle it well. And though Frank was always like an uncle to you, I should've talked to you myself."

Hunter's eyes widened with each word. He stood completely still, barely even blinking.

"You should be able to talk to me about these things. And I'm sorry I've come across as a father you can't talk to."

"Am I in trouble?"

That was all he wanted to know, whether or not he was in trouble? Damien crossed his arms. "Do you think you should be in trouble?"

"Um . . . I think . . . I'd like to explain."

Damien tried not to smirk. This ought to be good. "Fine."

"I know the rules, and I know I'm not supposed to be doing this. But you don't understand what I've been going through and how helpless I feel against everything."

Damien bit his lip. How to spin this? Spin it? No. This was real life, with a real kid. It was time Damien connected on a deeper level. He walked over to Hunter's bed and sat down, patting the empty space next to him. "Come sit down with me."

Hunter obliged, sitting next to his father with a slouch that made osteoporosis look healthy.

"Here's the deal. I do know what you're going through."

"You do?"

"Sure. What you're feeling is not unnatural. Every guy goes through this, and in and of itself, it's healthy. But when you take these urges and allow them to get out of control, by taking them places you know you shouldn't go, then you've got a problem."

"I'm not sure I'm following."

Oh, brother. How specific was he going to have to get? He glanced at Hunter, who was staring at him. He offered a small smile. "Okay, see, every guy is tempted with this. And with the Internet, it's so much easier to get. Back in my day, we had to actually have the nerve to go into the gas station and buy a copy. And then you had to try to hide it so your mother wouldn't find out."

By the expression on Hunter's face, Damien thought he was maybe saying too much. But what else could he say? He couldn't dismiss this or turn to anger. What good would that do? "All I'm trying to say is that it's normal to . . . It's just not okay to get involved in. Not in our house. Son, once you look at those images, you can never take them back. They're in you forever." Damien paused to take a deep breath and look at Hunter, whose face was still frozen with shock. "What? Am I being too forthright here?"

"What are you talking about?" Hunter asked.

"Pornography. What were you talking about?"

"The MySpace page I opened. I know I'm not supposed to have one, but I needed one."

Damien jumped to his feet, holding his stomach and his mouth at the same time. "That's what you were talking about?"

Hunter's eyes turned worried. "Can't I explain? Please?"

"Yes, of course." Damien tried not to sound as relieved as he felt. So the kid opened a MySpace page? Damien wanted to run around the room and do a little dance. But he had disobeyed, so Damien tried to look as stern as possible.

Hunter slid off the bed and slowly moved to his computer, watching Damien closely as if he was afraid of a sudden move or a possible lecture on the female anatomy.

Damien stood near Hunter as the kid typed something into the address bar. A page appeared.

"That's not you," Damien said. "And that's not your name."

"I just pulled a pic off the Web and made up a name."

"Why?"

More typing, then a new page came up. Hunter pointed to a block of writing. "Read this."

Damien scanned it. Something about a bratty girl. The

language was inundated with a lot of profanity and lewd comments. "What is this?"

Hunter turned in his chair, a serious expression on his face. "It's about Jenna."

"What?"

"They're talking about Jenna."

"Jenna isn't named."

"I know. You have to read more on this page to know it's her. But they're talking about her. All over the place. Smearing her name."

Damien looked at Hunter, then back at the screen.

"It's just a few girls," Hunter said. "I know who they are. They're the ones that hung out with the two that were arrested."

"So they're targeting Jenna because . . ."

"She told. They know she's the one that told the police where to find Gabby."

Damien stood upright, gasped. "How?"

"I'm not sure. I think it was mostly just a lucky guess. Jenna stopped hanging around them, and they decided she was the one that went to the police."

Damien shook his head, staring at the screen.

"But look what I've been doing." Hunter beckoned him closer. "It's like a cyber blast. I'm working to control the first page that appears on Google when Jenna's name is entered. So I've started blogs and a MySpace page and have linked up with any positive mention of her name, which is easy to do with alerts. Anytime her name is mentioned on the Web, I'm alerted. Then I sort of manipulate the information so that only positive remarks show up on the first page of Google. It's kind of a way to manage your online reputation. And I think it's working. Over the past few days, there has been way less activity. A lot of the people who were talking about her before are losing interest. But I'm not stopping until this thing dies down completely."

Damien quit staring at the screen. He couldn't take his eyes off his son. Emotions welled up as he watched him talk.

Hunter glanced at him. "What's wrong?"

His voice cracked. "I'm just proud of you. You're amazing."

Hunter looked away. "It's no big deal."

"It's a very big deal. Does Jenna know?"

"Yeah, I'm sure she does. It's hard to hide from this kind of thing."

"No, I mean, does she know what you're doing for her?"

"Please don't tell her. She'd freak out and get all emotional and stuff. And who wants a little brother handling your bullies, you know?"

Damien nodded. "I see what you mean."

"So this stays here?"

"I promise."

"Thanks. Oh, and I promise I won't tell anyone about your porn problem."

"What? No! No, there's no porn problem. It was just an example. Those magazines, that was a long time ago, like when I was younger, way younger." Damien took a breath. He was rambling.

An awkward moment passed. Hunter looked at Damien with a worried expression, indicating he thought there still might be some repercussions or perhaps new confessions.

"Finish up your homework," Damien said, then walked out, closing the door behind him. He leaned against the wall for a moment, catching his breath and chuckling a little. Well, at least he got the pornography discussion out of the way.

He listened for the shower. It had stopped. He walked the length of the hallway to find the bathroom vacant. Jenna's bedroom door was closed. He tapped lightly. "Jenna?"

No answer.

He hesitated before opening the door. He wasn't sure he could go another round of "It's pornography—wait, no, a MySpace page" again.

He nudged the door, cracking it open slightly, just enough to see the lights were off and Jenna was in her bed. She didn't even stir.

"Jenna?" he whispered.

She didn't respond. Her breathing was slow, peaceful.

He crept across the wood floor to the edge of her bed. He stared at her for a long time, remembering how he watched her sleep when she was a little girl, curled tightly around a giant panda he'd given her when she was four. He'd liked to watch her sleep, brush her tangled hair off her face, rub her cheek with the back of his hand.

He imagined, though, that now she was not quite the deep sleeper of her childhood.

Instead, he knelt down on the small, fluffy circle rug by her bed. As he clasped his hands together, the feeling of helplessness that caught him up in constant fear melted away. He knew he had no control over this situation, and there was nothing worse to feel than helplessness over a child.

But in the darkness of her room he was reminded that helplessness was often a portal to God, because rarely did the fragile, self-serving human pray for things in his complete control. He knew he'd been brought to his knees, and he willingly stayed there, his forehead laid against the side of her mattress. He prayed boldly, calling on the God he'd rarely thought about in the last few years. His small attempt at churchgoing was hardly enough to reconcile himself to his God. Yet he knew without a doubt, despite his absence, God would not be absent and that He was waiting even now to help.

"God help her," Damien whispered. "God help me. Help us. Help Marlo."

28

THE BRIGHT MORNING sun brought only dark thoughts for Damien. As the smell of rich, fresh coffee wafted through the offices, Damien sat in his chair, contemplating revenge.

And there was so much to avenge for, he couldn't quite wrap his mind around specifics for any of them. Instead, he played with the ideas, one after another, until he needed a refill on his coffee.

Walking to the break room, he remembered his prayer the night before, that God would help his daughter. He'd slept soundly, as if he were a small child handing over his biggest care to a parent. But with morning came a rush of anger and fear that had not left his side for a moment.

He'd thought he might talk to Jenna at breakfast, but she didn't look in the mood for conversation, so he stayed silent. They all did.

Damien couldn't just stand aside, though. He couldn't watch his daughter be brutalized by other people's words. As a kid who'd been bullied himself, he once wished they would've just beaten him with sticks and stones. It seemed far less painful than the words that followed him around like a torturing spirit.

It had lasted only one year, but it gave a lasting impression. In college he'd decided he would use words for good, not bad. That was the beginning of his journalism career.

Returning to his desk, he decided he was going to have to confront the principal and teachers and get this thing taken care of. Maybe these girls didn't tie another girl up, but the fact that they continued to defend those who did was almost as disturbing.

He wondered if he should consult Kay. She wasn't a confrontational person. But she also didn't like having her children messed with. He hadn't told Kay what he'd learned from Hunter. Not yet, anyway.

He grabbed his keys off the desk and lifted his jacket off the back of the chair. He couldn't wait a second longer. He couldn't watch his daughter suffer anymore.

His desk phone beeped, and a crackling voice came through. "Damien?"

"Yeah, Edgar?"

"I need you in my office."

"Look, I was just getting ready to—"

"Now."

* * *

Kay put on an aqua velour jogging suit. She messed with her hair for a moment and decided to take out her diamond earrings. She was not at all sure how to dress for this . . . whatever this was. She put on a small amount of makeup but no lipstick. She removed her watch and kept on only her wedding ring.

She lingered by the kitchen phone, wondering if she should call Damien, ask if this was the right thing to do. She picked up the phone but then heard a car in her driveway. Peeking through the kitchen window, she hung up the phone and grabbed her purse.

As Kay walked down the front steps of her home, her feet felt like lead. What was she doing? Why was she doing this? It seemed like such a bad idea, but here she was, opening the car door and sliding into the passenger's seat like they were going for brunch.

"Hi," Jill said with a sad smile.

"Hi." Kay closed the door and clutched her purse on her lap.

"I'm so happy you said yes," Jill said, reversing the car and backing out of the driveway. "I honestly didn't think you would."

Kay swallowed, trying to calm herself and rationalize this. Yet it still seemed like a bad idea. Perhaps it was curiosity that caused her to be here. Or maybe a hope that she could help solve Frank's murder.

Kay tried to get comfortable. She was glad the windows were tinted.

"You don't understand what it's been like for me," Jill said, staring forward as she drove. "Nobody will talk to me. People are leaving horrible messages on my answering machine, like I'm somehow involved. It's been hell."

"I'm sorry," Kay said softly.

"And I hate him." Her voice was steely, harsh. "I hate him so much."

"You think he did it?"

Jill's chin quivered. "Yes, I do. And that's what we're going to find out."

Kay tried to take a silent, deep breath. "I'm here for you. I want to help in any way I can, but I still don't understand why you asked me to come. How will this help?"

"You don't understand the kind of man he is. He's got this horrible, mean side to him. A side that's out for himself and only himself. It's what allows him to have this kind of affair without any regard for his family. It's what makes me think he's capable of doing what he did. But," Jill said, glancing at Kay for an unusually long few seconds, "he is also someone else. He can be very charming. Very convincing. I've fallen for this side of him so many times."

A pause in the conversation caused Kay to rethink this. She still had time to back out.

Then Jill continued. "I suspected, you know. That he was having an affair. I questioned him: 'Where were you? What took you so long?' But he has this charm. And so often it makes perfect sense. It only makes me look like a paranoid freak of a wife."

"So, you think me being there is going to help?"

"He knows he can play me. He knows what I want to hear. But he doesn't know you, so he doesn't know how to play you."

"I'm not sure I can be of any help," Kay said.

"You don't have to say anything," Jill replied. "Just be there with me. I need someone by my side."

It was a small thing to ask, to have someone stand by your side. How could she not? "Okay, sure. I understand."

For the next five miles, they drove in silence, without even the radio on. The only sound in the car was the cold north wind vibrating against the windows. Jill looked lost in her thoughts, and Kay wondered if she should even be driving.

Then Kay said, "I've been reading that Web site."

Jill glanced at her almost like she'd forgotten she was in the car. "What?"

"That Web site. I've been reading it. I think there are some things on there about me."

Jill smirked. "For sure?"

"No, not for sure. But I'm pretty sure. A former friend . . ." Kay wondered if she should mention it was the same woman who had the affair with Mike. Maybe later.

Jill's gaze stayed on the road. "Yeah, well, I know for sure there are things on there about me. Names me. People I thought were my friends."

"I know. I should stop reading it."

Jill nodded. "Could make you go insane."

Kay sighed and stared out the window. "I once said something really bad about someone." She felt Jill's attention, but she couldn't stop looking out the window. "I once had a good friend. She was married to my husband's best friend. We did everything together. The boys would go do their thing and we'd hang out, talk for hours. But I was always bothered by . . . the way she dressed."

"Dressed?"

"Yeah, low-cut blouses. A lot of low-cut blouses. I made a remark one day, offhandedly, to some people who knew her. It got back to her. She never spoke to me again." Kay bit her lip, trying to keep the tears from coming. "For a long time I blamed her. Thought she should dress differently. But I realize now . . . I'm the one that judged. My hang-up about how she dressed came from my own past, my own hurts." A certain heaviness lifted as she spoke. "One sentence changed my whole life. One sentence."

Jill reached over and took her hand. "It's okay. We all make mistakes."

Kay looked at her. "I've even judged you for how you dress. And I'm really sorry. I shouldn't jump to conclusions."

Jill laughed and squeezed her hand. "I know I dress like I'm eighteen. I guess I just felt Mike pulling away, imagining what pretty woman he was interested in, and I thought if I tried to make myself look younger, I might win his affection back."

Kay slumped into her seat. "See? A person never knows

another's motivations. How could I sit there and judge you for a tight tank top and not know what you're going through?"

Jill pulled into the large parking lot of the county jail, parked, and turned to Kay. "It's okay, my friend. Right now, how I look in a tight tank top is the least of my worries."

Kay stared at the building. It wasn't as tall as she'd imagined. They got out of the car and walked through the front doors. An officer behind a large black desk greeted them. They signed their names, emptied their pockets, and were led through several gated corridors until they came to a room with plastic tables and chairs. The floors looked warped and smelled like cheap Pine-Sol. One yellow sign alerted them to the wetness on the floor. They both stepped carefully toward the nearest table.

They huddled together on the far side of the room so they faced the door, their knees bumping each other with any small movement.

Kay glanced around, noticing the cameras and monitors. "I'm nervous."

"Me too."

"How's Natalie handling all this?" Kay asked, hoping to take her mind off the idea that she might very soon be staring into the eyes of a cold-blooded killer.

Jill shrugged. "Okay, I guess. She doesn't talk about it much. Hates school. I don't blame her. I don't know how to help her."

The sound of a large metal door opening, then shutting,

caused the women to sit up straighter. Kay could hardly breathe. She wanted to seem calm and cool, but she was certain she was not looking anything of the sort.

A tall, thin shadow crossed over the hard concrete. But the man who followed the shadow wasn't tall or thin. He was built much like Damien, with broad shoulders, a wide chest, and decent arm muscles.

Kay had seen his mug shot in the paper. He was clean shaven but looked disheveled in the picture, wild-eyed and scared.

This morning, though, even in an orange jumpsuit, Mike Toledo seemed pulled together as if he were wearing an expensive suit. He sat down with confidence, staring at Jill while acknowledging Kay with a small smile.

"This your lawyer?" he asked, a joking kind of smirk on his lips.

"This is my friend. I asked her to come with me."

Kay expected protest, but Mike simply regarded Kay with unassuming eyes, as if pondering the reasoning but not questioning it. He then focused on Jill. "I'm glad you came. I wondered when you would."

"Or if," Jill said.

"Baby, you don't think I did this, do you?"

Jill glanced at Kay, who could only widen her eyes with anticipation of the answer. "I don't know what to think. I know you had an affair. Don't even try to deny it. The police already told me that much."

Mike looked down. "I did."

"How could you? Especially after I forgave you for Cindy."

"It was a mistake. A terrible mistake."

Jill paused, pushing a tissue to the bottom of her nose. "I knew you were having an affair. I knew it. I even confronted you."

"This woman meant nothing to me. Absolutely nothing."

"And neither, apparently, did Frank Merret." Kay knew it came out of her mouth, but it was as if someone else spoke. There was no mistaking it, though. Both Jill and Mike stared at her. She tried to hold his steady, piercing gaze without falter. It was taking every ounce of her courage.

Mike slowly returned his attention back to Jill. "I can't discuss this. You know I can't. My lawyer has advised me not to talk at all, to anyone. It only protects you. The less information you have, the better." He leaned forward, his fingers touching the top of the table lightly. "How's Natalie?"

"How do you think she is?" Jill's tone was harsh enough that he pulled his cuffed hands off the table. "You've created a nightmare for us. And all you can think about are your legal rights?"

"I'm trying to think of all of us, trying to figure out things. I know this is a mess. But we'll get through it."

"There is no longer a 'we.' We are over."

Mike glanced between the two women. Then his stare landed on Kay. "Is this your idea? Putting thoughts in her mind about leaving me?"

Kay's breath caught in her throat.

Jill slapped her hand against the table. "This has nothing

to do with her. This is between you and me, and I'm telling you that we're done. Whether or not you killed that officer is up to the court to decide, but I'm not going through this anymore with you. We're over." She trembled from head to toe. Only Kay could see her hands, now tucked on her lap, shaking as if she'd plugged herself into an outlet. But the resolve in Jill's eyes was undeniable. And apparently unusual, judging by Mike's expression.

Suddenly, though, Mike's startled eyes turned scathing; his hot gaze drifted back and forth between Jill and Kay. "Well," he said, his voice smooth and calm, "I suppose when I get out of here after I'm proven innocent, we'll have to all three get together again. Talk through the facts. Clear up any . . . misunderstandings." He parked his stare on Kay. Then he grinned. "Right?"

Jill grabbed Kay's arm. "Come on. Let's go."

"So soon?" he sneered.

Kay and Jill made their way around the table. Kay thought the protocol was that the prisoner left first, but they were already at the door, ringing the buzzer to be let out.

Mike turned in his seat. "Jill, wait. Please. Let's talk. Just you and me. Why do you need her here anyway?"

"She's my friend!" Jill barked, ringing the buzzer again. The door swung open, and a guard appeared in the doorway.

Mike's menacing eyes followed them. "I wasn't aware you had any friends."

Kay took Jill by the shoulder and ushered her out the door, then glanced back.

Mike leaned against the back of the chair, raised both hands, and waved.

* * *

"Shut the door," Edgar said.

Damien studied Captain Lou Grayson, who stood near Edgar's desk. "Did you find any evidence linking Toledo to Frank's murder?"

Grayson glanced at Edgar, who gave a slight nod. Damien thought they were both acting weird.

"This is off the record for right now," Grayson said, "but yeah, we got the warrant, got in, and found some good stuff. But even better, our guys found a gun wrapped in a sack, thrown in a Dumpster about a mile from his house. We're running tests for a match, but it looks promising. He was denied bail." He urged Damien to sit. "But that's not why we're here."

Damien sat down. There was something in the air that surpassed the typical office tension that accompanied a busy day.

Grayson reached down and pulled out a folder from a briefcase that leaned against Edgar's desk. He dropped it onto the edge of the desk as if everyone should focus on it.

Instead Damien stared at Edgar, tried to read his face, but it remained expressionless. "What's going on?"

Edgar cleared his throat. "Frank's no longer on their radar for the Web site."

Damien sucked in a relieved breath. He smiled, nodding, eager for more information.

Edgar's attention drifted past Damien to Grayson.

"Damien, we're going to just come out and say it. No beating around the bush," Grayson said, his tone suddenly more formal. "We have reason to believe you're the one behind the Web site."

29

"WHAT?" THE QUESTION rushed out with too much air, making it sound like he'd whispered it. Damien felt small sitting in the chair, Grayson towering over him, Edgar's eyes narrow and critical. "What are you saying?"

"Are you the one behind the Web site?" Grayson said.

Damien's fingers curled toward his palms, his fingernails embedded in his flesh. "What are you talking about?"

"Answer the question," Edgar said.

"First you accuse Frank, the most honest man we know, who can't defend himself because he's dead, and when you can't prove that, you turn to me?" Damien jumped out of his seat, causing Grayson's hand to snap to his holster and Edgar to flinch. "You have got to be kidding me!"

"Sit down," Grayson ordered. "Now."

He'd known Lou for years, and never once had he talked to him this way. His tone didn't have a hint of familiarity. Damien glared at Edgar, whose gaze dropped to his desk.

Damien lowered himself into his chair slowly, his stare boring into Grayson. "What makes you think it was me?"

From the folder he'd set on Edgar's desk, Grayson pulled out a clipping from a newspaper. He turned it around and showed it to Damien, who took it and looked it over. It was a crossword puzzle. His crossword puzzle. Filled in.

"You published this puzzle this week. Yesterday, in fact. Is that correct?" Grayson asked.

Damien nodded. A chill crept down his spine. He was starting to understand where this was going.

"We found the answers particularly interesting. They seem to send a clear message." Grayson took out another copy of the clipping. "If you read from left to right, we have words and phrases like *important work*, *must continue*, and this one in particular caused some alarm bells to go off: *let their words kill them*. Not so cleverly disguised to be read backward."

Edgar looked terrified, as if he were sitting across from Hannibal Lecter.

Damien released his fingers and crossed his legs. He knew beyond a shadow of a doubt that this was not good, but there was no need for him to act guilty and afraid. He smiled. "Yeah, I can see where this looks bad."

"No kidding." Grayson grabbed a nearby chair sitting against the wall of Edgar's office, plopped himself into it, and was now eye level with Damien. It felt rehearsed, like somewhere in a textbook he'd read that if you sit across from a suspect and lean forward four inches, he'll confess everything. "Talk to me. Why did you decide to start the Web site?"

Damien rolled his eyes. "Give me a break. I did not start the Web site. I was trying to send a message to the person behind it. I wanted him to start up again, to prove that Frank was not responsible."

"Interesting," Grayson said, sounding not the least bit convinced. "Any reason you chose a crossword puzzle?"

"Why not write an editorial?" Edgar asked, a softness in his eyes indicating he really did want to know the reason.

Damien glanced at Edgar, then at Grayson, then down at his hands. He couldn't keep it a secret any longer. "The person behind the Web site contacted me."

Grayson's skepticism hung in the room like heavy, intrusive cologne. "Really."

"Really. He sent me a crossword puzzle. Here, at the office. When I solved it, it spoke of the Web site and for this person's need to continue."

"Except he hasn't continued, has he?" Grayson asked.

Edgar looked furious. "Damien, why didn't you report this? You should've told me!"

"I know. I know," Damien said. "I should have. I just thought since the person sent it directly to me, I could reach him, try to convince him to stop."

Grayson held up the crossword puzzle. "This doesn't sound like you want him to stop."

Damien shook his head. "I know how it looks. After Frank died, I wanted to clear his name. I wanted to prove he wasn't the one doing this. I thought if the person would start up again, that was a surefire way to clear Frank."

Grayson had a pretentious expression that begged to be slapped right off him.

Damien stood and went to the door. "I've got the original crossword the person sent to me."

Grayson and Edgar followed him out, Edgar hurrying to catch up with him. "You're in a boatload of trouble. You should've reported that to me."

"And to us," Grayson said. "We could charge you with hindering an investigation."

Damien remained quiet. What else could he say?

They arrived at his desk. Damien sat in his chair to better reach his briefcase, where he'd last put the crossword. It was buried between all kinds of useless things he kept in there. Behind a bulging green folder, he fished around for the thin, red one but felt nothing except vinyl.

Pushing his chair back, he knelt beside the the briefcase. With both hands, he removed three bulky folders in the way, tossing them hastily onto his desk. He stared at a wide-open space. No red folder.

"It's gone," Damien breathed. "It was here; I swear it. It was here." He looked at Edgar. "Did you take it?"

Edgar's eyes widened. "No."

"Maybe I should've asked, 'Did you write the original?'"

"That's ridiculous!" Edgar cast a disapproving look at Grayson.

"Really? Is it? Because as I see it, the only thing prospering from this stupid Web site is the newspaper."

"Prospering? The only thing this Web site has done—"

Edgar's gaze lifted like he was trying to ward off anger—"is make me understand how very few friends I have at this place." He turned and walked off.

Damien stared at the carpet. So that was why Edgar was acting so weird? He'd been hurt by it too? When was this going to end?

Grayson crossed his arms. "You've just become a person of interest."

* * *

Kay studied the Monopoly board, fingering her money.

"Mom, hurry up," Hunter complained. "You're taking forever."

"It's a game of strategy," Jenna said, but she didn't seem really present in the conversation.

Kay noticed Jenna staring at the mantel, at the eight-by-ten photo of Frank with the kids three Christmases ago. It had snowed ten inches that year, the first white Christmas either kid had experienced. They were outside for three hours and built four different snowmen.

Hunter sighed, toying with his silver car. "I thought Dad was coming home for dinner tonight."

Kay tried to smile, but she was worried. He had said he would be home early. When he didn't arrive, she'd called his cell phone. He answered and didn't give her time to speak. "I can't talk. I'll be home later." *Click.* She tried texting him an hour ago, but no reply came. She drew a card but barely paid attention to it.

"He'll be here when he can. Your move, Hunter." She caught Jenna's eyes, trying to look deeply into them, wondering what was going on behind that pretty face.

Jenna only smiled faintly, blinked peacefully, and reassured her with a pat on her wrist. She pointed to Kay's money. "You're really bad at this."

Kay laughed. "Yes, well, that's why your father handles all the money."

Hunter punched his hands into the air as he passed Go safely. "Sweet!"

The back door opened and Damien appeared, looking as haggard as if he'd walked all the way home from work.

Kay stood and greeted him. She took his briefcase and coat. "What's wrong?" she asked, trying not to sound urgent in front of the kids.

Damien stared at Kay, then at each of his children. He observed the table for a moment and looked at Kay. "You're not winning."

"I never do."

As though every move he made was an effort, Damien pulled out the chair at the head of the table and sat down. He folded his fingers together and stared at them as if they might do the talking.

Kay glanced at Jenna, then at Hunter, who both looked equally perplexed.

"Is it about Frank?" Hunter asked.

Damien shook his head. "I've become a person of interest in the Web site case. They think I'm doing it."

"What?" Kay gasped, though her hand hit her mouth trying to stop it. "What in the world? Why would they think that?"

Damien didn't answer at first. It looked like he was overcome by emotion but trying to hide it. "I made a bad judgment call."

"Damien, you're not involved in this, are you?"

"No, I'm not. And neither was Frank; I can assure you." He took a score pad nearby and a pencil. He doodled around the edges.

"Then what are you talking about, 'judgment call'?" Kay asked.

"I received a note at the office, a sort of encrypted crossword deal that I believe was sent to me by the person doing it. The mistake I made was that I didn't tell anybody. When the Web site stopped after Frank died, I decided to send an encoded message in the crossword puzzle in the paper. I just wanted to get whoever was doing it to start again so Frank's name would be cleared. Unfortunately, Captain Grayson is a crossword fanatic. He saw the clues a mile away and knew I'd put them there."

"So? Show him the crossword that was sent to you," Kay said. "Then he'll know."

Damien stared at the Monopoly board. "It's gone."

"Gone?" Kay asked.

"I had it in my briefcase. It's not there anymore. That's all I know. It makes no sense to me." Damien finally looked up. "The good news is that I haven't been charged with anything. They don't really have any proof, but I'm their best lead right now."

"That Web site has brought nothing but trouble!" Hunter suddenly yelled.

Damien said, "Calm down, Hunter. Please. We can't afford to get hysterical about this. Besides, as much as I hated it at first, I actually think it has done some good. I hear it in the break room. People are starting to talk about the power of words. People are listening more than they're talking." He broke the tip of the pencil and grabbed another one out of the game box. "Our dark and dirty secret has been exposed, and maybe we're better for it. I don't know. Life and death are in the power of the tongue, if you give the tongue all the power, I guess."

"Well, we'll prove your innocence," Kay said, her hands spread wide like a cat's paws on the table. "We won't stop until we do."

"It'll work itself out in time. I'm not really worried. I know I didn't do it. I wouldn't even know how to do it. Someone out there is the right person, and eventually he'll be exposed." Damien scribbled something on the pad of paper in front of him.

Kay leaned in. "What are you writing?"

Damien shrugged. "Just something I wrote yesterday. I planned on writing another op-ed. Seems ridiculous now, you know? I can't say another thing about it."

Kay turned the pad to read it. *Listen to all that is said from everyone you know. Listen hard and you will have understanding beyond the words.* "That's beautiful," she said, touching his arm.

Hunter stood, slapped his dad's shoulder, then hugged him from behind. "It's going to be okay. I promise. You're going to be fine."

Damien squeezed his hand. "Thanks, buddy. I know. It's all good. I have my family and that's what matters to me." He looked at him. "You got homework?"

"Yeah."

"Better get it done. The show must go on."

"What exactly can get me out of homework?" Hunter groaned as he trotted upstairs.

"Baby," Kay said, "let me get you something to eat."

"I'm not hungry. Ate a big lunch," Damien said, that smile emerging that was always supposed to try to put her at ease. "I think I'll go shower, relax, maybe read."

Kay watched him leave the room. The table was silent; then Jenna said, "I miss Frank."

"Me too."

"Frank was really brave. I mean, I always just saw him as Uncle Frank, but he didn't back down from a fight. He thought Angela was in danger and he didn't even pause. He just went right over there."

Kay nodded. "Yeah, Frank was brave. And honest. A good guy all around."

"He had good character."

Kay nodded again, eyeing Jenna. She wasn't one to normally wax so philosophical. But then again, she'd been through a lot, and that kind of pain can change a person.

Jenna looked at Kay. "I think I'm brave too."

Kay smiled, tears brimming her eyes. She touched Jenna's cheek. For once she didn't pull away. "Of course you're brave."

"Yeah, I am. I never thought of myself that way, but I am." She pushed her money to the center of the table. "I guess the game's over." She stood.

Kay stood also, embracing her.

"Dad prayed for me last night," Jenna said as she turned toward the stairs.

"Oh?"

"That's a good dad who will pray for his kid, right?"

"Yes."

"I think prayer works." She grinned, and light danced in her eyes. "See you in the morning."

Kay gathered the Monopoly pieces and put the game back in the box. She hadn't even talked about her day or what had happened at the jail. She knew Damien would not have approved of her going, and she would've heard about it for at least a few days.

Obviously he had enough on his mind.

But Kay knew she'd done the right thing. They had demonstrated strength in numbers, and as they had walked out of that jail, Jill started laughing. It was the first time she had ever heard the woman laugh. Kay knew Jill felt free, felt strong. Before they'd gotten into the car, Jill took her arm. "Thank you. I couldn't have done this without you."

"You're not alone anymore," Kay said, hugging her. "We're friends. I'm here to help you."

Kay loaded the rest of the dishes in the dishwasher and turned out the lights downstairs. As she climbed to the second floor, she had an overwhelming sense that everything was going to be okay.

30

DAMIEN BRISTLED AGAINST the cold north wind that snapped and snaked around the complex of condos. Even though his hands were shoved far into his pockets, he still couldn't find a warm spot for them.

He leaned against his car, hoping to block some of the wind, and waited. The individual condos boasted a variety of Christmas decorations, from out-of-sync blinking Christmas lights to oddly decorated palm trees on the balconies. Even with all the lights and decorations, it didn't feel like Christmas this year. Eight days away. Usually he'd be attending parties and buying gifts. But he couldn't get his mind or heart wrapped around the festivities this year.

He definitely wouldn't be hanging out in the cold, waiting for someone he had to confront in this way because the guy wouldn't talk to him otherwise.

He heard the opening of a door and stood upright, tugging at the bottom of his coat as he watched unit 105.

Soon enough, Gavin Jenkins rounded the sidewalk, adjusting his belt and holster and everything else that hung off him. He was so distracted by it that he didn't bother to look up.

"Gavin."

His head snapped up. He couldn't have hidden his shock any less had Damien been America's Most Wanted.

"I just need to talk to you," Damien said, holding out his hands for no apparent reason except it seemed like the appropriate thing to do in front of someone with quick access to a gun.

Judging by Gavin's expression, if he weren't wearing a certain badge of courage, he might've bolted. Damien could only guess that what kept him standing there was the uniform.

And it wasn't for fear for his life, either. Gavin knew good and well why Damien stood there waiting for him.

"What can I do for you, Mr. Underwood?" Gavin asked, his stance and demeanor instantly changing. "You're waiting outside my residence?"

"I didn't want to have this discussion at the police station."

"I imagine not. You're not a popular guy right now."

Damien looked away for a moment, trying to compose himself. He was no fan of Gavin Jenkins either. "I'm here to talk about Frank, but you already knew that."

"I can't give you any information about the case."

"I'm not asking for that, and I don't think you know

anything anyway, being a rookie and all. They don't tell you much, do they?"

"I don't think we have anything to say to each other," Gavin said, starting to walk away.

"You're wrong," Damien said. "I have a lot to say to you. Namely about how you could talk to your captain and make it sound like Frank had anything to do with that Web site."

"Look, I realize you're upset. We're all upset about what happened to Frank. I didn't spin it one way or another, though. I told the captain what I had observed. The fact is, whether you like it or not, Frank was on edge. Disappearing all the time. Obsessed with this Web site. Not over his divorce. Moody. I saw it firsthand. Whatever conclusions they drew from that wasn't up to me."

"Yeah, he was a little rough around the edges, but you know he was a man of character."

"I know."

"Then why not defend him? Why let his good name be dragged through the mud?"

Gavin just stared, still trying to maintain that stupid stoic expression on his face. "It doesn't look like it's his name anymore," he finally said, looking Damien in the eye.

Damien didn't flinch. "Well, better mine than his. At least I can defend myself." He looked down, wondering what the point was to all of this. Yeah, it felt good to confront the kid, but so what? What had that accomplished? "I just . . . he's my friend. He was one of the finest human beings I know. He went over to his ex-wife's apartment to try to save her life. He sensed she was in danger. That's the kind of man he was. He would've done the same thing for me. For anyone in my family. And even you. Do you know what his dying words were?"

Gavin shook his head.

"'She's worth fighting for.' Even as he lay there dying, he said that she was worth fighting for and always would be."

Gavin's expression changed. He looked curious.

"What?" Damien asked.

"He said that to me too. All the time."

"What?"

"'She's worth fighting for.' But he wasn't talking about his ex-wife. He was talking about Marlo."

Marlo?

Gavin stepped to the side and around Damien. "I have to get to work."

Damien watched him climb into an oversize, manhood-feeding pickup and drive away. Just when he was about to give up on this town, Frank reminded him, even from the grave, what there was to fight for.

He turned and headed into the cold wind.

*   *   *

Kay stirred her coffee, watching the cream swirl through the blackness. She took her mug and walked to the living room window that faced the street. A miserable cold spell had set in. The cloudy gray sky looked heavy and low. She'd not even changed out of her pajamas yet. Her mind, wrought with distraction, was having a hard time keeping pace with the usual schedule and doing such mundane things as combing her hair.

A certain comfort enveloped her, though, as she sipped the coffee and stared into the streets of her neighborhood. She couldn't quite identify from where it came, because so much was in disarray. But it was something in Jenna, something she saw last night and this morning too. A sense of fortitude and resolve. She held her head a little higher, stood straighter, looked adamant and determined. For weeks now, her shoulders had remained in a constant slump. But not this morning. This morning she had a gleam in her eye like nothing could stop her.

And Kay had gotten a lot off her chest. Talked to someone who could relate. Came to understand some things about herself and her past and how it had affected her all these years. How she'd mothered from a deep fear she hadn't realized was still with her.

She had a lot to share with her family, namely Jenna. A lot of forgiveness to ask for. A lot of confessing to do.

Kay wasn't sure how much time had passed as she leaned against the window, contemplating what life had delivered to her family. She was just about to get a refill on her coffee when a familiar blue sedan pulled into her driveway.

Jill.

At once, she panicked. She was in her pajamas, without a stitch of makeup on, and hair matted on one side of her head.

Jill opened her car door, struggling to get out with something big in her hands.

Kay started to rush upstairs but stopped. Why the vanity? Here was a woman who was at her most vulnerable state, with an adulterous husband in jail, charged with murder. What impression, exactly, was Kay worried about giving? There were no more impressions to be made. Only honesty and compassion.

She set her mug on the kitchen counter and went to the front door, opening it before Jill had even made it up the porch steps.

"Hi! My goodness, what is this?" Kay stepped outside and helped her with the box. "Come in. It's freezing."

"Are you sure? I was just going to leave it on the doorstep. I don't want to bother you."

"Don't be silly. You're no bother at all. You want some coffee?"

Jill came inside, her cheeks bright red from the cold. "That sounds perfect." She slipped off her gloves and coat and followed Kay into the kitchen.

"Cream? Sugar?"

"Yes, and lots of it." Jill smiled.

"So, how are you doing?" Kay asked, grabbing a mug from the cabinet.

Jill was quiet for a moment, her gaze moving along the lines of the kitchen. "Mike confessed."

"What?"

"They came in this morning with some deal. I guess they

have a lot of evidence proving Mike did it, so they came up with some deal that will keep them from seeking . . ." She pressed her lips together as if it was something she shouldn't mention.

Kay put the coffee mug down and came around the kitchen island, wrapping her hands around Jill's shoulders. "I don't even know what to say."

She nodded and shook her head all at once. Tears pushed onto the rims of her eyes. "He told them that he had gone to the apartment to confront this woman, Angela. Not to kill her. That he'd taken the gun to scare her. He thought she wasn't answering the door, so he used his key to get in. He wasn't in there long when he was startled by the police officer and shot him. Accidentally. But I don't believe him."

"What do you think happened?" Kay poured the cream and sugar in, sliding the mug to her.

"I think he went there to kill that woman. And I don't think he accidentally killed anyone." Jill took the coffee and sipped through the hotness. "But the prosecutors say that the fact that he killed a police officer will assure that he's in jail for the rest of his life."

Kay sipped her own coffee and watched Jill, still unsure what to say.

"I have to be okay. For Natalie's sake."

"How is she doing?"

"All right, I guess. We had a good talk last night about accepting what's happening and dealing with it in a raw and real way, instead of pretending that it's not there or that there's anything we can do to change it. Sometimes you just have to accept the reality of your life, you know? A couple of weeks ago we were worried about things like tryouts and the new uniform colors. Now . . ." She turned suddenly and stepped into the entryway, fetching the box she'd carried in. "I wanted to give this to you."

"What for?"

"For helping me through this. You didn't have to get involved in this mess. But I'm so thankful you did."

Kay pulled off the top of the box. Inside was a tall lavender candle encased within a hurricane lamp. Engraved at the bottom was the word *friendship*.

Jill said, "I hope I'm not being presumptuous. But I do consider you a friend."

Kay pondered a moment how drastically her impressions of Jill had changed. And how much she'd judged this woman, even unintentionally at times. "This is beautiful, and yes, I believe with all we've gone through, we are now officially friends."

Jill laughed and held up her mug. "Cheers."

"To a coming year filled with fewer complications and more blessings."

Jill nodded and they touched mugs. "Well, it doesn't look like things are going to get less complicated anytime soon with this town."

"Oh?"

"Haven't you heard? There was a new post this morning on that Web site. I haven't read it. I'm trying to cut back."

* * *

"You're late," Edgar said before Damien even reached his desk. "Busy morning?"

Damien cast a forlorn look at him and kept walking. He reached his desk and threw his coat over the back of his chair. Edgar was still on his heels.

"I wasn't even sure if I should come in today." Damien glared at his desk to keep from glaring at Edgar.

"Maybe you shouldn't have."

"So you're convicting me before I'm tried; is that it? Besides the fact that you've known me since I was twenty years old and know that I'm not capable of doing something so damaging. Why aren't you at least giving me the benefit of the doubt?"

"I did. I gave it an honest shot. I went home to Luanne, and we talked through it. I think I was more upset that you'd hidden the note from me than anything. But none of it made sense. I mean cerebrally, yes, I could see where your overzealous nature could lend itself to something like this. You're a passionate man, especially when it comes to our fine town. You're a person who loves words of all sorts. So connecting those dots was not difficult. But you have to take it a step further. You have to look at the man, his character, and I did that. I had to consider your ineptness at the computer. I even considered you were telling the truth about the missing note."

"But?"

"But then you go and do something stupid. Something unbelievably stupid. It's so stupid that I honestly can't imagine what you were thinking. You must think we're a bunch of morons around here."

Damien grabbed the back of his neck, rubbing it fiercely as he tried to ward off a headache crawling up the back of his skull. "Okay, yeah, maybe it wasn't that smart, but I couldn't let it rest."

"So you're saying you did it?"

"Yeah. I wasn't trying to hide or sneak around. But I had something to say. And I don't believe in hiding out and keeping my mouth shut, at least in most instances. So I went and confronted the jerk."

Edgar blinked. "What are you talking about?"

Damien sighed heavily. "You're not going to make me repeat myself, are you? I'm talking about that maggot Gavin Jenkins. He's the one who started that whole nonsense about Frank being involved in the Web site." Even at the mention of his name, Damien felt his blood pressure rise. He shook off thoughts of Gavin and looked at Edgar, whose face had frozen in an odd expression. "What?"

"You went and confronted Frank's rookie this morning?"

"That's what I just said and what you just said. What are we talking about here?"

"The Web site. There's a new post this morning."

"What?"

Edgar's eyes narrowed. "Now you're going to act surprised?"

"Yes, I'm surprised!" Damien's patience was growing thinner by the second. "Why wouldn't I be surprised?"

"Because it's about you."

"What are you talking about?" Damien sat down at his computer, hurriedly typing in his password. An error came up and he retyped, trying to slow down. Another error message.

"Stop." Edgar's voice was sharp.

Damien turned back around in his chair, feeling like a small child who had just been scolded.

"Get your things and get out of here."

"Edgar—"

"I mean it. You're on administrative leave until this has been resolved. And if you're involved in this, you can kiss this job good-bye."

"Wait—"

"I think you got your wish. Frank's name is about to be cleared."

31

DAMIEN STOOD IN the doorway to Frank's house with the key firmly gripped between his pointer finger and thumb. Except the door did not need to be unlocked. It was already wide open. A high-pitched, hollow-sounding whistle passed through the gaping hole.

Damien took a step in and saw a man walking through the back door.

The man looked up and noticed Damien. "May I help you?" he asked, wiping his feet on the small mat before walking to the front door.

"I'm Damien Underwood, Frank's friend."

"Damien, yes. We spoke on the phone. Duane Morley, Frank's landlord." He shook Damien's hand. "Listen, I've got to get this house ready for rental again. And nobody has called to claim this stuff. Any idea what he'd want done with all of this? I'm going to have to do something with it."

Damien scanned the room, each piece of furniture, each

knickknack, each piece of technology ushering in a different memory. There were so many. Damien gazed at the coffee table that had held heaping piles of hot wings and various boxes of fast food. The television, dark and dusty, seemed the perfect symbol for Frank's passing. That TV had probably never been turned off since it arrived at the house four years ago. Damien remembered the day Frank bought it. He'd helped him move it in. He'd been so proud of his flat screen.

"Mr. Underwood?"

"Yeah, sorry. Um, Frank would want this all donated to charity. He was that kind of guy, you know?"

"Sure. Of course. I really liked Frank. He was one of my best tenants." Duane headed toward the door. "Tell you what. I'll start getting this stuff moved out this weekend. That'll give you some time to look through everything, see if there's anything you want to keep."

"Thanks."

"Just make sure everything is turned off before you leave."

Duane left and Damien walked quietly through the house, gazing at dusty picture frames and books lining the small bookshelf. Kay had come over and cleaned out the refrigerator and pantry so the rodents wouldn't get any ideas.

There was the obvious absence of Christmas decorations, which Frank had purposely protested since his divorce.

He made his way to the basement, clicking on the light. The computer, set atop an old desk he'd found at a flea market, was still on.

Sitting down and leaning back in the ergonomically correct chair, he stared at the beams supporting the ceiling, wondering how Frank would tackle this problem of being wrongly accused.

First of all, Frank would want to know what was posted. Damien's stomach turned at the thought that someone had been listening to his conversation. And, it seemed, someone deliberately posted his conversation, knowing full well he was a suspect. It couldn't be coincidence.

He'd gone to the library and printed out the conversation but hadn't had the guts to read it. Not yet. He took it out of his back pocket but couldn't get himself to unfold it.

Did he really want to read it? No. He did not. But he was going to have to find the courage to read it anyway.

He carefully unfolded the paper. Frank had done the same thing, read a conversation, and it had ended in his death. What would this bring for Damien? for his family?

Damien chuckled, remembering Frank lecturing him about how archaic dial-up was. Now he was down to hard copies. Damien looked away for a moment to compose himself, as if the words were alive and were taunting him with ill-intentioned eyes.

Then he looked it right in the eye and read.

"I've become a person of interest in the Web site case. They think I'm doing it."

"What? What in the world? Why would they think that?"

"I made a bad judgment call."

"Damien, you're not involved in this, are you?"

"No, I'm not. And neither was Frank; I can assure you."

"Then what are you talking about, 'judgment call'?"

"I received a note at the office, a sort of encrypted crossword deal that I believe was sent to me by the person doing it. The mistake I made was that I didn't tell anybody. When the Web site stopped after Frank died, I decided to send an encoded message in the crossword puzzle in the paper. I just wanted to get whoever was doing it to start again so Frank's name would be cleared. Unfortunately, Captain Grayson is a crossword fanatic. He saw the clues a mile away and knew I'd put them there."

"So? Show him the crossword that was sent to you. Then he'll know."

"It's gone."

"Gone?"

"I had it in my briefcase. It's not there anymore. That's all I know. It makes no sense to me. The good news is that I haven't been charged with anything. They don't really have any proof, but I'm their best lead right now."

"That Web site has brought nothing but trouble!"

"Calm down, Hunter. Please. We can't afford to get hysterical about this. Besides, as much as I hated it at first, I actually think it has done some good. I hear it *in the break room. People are starting to talk about the power of words. People are listening more than they're talking. Our dark and dirty secret has been exposed, and maybe we're better for it. I don't know. Life and death are in the power of the tongue, if you give the tongue all the power, I guess."*

"Well, we'll prove your innocence. We won't stop until we do."

"It'll work itself out in time. I'm not really worried. I know I didn't do it. I wouldn't even know how to do it. Someone out there is the right person, and eventually he'll be exposed. Listen to all that is said from everyone you know. Listen hard and you will have understanding beyond the words."

Every word stopped his heart. Damien knew exactly where this conversation had taken place. Right at his dining room table, where his family had played Monopoly.

What was this supposed to be? Some confession to his guilt? He read it carefully. On the contrary. He was talking about how he didn't do it, but it still made him look stupid. If he were the one doing the Web site, this seemed like a lame attempt to cover his tracks, especially since nothing had been posted until now. It made no sense. What was the purpose of it?

Damien blew air from his cheeks, along with a sense of resentment that had bubbled inside him. He'd never felt so violated in his life. This was his family. This was a private conversation. It had no business being listened to by anyone else.

He let himself seethe a little longer, then decided he had to push his emotions aside if he was going to figure out who was behind this.

He stood and paced. First, the crossword puzzle. Someone at the office had access to it. He usually left his briefcase under his desk when he went out for lunch or on break. Maybe someone had a complaint against him, wanted to get even for something. He seemed generally liked, and though several of his colleagues had voiced disagreement about some of his op-ed pieces, nobody was hostile. It just made for lively conversation.

At least that was what he thought.

In five minutes of hard thinking, he could not come up with a single person who held a grudge against him enough to do this.

Damien tried to move on. A citizen of Marlo, perhaps? They already knew it was someone within the community, but who would want to set him up like this? Who would go to this much trouble? And who knew enough about him to know he was in trouble at work?

His mind wandered to the police department. Perhaps someone there knew he was being investigated. But again, why the grudge? Why take the trouble to record a conversation he had with his family? How long had this person been listening? all night? Was he watching the house?

His heart jumped at the thought of Kay. She was supposed

to go to work today. He took out his cell phone, dialing her number.

"Hello?"

"Hey, babe. Are you at the house?"

"No. I'm in town. Getting ready to show a house. Why?"

"I don't want to scare you, but . . . just be careful. Watch your surroundings. Lock the doors when you're home. And watch what you say."

"What? Why?"

"Our conversation was recorded last night. At the table."

A long stretch of silence. "What are you talking about?" Her voice was now a heavy whisper.

"I don't know what's going on. I'm trying to figure this thing out. But I'm somebody's target, and I have to find out who's trying to set me up. I want you to be vigilant, with yourself and with the kids."

"Both the kids have something after school. Jenna's got a class project she has to work on, and Hunter has to stay late to complete his science fair essay. I'll pick him up at five."

"Okay, that's good. I don't want to frighten them, and so far whoever is doing this doesn't seem the violent type, but we can't be too careful."

"I'm scared."

"I know. I am too. But we're going to get through this. The truth will come out."

"I want to call Reverend Caldwell. Tell him to pray for us."

"I think that's a good idea."

"I love you."

"I love you too."

"Call me soon, okay?"

"I will." Damien put the phone back in his pocket.

Think. Think.

He sat back down at the computer, scrolling through the previous conversations that were recorded. He studied every word, every sentence, trying to get an idea of some kind of unobvious agenda.

"I've never liked the man."

"Come on. We hardly know them."

"You can sense weirdos, and he's a weirdo."

"You've never said a word about this guy."

"Yes, well, that's before he went nuts."

"You have no proof that——"

"I don't need proof. I can see it in the man's eyes. Tell the kids not to talk to him. Or his wife. We're going to stay the _____ away from him."

"Do you really think she's having an affair?"

"_____, yes."

"I mean, I wouldn't put it past her, but——"

"It's written all over her. First of all, she's late all the time."

"But is it an affair? With a married man?"

"Of course it is."

"How do you know?"

"Because I know her, and normally she'd be talking the thing to death."

Something struck him. There were blanks where curse words should be. Without exception, every place a curse word looked like it should fit, a blank line was drawn. It had been like that from the beginning of the Web site.

Damien leaned forward, feeling like the ultimate sleuth. That had to mean something. He was certain it meant something to Frank, though Frank had never mentioned it. For Damien, it meant that whoever this was had an aversion to curse words. Which meant they were probably religious. Yes, so, it was the local nuns?

Or . . . Reverend Caldwell? The guy liked to pop up unexpectedly.

Damien filed the thought away and continued to scroll, looking to pick up more clues. It all seemed pretty random. Some conversations were more damning than others. There didn't seem to be a pattern of trying to target one person over another. It seemed like this person was just a simple observer, reporting the facts.

Kind of like an investigative reporter.

Damien shook off the thought and continued to read but still didn't find anything that stuck out to him.

He scrolled back to the top and decided to read the conversation about him. It hurt. He found himself blinking at every word, as if it were slapping him across the face. But he kept reading over and over. The more he read, the less painful it became, and he was able to read with a more critical eye.

And then . . .

Damien slammed himself backward in the chair. His heart hammered inside his chest. He shot to his feet, accidentally kicking the chair, then slapped his hands on the desk and put all his attention on the sheet of paper. He read. He reread. Again. And again.

"No," he whispered. "I don't understand. . . ."

He grabbed his keys and jacket and bolted up the stairs. He ran out of the house, not bothering to shut the front door.

32

KAY TURNED UP the heat in the SUV. Exhaust filled the space behind the bumper. Even with the heater running, it still felt frigid. Her windows were fogging over too.

Normally she would let Hunter walk home but not today. Not after Damien's phone call.

The parking lot looked fairly empty, and only a few cars had pulled to the curb. Hunter wouldn't be happy seeing his mom's SUV idling out front, but she didn't care at this point. She just wanted him home safely.

She'd texted Jenna earlier and tried not to sound frightened. Instead she said, *Checking in. Doing okay?*

Jenna's response: *Doing fine.*

That was all she needed to hear.

Now she just needed to see her son walking out the front doors of the school.

She swiped her hand across the windshield and checked her watch. She knew she was on time. He'd been staying late for a few weeks working on his science fair project.

She got out of her SUV and stood on the curb, glancing back and forth to make sure she hadn't accidentally missed him.

A few kids straggled out. She didn't recognize them, though admittedly, she didn't know many of Hunter's friends. She'd been so consumed with the whole cheerleading scene she had let those kinds of details slip lately. But Hunter had never had trouble making friends, and usually they were the good kids.

She blew into her gloved hands and wiggled around in her coat, trying to keep herself warm.

Where was he?

A nervous chill managed to snake its way up her spine, colder than what this wind was causing.

She couldn't have missed him. The kids always came out the front door to walk home. The back of the school was fenced in and there was no other way to go.

She took out her cell phone and called Reverend Caldwell. His voice mail picked up. "Hi, this is Kay Underwood. Our family is going through a lot right now, and I wanted to say thank you for your kindness. I'm so glad Gabby is okay. If you could just say a prayer for us. Thank you." Kay shut her phone and thought that perhaps she could say a prayer herself. She hadn't prayed in years besides the occasional blessing at the table on a religious holiday.

She wanted to pray, but she couldn't get her mind off Hunter.

He was going to kill her, but at this point she was willing to take the risk, since she felt like she was going to die from a combination of fear and hypothermia.

"Don't panic," she said as she started toward the school. She realized she'd forgotten to turn off her SUV and take the keys out. Her purse was on the floorboard. She paused but couldn't get herself to turn back. With brisk strides she swung open the heavy glass door of the school.

The halls were empty and dark. Her heels echoed dully against the laminate. A janitor swung his mop back and forth a few feet ahead. "Excuse me," Kay said. "I'm looking for Mrs. Patterson's room."

"Straight that way, at the end. Room 110."

"Thanks."

Kay hustled forward, nearly in a run. She found the room and grabbed the handle, but it was locked. She peered through the small window on the door. Heavy shadows, long against the floor, clung to the last bits of light filtering through the outside window.

Kay turned, her back against the door, each breath hard to take. She hurried to the center of the building, where the office was and hopefully the teachers' lounge.

She heard a few voices and followed them into a long room with tables, a sink, and a coffeemaker. She couldn't even remember what Mrs. Patterson looked like.

A few teachers looked up as she cleared her throat. "Sorry to bother you. I'm looking for Mrs. Patterson?"

"Yes, that's me," said a slender woman with long, straight

hair. She didn't really fit the profile of a science teacher. "What can I do for you?" she asked, walking toward Kay.

Kay lowered her voice and tried a pleasant, calm smile. "I'm sorry. I'm just looking for my son, Hunter Underwood."

"I haven't seen him since school today."

"He was staying late after school for that project."

"What project?"

"For the big science project he's been working on."

Mrs. Patterson shook her head. "I don't know what you mean."

"He said there was some science project he was doing. He's been staying late after school. Today he was working on the essay."

"I'm sorry. You must be mistaken. I have assigned nothing like that, and nobody from the class has been staying afterward."

* * *

Damien peeled into the driveway, punching his garage door opener. He sped into the garage and got out. The metal garage door rumbled closed. He unlocked the door that led into the laundry room, irritated it was locked although he'd been the one to suggest the extra precaution.

The house was dark and empty. Somewhere he thought he smelled a candle recently burned. Was it lavender? Damien stopped in the kitchen, trying to catch his breath. He had to get a grip. He had to try to think clearly, not panic, no matter what the outcome was.

He slipped off his coat and stuffed his gloves into the pockets, then threw his cell phone on the counter.

His legs felt as if he were walking on unstable ground, as if at any moment his feet might sink into an unseen hole. Both hands were flat against his chest as he made his way to the dining room.

There it was, still sitting on the table, closed up and ready for another family game night. He turned on the chandelier. Its sparkling light caressed the room, but there was nothing to calm Damien's dread.

He pulled out a chair and sat down, then moved the box toward him, staring at it for a long time. It took several tugs, but he finally removed the box top. Inside, the game was put back nice and tidy, with all the money lined up in neat stacks. Kay must've done it.

He removed the game board, the pieces, and the money. He took a deep breath as he lifted out the pad of paper he'd doodled on the night before. He flipped it over to where he'd jotted down a line from the op-ed piece he'd been working on for the newspaper.

> *Listen to all that is said from everyone you know.*
> *Listen hard and you will have understanding beyond*
> *the words.*

These sentences had been recorded in the conversation and posted on the Web site. Except Damien had written them down, not spoken them.

He had not spoken them.

Whoever recorded the conversation had to have been in the room, close enough to read it.

At the table.

Damien sat there, unable to react to the sobering realization of what was before him. His fingertips traced the letters of each word he'd written. His heart broke. He now had understanding beyond the words.

His fingers pressed against his lips to keep them from trembling, but he knew what he had to do. Shoving himself away from the table, he stood and walked to the stairway. He used the rail and took his time with each step. It didn't seem real. It seemed impossibly unreal.

At the top he hesitated. What he might find could change his whole world in an instant and would prove everything wrong that he'd believed. It almost seemed as if he'd just been given news that he would die, and he had a few minutes to ponder it. There was nothing to do in a few minutes except to briefly reflect on what could have been.

He walked toward Hunter's room. The door was shut. He turned the knob and opened it, almost expecting the young man to be diving toward or away from something.

But the room was quiet and peaceful. Neat, even. But odorous in a way only a teenager can manage. It felt awkward to be in here without Hunter. He couldn't even remember the last time he'd been in his son's room alone. It felt like trespassing.

There was no use just standing around and thinking about

it. He first went through his desk, searching through a bunch of unorganized papers, spirals, and folders. Nothing.

Next he went to the closet, where he scooted clothing across the bar, digging behind boxes and junk, trying not to think of the implications of what would happen if he found what he was looking for.

He walked out of the closet empty-handed and glanced around the room. There wasn't a great deal of hiding space in the room. He walked over to the bed and dropped to his knees. The floor was cold even with the rug.

He lay flat on his stomach and reached through the shadows, a little afraid of what might jump out and grab him. He groped around. A few papers. A couple of old toys.

Then his fingers touched something cold, firm, folder-like. Walking his fingers across it, he tried to scoot it across the rug. When it didn't budge, he nudged his thumb underneath it and pulled.

Out slid a bright red folder. Damien pushed himself to his knees. His hands shook so badly he could barely open it, but when he managed to, his heart sank with grief. There in the folder sat the original letter that had been sent to him from the person responsible for the Web site.

His son.

Damien fell with his face to the floor, crying against the folder . . . against the evidence.

Damien was unsure how long he'd lain on the carpet when he heard a loud knock downstairs at his front door. He couldn't move and didn't want to. But the banging continued, and now he heard a strong male voice. "Damien! We know you're in there!"

He looked at the folder, unsure what to do with it. So he carried it downstairs with him. Through the thin curtains of the side windows, he saw three men. He set the folder down and opened the door.

Captain Grayson stood in full uniform. Next to him an officer Damien didn't recognize. And Detective Murray.

"You're under arrest, Damien, for violations of state privacy laws." Grayson took out handcuffs. Damien went numb as he offered his wrists. "You have the right to remain silent. . . ."

But Damien didn't care anything about his own rights at the moment. He wondered what he should do, whether he should turn over the evidence against his son. He stared blankly past the officers, past his front yard, into some unknown future that looked bleak.

"Damien?"

"What?"

"I'll tell you up front that we have linked your credit card to the Web site. That's the evidence we needed to make the arrest."

Damien nodded.

Grayson then handed him over to be taken to the patrol car. Damien's elderly neighbor across the street stood in his coat, watching the entire scene.

In an instant Damien could show them all he had, turn

Hunter in. The folder lay right inside. But as they pushed him into the patrol car and as the officer reached across him to buckle him in, Damien didn't say a word.

* * *

Kay, her skin now numb to the cold, returned to her SUV and turned it off, pulling the keys from the ignition. She closed the door and punched the remote lock.

Where was her son? The path that Hunter took home could not be followed in a vehicle. He always cut through the park and then through a heavily populated neighborhood that did not have fences.

She hurried toward the park, cursing as she thought about him not having his stupid cell phone. What if he was in trouble? Why did she have to ground him from that, when he might need it the most?

Then wind stung her eyes, blurring her vision. "Hunter! Baby! Hunter!" Tears blew from her face. "Hunter!"

She wasn't exactly certain of the path, but she knew she was close. She continued to call his name over and over. The walk home was a little less than a mile, and she'd run the entire thing in less than ten minutes, calling his name all along the way. She even stopped some people to see if they had seen him.

But nobody had seen her precious boy. She came within a block of their house. She could see the driveway. The house looked empty. All the lights were out, except the dining room light, which she must've left on. If Hunter was there, every light in the house would've been glowing. He had a bad habit of leaving lights on everywhere.

She turned and started the long run back to her SUV.

33

At home, Kay parked the SUV in the driveway and hurried to the front door, unlocking it with shaky hands. Her mind rattled with all sorts of possible scenarios. She dialed Jenna's cell phone again.

"Hello?"

"Have you seen Hunter?" Kay kept her voice light.

"No. Can I call you back? I'm in the middle of something."

"Don't worry about it. I'll talk to you when you get home." She hung up and dialed Damien's cell phone. She didn't want to worry him, and she was having a hard time trusting her gut instinct right now, but something told her not to blow this off.

She turned suddenly, because as she heard the phone ringing in her ear, she also heard Damien's phone ringing somewhere nearby.

There, on the kitchen counter. Next to a red folder. She

shoved the folder aside and stared at the phone as it blinked and vibrated.

Damien had been home? Maybe he had Hunter. Yes, that had to be it. She'd never known Damien to forget his cell phone, but he had a lot on his mind.

It made sense, but she wouldn't rest easy until she knew they were together for sure.

She went to the dining room to turn off the light. Scattered across the table was the Monopoly game. They must've played a quick game after school. She smiled, though. It definitely meant they'd been together because who plays Monopoly by themselves?

She managed a few deep, thankful breaths of relief and opened the freezer door. Wherever they were, she knew they'd be home for dinner, and she'd have it ready for them.

* * *

Grayson apologized for the cuffs, saying it was procedure and that they cuffed everyone.

Damien didn't say anything as he stared out the window of the patrol car, watching his town pass, street by street, house by house, door by door.

The general mood seemed subdued like the crowd after a holocaust movie. But why not? Many of them had their private words splashed across the Internet. Others read the ugly words spoken about them. The ugly words they'd used themselves.

It made Damien wonder if the words had any power

before they were printed for all to read. Did they change the world when spoken, or did they change the person speaking them?

The short drive to the jail was over. The patrol car pulled to the side of the jailhouse into a small, underground parking garage. Grayson helped Damien out of the car, guiding him along as if he were a dinner date, with his hand on his back and his attention to detail, like opening doors and gesturing which way to walk.

"Sit here," Grayson said. "I have to get paperwork."

Damien sat in a metal-and-vinyl chair, watching the activity in the jailhouse. It wasn't particularly busy. A few people glanced at him, but other than that he was left alone.

So he pondered whether or not he would face the consequences of his son's actions. Would he be willing to spend time in jail for Hunter?

He couldn't fathom why his son would do such a thing, yet he knew there had to be some good reason. Hunter was not one to cause chaos and destruction for no general purpose.

Through a nagging headache, Damien tried to find the strength to analyze the situation apart from his emotions. But he found it nearly impossible.

And so he sat there, his cuffed hands limp in his lap, waiting for whatever might come. He could do nothing, so he did nothing. He shoved it all out of his mind and stared at the linoleum, a dull gray but clean. He'd once done an op-ed column about the conditions of the jail. Looked as if they'd taken his article to heart.

* * *

Jenna had texted, said not to wait on dinner for her. Kay sighed, watching the oven as if something exciting might happen. She'd fixed a simple Mexican casserole, a sure winner. It was bubbling and ready to be served, with no one to serve it to.

Kay turned down the oven temperature and leaned against the counter, fiddling with a dish towel. She wondered what her parents had felt like when she was a teenager and there was no way to touch base with her. Maybe they were forced not to worry until there was confirmation that something was wrong.

She actually had quite a bit of assurance that everything was okay, but her motherly instinct still wouldn't rest easy.

She tossed the salad for the fourth time and decided to go ahead and fill the water glasses with ice. The phone rang.

She snatched it up before it even completed the full ring. "Hello?"

"Kay? Are you okay?"

Kay caught her breath. "Jill?"

"Yes, it's me. What's the matter? You sound worried."

"Um . . . no. I'm expecting a call; that's all. Why do you ask?"

"Just because, you know . . ."

"Know what?"

"The Web site."

Kay gripped the dish towel. "I thought you were cutting back."

"Natalie told me." She paused. "I didn't realize Damien was a suspect."

"He's not. I mean, he is. But it's ridiculous. They don't have any proof. They're grasping at straws. We're fine and . . ." Her voice cracked, and she couldn't get the rest of the sentence out. Fine? She wasn't fine, judging by how she wrung the towel like there was water to squeeze out.

"I'm coming over."

"No, that's not necessary. I'm . . . Jill?" The line was dead.

*   *   *

Damien watched the plump and disengaged woman behind the desk take the man's fingers one by one, pressing the tips into a pad of dark ink, then rolling them from side to side inside little white boxes. He looked like a criminal. Disheveled hair. Dirty hands. Torn clothes.

She handed the man a wipe, as if he might be concerned about a stain on his fingertips.

Damien remained in his seat, where he studied his own fingers. He wondered why he hadn't done that yet.

He sensed someone standing above him. Grayson. "You get one phone call. You can make it over at that empty desk." He talked like there was nothing unusual going on. Just a regular day. "I'm not charging you yet. I want to give you every opportunity to clear this thing up. We're going to hold you here for seventy-two hours. As we continue the investigation, we'll be able to ask you to clarify things for us as they develop. I hope you understand."

Damien wondered whom he should call. Kay? He knew if he heard her voice, he couldn't lie to her. He'd have to tell her everything. Should he call a lawyer? What was the point? It was his decision to take the fall for his kid or not. Plus, it just made him look guiltier. A friend? And which friend would that be? He didn't have any close friends except Frank. These days he wasn't sure where he stood with his coworkers.

"Damien?"

Maybe it was safer for everyone involved if he sat in jail. He needed more time to think things through. "I'll pass."

"You'll pass?"

"Yes."

"Fine." Grayson took him by the arm and led him to a holding cell. "Bail will not be set until we file official charges. For now, you'll be here until we figure some things out."

Grayson stepped aside and let the officer working the jail holding area lock the door. The cell was a reinforced concrete box. Damien estimated about six feet by eight feet with a sliding door made of heavy bars. There was a slot, presumably for food. A stainless steel sink and toilet were bolted to the wall. There were two cells on either side of the expansive room. This jail was built in the late forties. Not much about it had changed, except the decor and the floor.

"I don't know what to say." Grayson stared at the floor, the sounds of the police holding area whispering between them. He finally looked up. "I don't suppose you have anything to say?"

Damien answered him by sitting in the single chair near the back wall. He couldn't look him in the eye for fear that Grayson might read his face and know he was hiding something more than what Grayson perceived as guilt.

Grayson sighed and left.

Damien sat still, his chest barely lifting to breathe, and closed his eyes, remembering the day Hunter was born and the first words he whispered into his tiny ear: *"I will always protect you."*

34

"I JUST WISH I knew where they were," Kay said. She'd taken the casserole out of the oven and served them both a plate, but she couldn't taste the two bites she'd tried.

Jill noticed. "You're sure they're together?"

"Yes. Monopoly was out and they love playing it together. But where they went after that, I don't know." She couldn't tear her gaze away from the cell phone on the counter. "I really wish we wouldn't have grounded Hunter. If he just had his cell phone with him."

Jill reached across the breakfast bar for her hand. "I'm sure they're fine. Like you said, you know they're together."

Kay smiled. "I bet right now Damien is realizing he forgot his phone and he's kicking himself."

"He knows he's going to be in big trouble when he returns." Jill let go of her hand and returned to eating her portion of the casserole. "Maybe we should pray."

Kay was certain her eyes appeared startled. It seemed like

prayer occurred more often when there was a crisis to pray for. Was there a crisis? "We, um, we don't go to church much. I mean, we haven't, you know, for a while. We did recently. Once. But not regularly."

"And what's that got to do with the price of tea in China?" Jill rose and came around the bar, sitting on the stool next to Kay. "When Gabby was missing, I just remember thinking how easily that could've been my Nat. I'm sure your family is fine. You already talked to Jenna. And you know Damien and Hunter are together. But let's pray anyway. If anything, for your sake."

Tears dribbled down Kay's cheeks. "Why would God listen to me? or any of us? Look what this town has become."

Jill smiled gently. "It's what we've always been, I suppose. It's no surprise to God."

"I didn't realize you were religious."

"I used to be, you know, years ago. I actually met Mike in church. I haven't talked to God in a really long time. But let's just say I've been brought to my knees by circumstances beyond my control."

Kay laughed. "Yeah. I guess you have."

She took Kay's hand and began praying. Kay had to tune out all the noises of the house. The living room fan's hum. The oven's ticking as it cooled. The branch near the dining room that scraped across the window. The heat kicking on. So much distraction.

The prayer seemed to end as quickly as it began. Kay opened her eyes, blotting them with her napkin. Jill's eyes gleamed too. They both offered comforting smiles to one another.

Jill's cell phone sprang to life with a disco tune. "Text message from Nat." She plucked it from her purse. "Oh, wow."

"What?"

"Another post has been made on the Web site. Nat said I have to see it to believe it."

Kay groaned. "Oh, brother. What is it this time? Someone dyed their hair the wrong color?"

"Can I use your computer?"

"Sure," Kay said, pointing to the nearby office. She didn't really want to look. She was so tired of this mess and all that it had brought to her town and her family.

She helped Jill log on and then headed to the garage for more trash bags.

"Oh!" Jill gasped.

Kay tried to hide her irritation and kept walking to the garage. She was done with that stupid Web site. She opened the door, hoping not to let too much cold air in. The garage was drafty and always had . . .

Kay stumbled backward, nearly tripping herself. She hit the door with her back, throwing herself off-balance. She toppled to the floor, jamming her elbow. A fiery pain shot up her arm. "Jill! Jill!"

Pattering footsteps rushed toward her. "What is it?"

Kay's shaking hand pointed to Damien's car. "His car is here!" She turned to Jill, sinking into her arms. "Where are they?"

* * *

Damien wasn't sure how much time had passed. There was a digital clock high on a wall in the jail, but he could see only the hour, not the minutes. It was starting to give him a good sense of what jail was going to be like, where time becomes meaningless and precious all at once.

His hand stroked the day-old stubble that had sprouted from his skin. He hated the prickly feel of it and usually shaved every weekday. He wondered if he would shave in prison. He wondered if he would even serve in prison. He had no idea if what he was charged with carried jail time. Yeah, he should probably call a lawyer.

Maybe tomorrow.

He needed more time to think.

What he couldn't quite wrap his mind around was telling Kay. He didn't want her to see him like this. But it was inevitable. And what would Hunter say? Would he let Damien take the fall? Knowing his son, he doubted it. But it might be necessary. He wasn't sure he could live with the idea of his kid in juvie with all sorts of messed-up teens. He didn't want Hunter introduced to the dark side of life that way.

The reality of it wasn't sitting well because so far he hadn't nailed down exactly what that reality might be. Did he really think he could make up his own reality here? take the fall for his kid? Was that in Hunter's best interest?

If he could just talk to Hunter, ask him what this was all about. But right now he knew Hunter was safe at home with

Kay. She'd picked him up from his after-school stuff. That was where he wanted everyone. By late tonight, he was sure they would find out where he was. Maybe they already knew. Maybe Grayson paid them a visit. Maybe the neighbor came over and expressed concern.

It was weird having absolutely no control over anything. No matter what he wanted to do or what he thought he wanted to do, he could do nothing but sit. Unnerving yet strangely freeing.

A noise caught his attention. The jail had come alive with a small flurry of activity. People who'd been previously sitting were now on their feet. Small groups of three and four were huddled around computers, murmuring just out of earshot.

Someone in uniform passed by.

Damien jumped to his feet and clung to the bars. "Hey, what's going on?"

He was ignored.

* * *

"I'm driving and that's final," Jill said, whisking Kay down the front steps of the home she didn't bother to lock.

Kay ran to Jill's car, tugging at the handle until Jill unlocked it. Kay noticed their neighbor across the street staring for no particular reason.

Jill started the car and slammed it into reverse, barely looking back as she skidded out the driveway. Kay tugged at her seat belt before it finally unlocked enough for her to get it around herself.

Jill's attention was divided between the road and Kay. "Here's what we're going to do. We'll go file a missing person report. Reports."

Kay nodded, swiping at tears, trying to calm herself down.

"But the likelihood is that they're together," Jill continued, floating through a neighborhood stop sign. "We have evidence of that. And that's a good sign."

"But where would they walk to? What would they be doing?"

Jill stared forward, her face frozen with what looked like an important thought.

"What is it?" Kay asked.

"Maybe . . ."

"What?"

"I told you there was a post on the Web site, right? A new one?"

"Yes?"

"It was a note from whoever is responsible for the Web site. He said he'd reveal himself. It's going down in like fifteen minutes." Jill concentrated on the clock. "Maybe that's where they went."

"Where?"

"Old Morgan Road. There's nothing really out there."

"An old abandoned dog-food factory."

"Yeah. And a dump." Jill glanced at her. "They could've gone there."

"On what? A bike? It's like five or six miles from our house."

"Maybe they rode with someone."

Kay tried to swallow that possibility. "Yeah. That's true. Someone could've picked them up." She grabbed Jill's arm. "I'm totally overreacting, aren't I?"

"There are a lot of possibilities here," Jill said. "But I don't think it's bad that you alert the police. You can't be too safe, especially with how nutty this town is getting."

"I just feel in my gut . . . something. Something's not right." She pressed the side of her head against her window, gazing out at the evening traffic. "Hunter lied to me. I think. I might've misunderstood him, but I don't think so. He told me he was doing some after-school activity, and the teacher said there's nothing going on."

Jill patted her leg. "Okay, then that's possibly good news."

"How?"

"He's maybe up to something, but at least it means he's not involved in some freak accident. He might be lying to you, but he'll be coming through that front door, probably with some story he'll try to sell. And you'll never be so happy to have a story sold to you."

"Yeah. You're right. So maybe we shouldn't panic." Outside, leafless trees and yellow grass dimmed against the fading light. "I miss Frank. He would know what to do. He would tell me what to do." Kay sank in her seat, watching the streetlights pop on one by one. "Maybe it's foolish to go to the police."

Jill's expression solidified into determination. "No. We're going to the police. Definitely going to the police."

*   *   *

Damien continued to stand at the bars, wondering what the commotion was about, trying to get the attention of anybody who seemed willing to spill the beans to a guy they thought might be capable of posting it on the World Wide Web. A couple of times a few people who were hunched over the computer turned and looked at him. What? Was some indecent picture of him circulating now?

Weariness drew him back to the chair. He wanted to curl up on his cot and drift into unconsciousness. But the strong smell of urine kept him from doing anything but sitting straight up.

He noticed, though, that the attention of all the people in the middle of the room suddenly drifted to the front doors. Captain Grayson entered, trailed by two officers. He stopped and talked to someone, then focused his attention in the direction of Damien.

Damien stood, greeting him at the bars. "What's going on?"

"Why do you ask?"

"I'm pretty observant. I can tell something big is going down." He nodded toward the open floor of the police station.

Grayson looked excitable and relieved. His face was trying to tell some sort of story, perhaps favorable if Damien was being granted a wish or two. "We're releasing you."

"You are?"

Grayson's smile spoke first. "We have new evidence that someone else is behind this." His smile dropped. "What's the matter?"

"What kind of evidence?"

"A post just showed up on the Web site. Whoever is doing this says he plans to reveal himself out on Old Morgan."

"Old Morgan? There's nothing out there but an abandoned factory."

"You're not off the hook yet, okay? Your credit card is still involved, though it may have been stolen. But there is stronger evidence now pointing to you not being the person we're looking for. Whoever this guy is, it looks like he wants to be caught. Our intention is to bring him in tonight, peacefully and without resistance." Grayson's radio crackled with a voice, and he turned it down. "Of course, this whole thing could be a setup. We don't want to have a suicide-by-cop incident, either."

Damien's nerves sizzled with panic. Suicide by cop?

"We're not taking any chances. We have no idea what kind of person we're dealing with. But the good news is that you get to go home to your family tonight." Grayson started to walk away.

"Wait! Please! Unlock the door!"

Grayson turned back toward Damien. "Calm down. There's a procedure we have to go through. Like every good government establishment, there's mile-high paperwork. You'll be out of here by this evening, though."

"Lou! Wait! Please!"

Grayson looked irritated. He rejoined Damien at the bars, his voice low. "Let me give you a piece of advice. I realize this whole thing could be a potentially big story for you. Your reporter instincts are going crazy. You want to be there when the news breaks. But as a family man myself, my advice to you is to go home, be with your family. I say this with deep conviction: your family's the most important thing you've got on this green earth. Focus on that tonight, all right?" He turned and marched straight into a group of deputies waiting near the front entrance.

Damien grabbed at the bars, wanting to scream, but all he could do was helplessly watch. *What's Hunter doing?*

Through a nearby crackling radio, Damien heard the words *SWAT team.*

35

"SIR, THERE'S PAPERWORK. We're waiting for a fax from the DA's office." The plump woman behind the desk turned at the sound of a fax machine nearby. "Don't have a cow. I'll go look."

Damien watched her take her sweet time as she wove around three desks to get to it. She pulled the paper off the machine, took a long look at it, and then nodded. She ambled back over, accompanied by a skinny man and his superlarge key chain. Without much effort, he picked the right key and unlocked the cell door.

Damien's heart raced as if he'd been running for miles, except all he'd been doing was standing at the bars, gripping them as though he might be able to break through. His ears burned bright red. His fingertips tingled.

The woman gestured. "Right this way, sir. We need you to fill out—"

"Where's my stuff?"

The woman made no attempt to hide her annoyance. "Sir, just sit down here. We're working as fast as we can. This isn't the Marriott." She headed toward some file drawers but got sidetracked by a fellow jailer. She stopped to chat.

Damien realized what he was about to do was probably the stupidest thing he'd ever done, but at the moment he seemed incapable of being rational. *Suicide by cop, SWAT team, be with your family*—the words throbbed and pulsed like a bad headache.

It was almost like watching himself in a movie. He bolted from his seat and ran toward the front door, half-expecting a group of people to pounce on him. He was a free man, but was it before or after the paperwork?

He heard the woman shouting, "Sir! Sir!"

He shoved the front doors open and rushed down the irritatingly long front steps of the police station, his feet moving like he was running tires at football practice.

Old Morgan Road was at least five miles from the police station. He didn't have a car or his wallet. He didn't even have a coat. He was going to have to hitch a ride. Squeezed into his half-baked plan to get to his son was a frantic prayer to God, with no real words able to express what he needed. Still, he was pretty sure it was coming in loud and clear.

He glanced behind him. Nobody was coming out of the police station after him. He turned and headed south toward Old Morgan Road.

* * *

Kay tried one more time to text Jenna. She pushed Send, then stared at her phone. She'd tried calling minutes before, but there was no answer. Now she was unable to get ahold of a single person in her family.

"I'm so afraid," Kay said between the sobs. "I feel like something is really wrong."

Jill stretched her hand across the car and grabbed Kay's. "I know. But it's going to be okay. We have to trust God that—"

"Damien!" Kay gasped. "Jill, slow down!" She unsnapped her seat belt and leaned toward the dash of the car, peering out into the cold, black night. Someone was running toward them on the side of the road. When the car's headlights bounced off him, she swore it looked like Damien.

Jill pulled to the curb. Kay opened her door.

"Kay!" Jill yelled.

But Kay ignored her, hurrying toward the dark figure approaching them. She could tell it was a man and his hand was now in front of his eyes, shielding them from the headlights.

"Damien!" Kay rushed into his arms, crying. "Where have you been?" She backed away from him and looked him over. His somber expression terrified Kay instantly.

"The kids? Where are they?"

"I don't know," Kay cried. "I thought maybe Hunter was with you. I went to pick him up after school, and he wasn't there. The teacher said there was no science fair project going on."

"Get in the car!" Jill yelled. "It's freezing!"

Damien held up a finger to Jill and looked at Kay, his thumbs stroking her cold, wet cheeks. "They arrested me tonight. I've been in jail."

Kay was nodding but not really understanding.

"They just released me because the person doing this said he'd reveal himself tonight on Old Morgan."

"I know. What does that have to do with us?"

"I don't know how to say this, so I'm just going to have to say it, okay?"

"Okay." The strength that Kay had felt only moments ago upon seeing Damien now slid right out the bottom of her feet. She was pretty sure all that held her up were Damien's hands, now holding each of her elbows.

"Hunter is the person behind the Web site."

Kay was nodding again, not because she understood, but because she was trying to digest it while thanking God Damien hadn't just told her one of their children was dead. Yet as the words sank in and as Damien looked deeply into her eyes, the gravity of what was spoken hit her hard. "Hunter . . ."

"We have to get to Old Morgan Road. I don't know what Hunter's planning."

"You're sure it's Hunter?"

Damien took her by the shoulders and helped her into the car. He climbed into the backseat. Jill had the heat cranked but Kay couldn't feel her hands or feet, and she didn't think it was because of the cold.

Kay turned to Damien. She didn't say anything. She couldn't. They stared at each other until Jill said, "Damien, I'm so glad you're—"

"Take us to Old Morgan Road. And hurry."

* * *

"The whole town showed up," Damien whispered as they pulled to the side of the road. The abandoned factory, which looked more like a warehouse, glowed in the darkness from all the car lights shining on it. It seemed hundreds of cars surrounded the warehouse.

Damien jumped out of the car and opened Kay's door, pulling her out. "Come on!"

He held her hand as they hurried toward the large crowd. Eight police cars were parked nearby, their blue and red lights silently strobing.

Damien pushed his way through the crowd, trying to get to the front. Whatever was happening, it was going down fast.

Captain Grayson shouted through a megaphone, "Come out with your hands up!"

Kay gripped Damien's arm. "Don't let anything happen to him!"

"I know," Damien said, pulling her through the tight crowd. He had to shove a few people out of the way just to get through. He bumped into a large shoulder.

"Damien," the man said.

Damien looked over at him. Bruce, from work. "Sorry. I need to get by."

Bruce nodded, then pointed to the warehouse. "I'm sorry. I'm really sorry."

"Why?" Heads were still in the way to a clear view of what was going on. He let go of Kay's hand and used both hands to part a way for himself. He emerged from the sea of people being held back by police tape and noticed first Grayson and his team of cops with their guns drawn. Four had SWAT team jackets on, the only ones in their town. Damien had once written an editorial raising the question, *Do we need SWAT?* And then reversing the dilemma: *Don't we need more?*

"Come out now!" Grayson hollered.

Damien glanced toward the factory, searching frantically for Hunter. He prayed Hunter would come out, give himself up. And not do something stupid like come out with a gun. Where in the world would he get a gun? From Frank?

He wanted to make it over to Grayson, tell him it was Hunter and to not shoot. But he was squeezed between people and police tape and police officers, all trying to control the crowds.

A few people down, on the left, was Reverend Caldwell, his Bible clasped in his arm.

Kay came up behind him and gasped, just as Damien noticed what everyone was staring and pointing at. His gaze stopped on the spray paint across the large brick wall of the factory. Expansive purple and green letters glowed against the light. They might as well have been written in blood.

Jenna Underwood is a virgin.

A list of words went on with such vulgarity that Damien's stomach turned over.

Kay gripped his arm, crying. "That's what this has been all about? That Jenna's a virgin? They're crucifying her for being a virgin?" She covered her mouth. "And this whole time I thought . . . she wasn't."

"Stay here," Damien commanded, then shoved past the police tape.

The nearby officer caught him with a strong arm and his stick. "Get back!"

Damien tugged against his strength. "That's my daughter! Jenna! Where is she?"

The officer let go of him but grabbed his shirt. "Sir, calm down. We don't know what's going on yet. Nobody has come out, but we saw movement inside just moments ago."

"That's my daughter," Damien repeated, staring again at the crude words spray-painted around her name.

"Sir, have you seen your daughter today?"

"Not since she left for school."

Grayson suddenly noticed him. No words needed to be exchanged. They instantly understood each other. Grayson issued a signal with his hand, and the men in bulletproof vests and helmets began inching forward, their automatic weapons poised to strike.

Damien found himself unable to watch. He turned his

head, scanning the crowd for Jenna, hoping she was not inside. Then he saw him.

Hunter.

He stood on the other side of the large crowd, pushed against the police tape, bundled up in a hat and coat and gloves, watching with a somber expression. There was too much chaos to call out to him, and he was too far away anyway. Police movement kept impairing Damien's view. He was even afraid to blink for fear he would lose sight of his son.

"Stop right there!"

Damien's attention jerked toward the warehouse. He tore away from the officer's grip but stayed next to him, watching, with the rest of the crowd, as two shadowy figures emerged from the gaping hole that was once a large door to the factory. Their silhouettes were created by the car lights shining in through the broken windows at the back of the warehouse.

Their hands were raised over their skinny bodies, and soon they stepped into the light provided by the police and the other nearby cars.

"Is one of those your daughter?" the officer asked.

Damien shook his head. He recognized one as a cheerleader. He thought her name was Madison. The other girl didn't look familiar.

"Get down on your knees!" Grayson shouted at them through the megaphone.

They both dropped quickly, keeping their hands up. A group of police rushed toward them.

Damien tried to find Hunter. He still stood in the crowd,

watching. Was he wrong? Were these two girls responsible for the Web site? Or was something else going on?

"Damien! Where's Jenna?" Kay cried from the front of the crowd.

Damien intended to find out. Without any more hesitation, he bolted for the factory. He heard Grayson shouting at him, but he didn't stop. What were they going to do? shoot him?

He stumbled over the gravel, barely keeping his balance, twisting his right ankle. Pain shot up his leg, but he didn't slow down.

"Underwood, get out of the way!" Grayson yelled.

But Damien ran right up to the girls, who were still on their knees, their hands raised, their bodies shaking in the cold. Both grew even more fearful as Damien approached.

The girl on the right, with her pink-streaked ponytail and overdone makeup, boasted a dark purple bruise on the side of her face, which bled into a greenish yellow toward her mouth. The other girl didn't look much better. Her bottom lip was split open. Dried blood trickled down her chin.

Suddenly Damien was shoved out of the way, thrown to the ground by one of the SWAT guys. Grayson stood over him.

"Where's my daughter?" Damien called out to the two girls, who'd been yanked to their feet and were now being frisked. "Where's Jenna?"

Neither answered. One glared at him as if he'd spit at her.

Damien turned his focus toward the factory.

A hand grabbed his shoulder. "Damien, don't. We haven't secured the building. We don't know who or what else is in there."

"I can't stay here, Lou, and wonder—"

Both men saw it at the same time. A crackling, breaking sound, then a flash of orange.

"Fire!"

"It's not safe," Grayson said. "We don't even know if she's in there!"

Damien took one more look at the girls' bruised and bloodied faces. "She's in there." He ran through the open factory door. Thick, black smoke climbed the walls, blocking the car lights that had once streamed through the open windows.

Grayson came up beside him, covering his mouth with his jacket.

"She could be anywhere," Damien said. He didn't have one clue which way to go. Above him, fire danced across the beams. They ducked against loud popping.

"Jenna! Jenna!" Damien choked on the thick smoke. He wrapped his arm across his mouth and tried to look for any movement or hear any sound besides the strange and low groan of the fire.

"Dad!" Her voice was distant, muddled.

"This way!" Damien shouted to Grayson. They made their way along a wall where a tiny sliver of light led the way. Deep against the shadows of the far corner of the building, Damien saw movement. "Jenna!"

"Dad, over here!"

Flames roared nearby. The heat, though a few feet away, seemed to scorch his face. Damien made it to Jenna, who was huddled in the corner. He pulled her to her feet. "Are you okay?"

She nodded and cried, pointing to a boarded-up window. "I tried to get out this way, but I can't get the wood off the window!"

Grayson handed Jenna his flashlight, and he and Damien tried to pry the boarded-up window.

"It's not budging!" Grayson yelled. "Let's go back the way we came!"

They all turned, but the fire had shifted and now blocked the path they'd used to come in.

"Is there another way out?"

Jenna shook her head. "That door over there is steel, and it's locked."

Grayson hurried over, tried to kick it in, but with no luck.

"I'm sorry." Jenna clung to Damien. "I'm so sorry!"

"We're going to get you out of this. Lou, over here! Let's try this board again!"

The smoke hung low against the ceiling. Damien coughed as he tried to breathe. Each man grabbed a side and they tried to pry it again, but it wouldn't move. Damien turned, grabbing the flashlight from Jenna. He scanned the floor for anything that could help. Then he saw a small steel pipe near the wall.

He rushed over and grabbed it. His hand sizzled. The fire was three feet away from it, but it had already acquired its heat.

Damien handed over the flashlight. Grayson lifted the wood just enough to slide the metal bar in. With every ounce of muscle he had, he pried the wood. Within ten seconds, the board popped and now hung by only two screws. They easily pried off the other side. Damien shouted for Grayson to climb through and help Jenna out. He lifted Jenna and dumped her through the window. Grayson caught her and then reached for Damien's hand.

But suddenly a searing pain shot up Damien's arm. He caught a glimpse of Grayson's eyes, wide with fear. He lost his footing. Tried to scream. A horrendous smell and unbearable heat stopped his breath. He reached for Grayson but instead fell backward. As he hit the ground, he saw it . . . his arm was on fire.

But his baby girl was safe.

And even as agony like he never imagined existed overtook every one of his senses, Damien knew he could die with peace. He wanted to say good-bye, but there was no time.

He closed his eyes. The pain fled.

36

"Dad?"

The sound of his name pulled Damien from a deep, dark, safe place.

"Dad?"

He opened his eyes, searching for her. "Jenna?" All that came out was a whisper.

"I'm right here."

His family's faces came into focus.

Kay leaned toward him. "You're at the hospital, sweetie. Your arm is burned, but you're going to be fine."

Damien stared at it, wrapped tightly in white gauze. His mind swirled in a strange, dizzy state. Maybe pain meds? An IV methodically dripped above him. "How bad is it?"

"You're probably going to need some skin grafts." Kay stroked his hair.

Damien tried to move, but pain stabbed through his arm. He looked at Jenna. Dark blue bruises swelled against her cheek. With his good arm, he reached to her face and touched her cheek.

Jenna actually smiled. "They got one punch in, but I really stood my ground. I got Madison right across the face. In self-defense of course. She fell down."

"Did they start that fire?"

"No. I'd brought a lantern from the garage. It was on the ground, and in the fight, I accidentally kicked it over." Jenna stared at her hands. "I didn't go there to fight. I went there to tell them I forgave them. You should have seen the look on their faces when I said that. But then Madison got mad, and that's when I had to hit her."

Damien searched her face, trying to find answers, trying to comprehend it all. "How did you end up there?"

"A little bit of courage goes a long way." She glanced at Kay.

Damien took her arm. "There were some really horrible things written on the walls, and there are a lot of people out there—"

"I know. It's okay." Jenna sat on the edge of the bed. "I knew what they were planning and I came anyway, because . . . of Frank."

"Frank?"

"Yeah. He always stood up for what he believed in, so I decided to have courage like him. Stand up for myself. I hadn't done that. I'd just let them say what they wanted about me, but I never stood up for myself." Tears glistened in her eyes. Kay wrapped her arms around her. "But not tonight. Tonight I fought back. With truth. I don't care what they say about me."

Captain Grayson entered the room, looking weary but relieved. "You gave us a scare. Both of you." He touched Jenna's shoulder. "You okay?"

Jenna nodded.

"How about you, big guy?"

Damien grinned. "Besides having my arm melted off, I'm great."

"These girls are going to have a lot to answer to." Grayson faced Jenna. "I'll need a statement from you. Tonight if possible."

"No problem," Jenna said.

Hunter entered, carrying a can of soda and what looked like a heavy burden. "Can I talk to you, Dad, for a second? Alone?"

The three of them started to move out of the room, but Hunter looked at Grayson, who stopped and returned to the bed.

Damien's gaze shifted between them. Then he said to Hunter, "That must've been tough to watch out there. To read. I'm sorry you had to see it."

"Nobody believes that," Hunter said, lowering contemplative, withdrawn eyes. "Everyone knows what those girls are about."

"There was a post saying that whoever was behind the Web site was going to reveal himself tonight."

"Dad, there's something I need to tell you."

"I think someone caught wind of what was going to go down tonight and knew the town was very caught up in this Web site, and that could be a great way to save a sister in danger and get some very misguided girls caught. How can you run away from an entire town showing up?"

Hesitancy flashed across Hunter's expression.

"It's you, isn't it?"

Hunter looked Damien right in the eye. He nodded so slightly Damien wondered if he'd seen it. But then he said, "I'm the one doing the Web site."

Damien was surprised by how quickly his emotions showed their hand. "Why?" he whispered.

"At school we were talking about social experiments and about people who risked a lot to make a difference, and I just came up with this idea one day. I hear things at school. See things. How people talk and the damage that it does." Hunter looked like he was on the verge of tears too. "You always taught me the power of words, and I wanted to show what they can do when misused. It sort of got out of hand. I didn't expect everyone to go all nuts. But I couldn't stop either. There was a point to be made. And then I heard there was this plot against Jenna because she told the police . . ."

"Son, I know your heart, and I know your intention was good. That's all that matters to me. Whatever the consequences, we'll face them together, right?" Damien glanced at Grayson.

"He confessed just a few minutes ago," Grayson said. "Even brought his own evidence."

Hunter pulled out a long, telescope-looking gadget from the backpack on the floor. "I brought this to show the police that it's really me."

"You planned on turning yourself in tonight."

"After I knew Jenna was safe, yes." He fingered the gadget, looking at it as if it were a good friend. "Frank knew, you know."

"What are you talking about?" Damien asked as he and Grayson exchanged glances.

"He caught me one day, behind a house, as I was preparing to listen. He asked me what I was doing. I made up some stupid story he didn't believe. Later I went to him and sort of spoke vaguely. I just wanted to know what he thought. Before he died, in front of our house actually, he told me that it was time I stopped. I told him I would . . . but all this stuff started happening. Then Frank died. Then they thought it was you."

"That's when you posted our conversation. You wanted to prove I wasn't behind this."

Hunter nodded. "Plus, you said some really profound things, things I think this town needed to hear."

"And you sent the crossword puzzle, then took it back?"

"Yeah. I thought I was protecting you. I went through your briefcase one day. It was right there in the center pocket."

Damien's heart swelled with love for his son, even as his body tensed with waves of pain. The courage and compassion his children showed overwhelmed him. But now what would happen?

37

THE BLOODY STAIN

By Damien Underwood, staff writer

On a cold Thursday in December, only days before Christmas, Marlo collapsed under the weight of its own words, never to be the same again. What began with thoughtless words ended with a consuming fire.

Though Marlo would always be marred by the bloody red stain of disgrace, I had hoped it might welcome the painful cutting out of its deepest regret. A long scar would remain, but it was that scar that could cause Marlo to fight harder for innocence and goodness.

Months later, people walk the sidewalks again but rarely wave at neighbors, shake hands with those whom they have much in common, and trust one another. It has become evident that trust begins with words. Trusting someone to speak kindly when you are not present means trustworthiness in many more countless ways. To know trustworthiness first with words, then with actions was to be this town's richest attribute, the most desired character trait.

Except Marlo could never quite forgive what it had done.

Ideally, the power of words was never to be taken for granted. Everyone in town might have vowed to never be undone by their own words again. If there was something to be settled, it should be done face-to-face. If there was a grievance, then courage would find them talking openly about it.

But instead, Marlo continues to reel and rage, reminding one another of the sins committed.

Only forgiveness can stand now. Only forgiveness can wipe the slate clean. Who is willing to stand up for that?

On March 13, my son, Hunter Underwood, stood before a judge to receive his sentence. On his way to the courthouse, people taunted him. Yelled at him. Booed him for invading their privacy. He took it like a man, because he had done what they accused him of.

Inside the courthouse, he held his chin high, ready to accept the consequence of his actions. For the first time he was dressed in a suit. He looked handsome and mature. And scared to death.

The judge sat high, cloaked with the authority of the robe and the title. She gave a brief lecture on the law and how many laws he'd broken. Hunter nodded, understanding full well that no matter any good he had done, he still had to face the law.

But then, to everyone's surprise, the judge told Hunter

that in the right situation, mercy is oftentimes more powerful than punishment. The stain can be a reminder but not always a verdict. So she sentenced him to community work and a lifetime of sharing his passion for the power of words.

He did just that. In July, his essay "The Power of Words" was published by *Time* magazine, and the story of Marlo was told in *People*. Hunter finished his community service three weeks ago.

On Sunday, our pastor taught from Genesis, which recounts a loving God who speaks the world into existence. I found myself thinking about how true it is that our words have the power to speak life—and also death—into whatever they touch.

Life and death are indeed in the power of the tongue. And words are as permanent as ink pen on a crossword.

It is with deep sadness that I tell you this is my last column for the *Marlo Sentinel*. My family and I are moving away to heal and find joy inside community. For community has richness and fulfillment to offer. And our family has much to give.

We've committed ourselves to taking care of my good friend Frank's sister, Meredith, and providing whatever she needs for the rest of her life. It is the least we can do for a man who fought hard to save the town he loved.

Our hearts will always be close to you, Marlo. We will pray for you daily. Speak kindly. Love powerfully. Listen fully.

"But a tiny spark can set a great forest on fire. And the tongue is a flame of fire. It is a whole world of wickedness, corrupting your entire body. It can set your whole life on fire, for it is set on fire by hell itself."

—JAMES 3:5-6

Discussion Questions

Use these questions for individual reflection or for discussion within your book club or small group. If your book club reads *Listen* and is interested in talking with me via speakerphone, please feel free to contact me through my Web site at www.renegutteridge.com, and I'll do my best to arrange something with you. Thanks for reading!

1. Do you believe words have power over you? What about the words you speak in private? Do they still have power? over you? over someone else?

2. Can you recall an instance where words changed you, either for better or worse?

3. Kay's life was changed by words when she was young, but the pain it caused her and others continued into the next generation. What steps can we take to make sure painful words do not continue to cause harm through more generations?

4. Why do you think Frank kept his sister a secret, even from his best friend?

5. If you were the one who discovered who was behind the Web site, would you turn them in? What if it were a friend or family member? Would you try to protect them from the consequences?

6. How have social networking sites and other techno-logical advances—like texting and Twittering—changed what we say about ourselves and others? Do you think people feel freer to share personal details? What issues can this present?

7. If you have a damaged or estranged relationship in your life, and you were asked to write the person a letter, could you do it? Why or why not? What would make it hard or easy?

8. What are three words you'd like to have spoken about you?

9. What do you think are five of the most powerful words in the English language? What makes them powerful?

10. The Bible has a lot to say about the power of the tongue. For instance, Damien quotes James 3:5-6 in his letter to Marlo. Read and discuss the following verses: Psalm 34:12-14, Proverbs 13:3, and Proverbs 15:4.

About the Author

Rene Gutteridge is the author of sixteen novels, including the Storm series (Tyndale House Publishers) and *Never the Bride*, the Boo series, and the Occupational Hazards series from WaterBrook Press. She also released *My Life as a Doormat* and *The Ultimate Gift: The Novelization* with Thomas Nelson. Rene is also known for her Christian comedy sketches. She studied screenwriting while earning a mass communications degree, graduating magna cum laude from Oklahoma City University and earning the Excellence in Mass Communication Award. She served as the full-time director of drama for First United Methodist Church for five years before leaving to stay home and write. She enjoys instructing at writers conferences and in college classrooms. She lives with her husband, Sean, a musician, and their children in Oklahoma City.

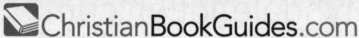